Nicole stood frozen in the center of her bedroom...
her violet eyes dark stains of fear, her mouth trembling
with unspoken protest. Valentin towered in her
doorway, his unruly blond hair tumbling over his
forehead and his eyes blazing with cold blue fire.
Though his clothes were dirty and mud-spattered, he
swept Nicole an elegant bow. *sheet*

"You cannot come in here," Nicole whispered.

"It would seem I already am in here, ma'am.
I was given to understand that you *insisted* upon my
presence." *Pretty good +9*

"But not at such an untimely hour. This is
quite improper."

"What, my dear, did you expect from a
'fortune-hunting rake'?" Nicole's former rash words
were flung in her face with quiet contempt; and as
the Viscount stepped toward her, she thrust out
her hand as if to ward him off. With a quick
movement, he pulled her into his arms.

"What are you doing?" she gasped.

"Getting acquainted, my dear, in keeping with
your charming request of my mother. What better
way to settle matters and insure our forthcoming
nuptials than by forcing your hand?"

Sweet Bravado

by Alicia Meadowes

WARNER BOOKS

A Warner Communications Company

Some historical details have been altered to
fit the needs of the story.

WARNER BOOKS EDITION

ISBN 0-446-89936-4

Cover art by Walter Popp

Warner Books, Inc., 75 Rockefeller Plaza, New York, N.Y. 10019

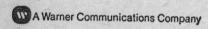 A Warner Communications Company

Printed in the United States of America

Not associated with Warner Press, Inc., of Anderson, Indiana

First Printing: February, 1979

10 9 8 7 6 5 4 3 2

To Dan and Mary Gallina.
Home is where the heart lies.

Prologue

"Damn!" The angry Viscount of Ardsmore strode across the room to pour himself another glass of port. "A nice homecoming this has turned out to be." He turned his blazing blue eyes on his mother who was seated across the room from him. "First a funeral and now this blasted will. I still can't believe Aunt Sophie did this."

"That old woman must have been senile," Lady Eleanore fumed.

"Nasty business," Perry Harcourt sympathized.

"Sylvie Moreau!" Lady Eleanore exclaimed bitterly. "That ballet dancer has had the last laugh after all."

The Viscount stared at her thoughtfully. "That is hardly to the point, madame. It is the daughter who concerns me, not the mother."

"But the daughter of a *ballet* dancer," his mother protested.

"What are you going to do, Val?" Perry asked.

"Marry her," the Viscount replied curtly. "Do I have a choice?" He looked from his mother to his brother, mocking their dismay. "Unless the lot of us decides to take up residence in Newgate." He laughed at the horrified expressions on their faces.

"Bad as that?" Perry questioned.

"Worse. You know the Harcourt talent for spending money as well as I do," Valentin drawled. "One might say Aunt Sophie has come to the rescue despite her damnable scheming. The old girl's fortune is going to save our spendthrift skins." The Viscount cast a bold glance toward his mother and winked slyly at Perry. "I have some rather pressing . . . er . . . expenses that can no longer be staved off with my infinite charm," he said, mocking himself.

"Know what you mean, old man. The Von Hoffman woman was flaunting some pretty fancy emeralds at Vauxhall . . ."

"Mind your tongue, you young blockhead!" the Viscount snapped at his hapless brother, who flushed a deep scarlet. "Will you never learn discretion?"

"My son." Lady Eleanore came to him clutching at his arm. "I know the sacrifices you are making."

"Spare me the speeches, madame. We have much to discuss, since I return to France in the morning. First we must instruct Dilworth to find the girl, then—"

"I say, Val," the heedless Perry interrupted. "Don't mean to throw in a damper or anything, but just suppose Nicole won't have you?"

"What!" Lady Eleanore cried. "Your brother, the Viscount of Ardsmore, and that little French nobody! She would not *dare* refuse!"

"And there you have it, Perry. A marriage made in heaven." Valentin Harcourt laughed sarcastically, then raised the port and downed it.

Chapter I

"C'est barbare! Our wits shall be jolted from our brain-box before we reach Paris in this tumbril of a coach," exclaimed the agitated little Frenchwoman accompanying the young girl beside her.

"Come, now, madame. Do not give in to your fears," the young woman responded in an effort to keep up her spirits. "You will cast us both into such glooms that we will be quite undone. Let us consider my good fortune. It is not every day that a pauper such as myself is turned into an heiress overnight."

"Hélas, mon petit chou. That is what troubles me most about this mad adventure. This marriage with that English devil! He will eat you alive, that one. I remember him at your dear papa's funeral. So arrogant. And those wild blue eyes like Satan . . ."

"Madame!" The sharp command silenced further babble from her companion but stirred up a veritable storm of unrest in the girl's breast. She schooled her facial muscles into a mask of calm repose, but the frantic thoughts leaping wildly in her mind could not be subdued.

Nicole Harcourt had met her frightening cousin Valentin, the Viscount of Ardsmore, only a few times during her childhood. She was thirteen years old the last time she saw him. Almost eleven years had passed since her father's funeral, and yet the memory of Valentin Harcourt remained vivid in her mind. It was those fiery blue eyes that haunted her dreams and seemed to watch her haughtily through the accumulated fantasies of her adolescent years that she recalled most of all. Now she was on her way to meet Lady Eleanore, the Viscount's mother, to make the arrangements to marry him. Could it be true? She—the wife of that blond god she had worshipped in the secrecy of her heart all these years?

The presence of an inheritance had come as a shock. Aunt Sophie had remembered Nicole and made her, as well as Valentin, the joint heirs to her vast riches. Only four months ago Mr. Dilworth, a solicitor representing the Ardsmore interests had arrived at the small cottage in Beauvais where Nicole lived with Madame Lafitte and informed them of the will. Until Mr. Dilworth's arrival, Nicole's had been a life of quiet anonymity since the death of her mother three years before. Mr. Dilworth explained to the girl the incredible stipulation of her great-aunt Sophie's will; that Nicole must marry his lordship, Valentin Harcourt, Viscount of Ardsmore, or the inheritance would be lost to the entire family. This was Aunt Sophie's last attempt to reunite the two branches of the Harcourt family.

Eleven years ago Aunt Sophie came to France searching out her favorite nephew, Rupert Harcourt, Nicole's father. Aunt Sophie was determined to see her nephew reconciled to the Harcourt family, but her plans unravelled with the untimely death of Nicole's father.

His death left Nicole and her mother in difficult financial straits, and almost completely isolated. They were alone in the world, except for a sister on her mother's side whose tie to them had never been strong. Nicole's aunt, Lorette Beauchamp, and her son, Phillippe, came to the funeral merely out of duty but offered little comfort to the lonely pair. In fact, Phillippe had snickered as the priest intoned prayers for the dead. It was Madame Lafitte who was their one rock of support throughout the trial of Rupert's death and burial.

Reluctantly, Sophie had supplied a small pension for Rupert's widow, Sylvie Harcourt, and requested that Nicole be allowed to return to London with her and be raised in a manner suitable to a child of aristocratic lineage. But, unbeknownst to Nicole, Sylvie had spitefully declined. She refused to let the Harcourts have any further opportunity to dominate her affairs, even though it meant denying Nicole her place in English society. Sylvie could never forgive nor forget her frigid reception by the Harcourt family. When Rupert presented Sylvie Moreau, former ballet dancer from the Opéra de Paris, as his wife to that arrogant dynasty, they closed ranks in frozen hauteur. He had committed the unpardonable. Rupert, to his chagrin, found he was unable to disguise the vulgar ambition of his lovely dancer-bride and force her down the unwilling throats of the English *ton*. He eventually retreated from London to eke out a ramshackle existence in pursuit of faro and chemin-de-fer. In 1803, with a temporary cessation of hostilities between England and France, Rupert took Sylvie and Nicole to the Continent where he continued his unstable quest of Lady Luck.

Although Nicole's father had cut himself off from the

family, he nevertheless communicated with Aunt Sophie. He refused all efforts on her part to mend the family breach. However, when Sophie heard of Rupert's abrupt departure from England, she followed him with the intention of forcing him to comply with her wishes for peace, but it was too late. Rupert was fatally ill. Sophie attended the funeral accompanied by her great-nephew, Valentin, whom she had brought with her.

A new idea to further her plans for reuniting the family struck Sophie as she studied Nicole standing next to Valentin, but it would have to wait. Sophie returned to England with Valentin, and the resumption of hostilities between England and France put an end to further contact between Nicole and the Harcourt family.

It was still early afternoon, and snow was falling heavily as Nicole Harcourt and Madame Lafitte arrived at an imposing residence on the Boulevard St-Germain. The coach pulled into the courtyard before the Hotel Belmontaine, relinquished its passengers, and continued on its way. Madame Lafitte and Nicole stood in the courtyard, looking about in bewilderment and wondering what was to happen next. However, Madame Lafitte was not one to lose time in matters of wonderment. She sprang into voluble action, mounting the stairs and tugging Nicole along. She pounded the brass knocker forcefully and complained loudly at their lack of reception.

"C'est barbare!" complained the outraged Lafitte. "That not one member of the family should be here to welcome you. This is insupportable." She chose her adjectives freely from both French and English.

"It's insulting," Nicole agreed with heat.

At that moment the heavy oak door swung open and a poker-faced butler ushered them into the library. Again the pair stood looking about uneasily. This time they were in the middle of a room hung with quantities of red damask draperies that shut out much of the thin November sunlight. A small fire in the grate did little to relieve the heavy chill in the air, and the single branch of lighted candles was of little assistance against the wintry shadows filling the room.

"I suppose we may as well make ourselves comfortable," Nicole suggested and seated herself on the nearest straight-backed chair. "Come madame," she beckoned firmly. "Be seated here beside me." They sat in contemplative silence for a few minutes.

"I had hoped for more of a welcome from your relations," admitted Madame Lafitte as the minutes passed. "It does not seem they are overanxious to receive you."

"Receive me indeed! They should be waiting here with open arms to welcome me. Do not forget, Fifi, were it not for me, they would not have the prospect of great-aunt Sophie's riches before them," Nicole declaimed with much feeling of justice on her side.

"But *ma chère* Nicole, the reverse is just as true of you. You stand to benefit no less than they. Come now, you must admit it," chided Madame Lafitte, who had calmed down once she was quietly seated and removed from the discomforts of a jostling coach.

Irritated, Nicole snapped, "Oh, Fifi, do not be so fair-minded. They do not deserve it. Look how they treat me already! Apparently they do not care enough to make me feel welcome in a strange house. It is evident that their attitude has not changed over the years. I am my mother's daughter, after all, and they could never forget that she was a . . . a dancer. This sets the pattern, do you not think so?"

"Patience, little one," Madame Lafitte counseled.

Nicole jumped up to pace nervously about the room. With a sigh she removed her pelisse and shook out her dark-blue dress. She untied her bonnet and began smoothing her hair into a semblance of order. She wore her dark tresses simply, without benefit of the hairdresser's arts.

"Stop fussing, Nicole," Madame Lafitte broke through her thoughts. "You are quite presentable. Come, sit down."

"I feel better on my feet," Nicole replied.

At that moment Lady Eleanore, the Viscountess Ardsmore, swathed in sables and exuding self-importance, sailed grandly into the library trailed by her niece and companion, Cecily Fairfax. Nicole, noticing their elegant toilettes, felt at a disadvantage in her simple merino.

Lady Eleanore advanced toward Nicole, her thin lips pursed as she tilted her silvery head to one side and stared down her aquiline nose at the girl.

"My *dear* Nicole," Lady Eleanore finally broke through the frosty silence. "How happy I am to meet you again." She made no apology for her tardy arrival.

Nicole stood still allowing her cousin to brush her cheek with a cold kiss. "I too am happy to meet again after so many years, Cousin Eleanore." Nicole spoke through stiff lips.

"Cecily, dear, come meet Nicole Harcourt." Lady Eleanore addressed the young girl behind her.

Cecily examined the rather breathtaking picture Nicole presented and murmured her greeting. She viewed the silky luster of Nicole's blue-black hair and the smooth ivory of her complexion with a sudden flash of despair. This was an undeniable beauty. One look at Nicole's violet eyes and Valentin was surely lost to Cecily forever. Valentin was soon to take this gorgeous creature to wife. There would be no room for Cecily in such a union. Her hatred of Nicole sprang forth on the moment.

The Viscountess, viewing Nicole's beauty with the dispassionate eyes of the future mother-in-law, found her displeasure less in Nicole's appearance than in her credentials. The daughter of a dancer! Well, what cannot be changed must be endured. The girl certainly had a presence about her, and her exquisite figure in the proper clothes would command admiration. Nicole and Valentin would make a striking couple, no doubt of it. The Harcourts would carry off the affair with their usual *panache*.

This wedding, forced on her by Sophie's eccentricity, must be accomplished with all due haste. Valentin's expectations had held off creditors of every description far beyond their limits. The family coffers were bare and the situation was desperate, but there was no need for Nicole to be apprised of this. Such knowledge was sure to strengthen the girl's position. Only look how bold she appeared, standing silently before them, waiting for her to carry on the business of this meeting.

"Well, shall we put aside further display of amenities and get on with the business at hand?" Lady Eleanore suggested haughtily.

"As you wish, Lady Eleanore," Nicole answered quietly.

"We have ourselves just arrived from London and taken residence here at the Hotel Belmontaine. This house should afford us a suitable background for the wedding and all affairs attendant upon that event, don't you think?" The Viscountess did not wait for an answer. "I believe it will be to everyone's advantage to accomplish this *wedding* as speedily as possible. As a matter of fact, arrangements for a civil ceremony at the British Embassy have been scheduled for six weeks hence. That will give us enough time for fittings and completing your trousseau, as well as a few quiet introductions into society."

Nicole was surprised at the speed with which everything was being arranged. "But my dear cousin," Nicole interrupted her. "You go along too fast for me. I must inform you that I have not entirely made up my mind to this marriage."

The Viscountess stared unbelievingly. "What is that you say? *Not* made up your mind? Surely you are jesting," she exclaimed sharply. "You are here. You know the conditions of the will. What else is there?"

"There is another party necessary to fulfill the conditions of that will, I believe," Nicole answered firmly.

"But the Viscount has consented. He is *perfectly* amenable to great-aunt Sophie's . . . demands."

"Perhaps I would like some evidence of a more tangible nature. I have yet to set eyes upon my prospective bridegroom in person. Eleven years is a long time."

"But my dear girl, this is a marriage of *convenience*. Surely you do not expect the Viscount to go through the hypocrisy of a courtship?"

Her words stung Nicole cruelly. "Perhaps not a courtship, but at least he could give some time to our becoming acquainted."

Lady Eleanore turned her bewildered eyes to Cecily who shrugged her shoulders eloquently.

Nicole was enjoying her cousin's discomfort and sudden loss of grand manner. It assuaged a little that cold arrival earlier.

During the lull that followed, Cecily Fairfax could hardly sit still. Could there be some hope for her after all? Would this half-French nobody relinquish her claim to Valentin? She could barely breathe, so great was her agitation.

"My son is a member of the Duke of Wellington's staff engaged in delicate matters of state for His Majesty in Vienna. As such he is not at liberty to come and go to satisfy the *whims* of a romantic girl." The Viscountess picked up the attack again with alacrity.

"There is nothing romantic about my desire to reacquaint myself with Viscount Ardsmore, I assure you," Nicole lied nervously. "There are matters he and I should settle between us before marriage plans proceed further."

"What matters, may I ask?" Lady Eleanore demanded arrogantly.

Nicole faltered for a moment. What matters, indeed? She would die before admitting to her cousin the fears she felt about Valentin. Her fear that the idol of her dreams would find her wanting. That he would not love her with the same desperate devotion as hers—a devotion born of years of romantic fantasies in which Valentin pursued her, wooed her, rescued her, ravished her, protected her and loved her again and again. It could not be just a marriage of convenience!

"I would prefer to see the Viscount before we proceed further," Nicole replied with quiet determination.

Lady Eleanore recognized Nicole's intransigence. "Very well. I will post a letter to my son in Vienna this very night. I had hoped to spare him any unnecessary inconvenience, but I see you are *determined* to present obstacles. Nevertheless, I must insist that you remain with us at Belmontaine so that the preliminary fittings can be made. Even you must realize that a trousseau is not assembled overnight." Anger prodded the Viscountess to speak with unconcealed disdain.

Nicole bit back an angry rejoinder as Madame Lafitte grasped her elbow. Now that the gauntlet was flung between them, Nicole repressed a tremor of fear. Perhaps she had gone too far. After all, her cousin was only engineering the accomplishment of Nicole's dearest, deepest desire. What was she doing to be throwing obstacles in the way? She would marry Valentin tomorrow, were he to ask her. And even if he did not come to ask her, she would still marry him.

Lady Eleanore rang for the housekeeper. "Madame Dupré, please show my guests to their rooms." She turned to Nicole. "If you will follow Madame Dupré, she will see that your needs are cared for. You will find your boxes already unpacked. And now if you will excuse me, I will go write that letter." She swept from the room just as grandly as she had entered minutes ago with Cecily trailing in her wake.

Once they reached Nicole's bedroom, Madame Lafitte began to lecture her charge. Although the lady had voiced considerable criticism of the marriage and the bridegroom, she never doubted for a moment that Nicole would or should marry Viscount Ardsmore. She had accepted it as a foregone conclusion. The marriage represented a heaven-sent opportunity for Nicole's financial security. Madame Lafitte was conscience-stricken that she might have contributed through foolish babble to Nicole's possible rejection of this good fortune. But the girl proudly refused to listen to her.

Chapter II

A pale sunlight filtered into the breakfast room at the back of the house. There was a sideboard amply provided with eggs, ham and kidneys, but Nicole preferred the French custom of coffee and croissants for breakfast. Were it not for the cold winter light, the room surrounded by windows on three sides would be a cheerful retreat, providing, as it did, a charming view of the terrace and gardens to the rear of the house.

The bed chamber in which Nicole had just spent the night was a far cry from the homely little room of her girlhood in Beauvais. It was of immense proportions and luxurious appointments with blue satin paneling on the walls and matching velvet draperies at the tall windows. She had just bathed in comfortable warmth before a substantial fireplace and yet her temper was not that of one well pleased with her changed circumstances. Yesterday's interview with her cousin still rankled, and Nicole was not in a mood for appreciating her sudden change in fortune.

As soon as Madame Lafitte entered the breakfast room, she resumed her attack on Nicole. She had to convince the girl to accommodate the Harcourts.

"*Ma chère* Nicole, let me speak to you as your own dear mama would . . ."

"That is hardly the right tactic to employ, madame, since it is my own dear mama who suffered most at the hands of the cruel Harcourt family."

"*C'est vrai,* but . . ."

"But nothing, Fifi. My father was forced to leave London because my mother was scorned for being a ballet dancer. Do you think I can forget that? At last fate has dealt a few trump cards to this side of the family, and I shall play them well. Let them squirm a little. Revenge can be sweet."

"You sound bitter, Nicole."

"Why shouldn't I sound bitter?"

"You must forget the past, child, and think of the future. It could be rosy. Regard your changed circumstances, and furthermore, the young man who came to your papa's funeral was very handsome, *n'est-ce pas?*"

"Valentin is another matter," Nicole admitted. She could still see him standing tall and aloof at the graveside, a fugitive ray of sunlight glinting against the burnished gold of his hair. He had seemed a vision materialized briefly from a girlhood dream of the ideal knight, all strength and beauty and valor. Yet now he was to be hers for a mere nod of assent. It was Lady Eleanore, his mother, who stood in the way. That woman roused all Nicole's latent bitterness for those years when she and her mother were outcast Harcourts, denied recognition be-

22

cause they were beneath family consideration. That the Harcourts might have some justice on their side, considering her mother's low birth and questionable career, only lent fuel to the fire of Nicole's wrath.

A young serving girl interrupted Nicole's ruminations. "Excuse me, *mademoiselle,* but the Viscountess awaits you in the drawing room."

"Thank you, Lily. Tell my cousin I shall be with her directly." As the door closed behind the maid, Nicole turned to Madame Lafitte, a sly smile of satisfaction lifting the corners of her mouth. "Anxious, wouldn't you say?"

"Nicole, take that smug expression off your face," Madame Lafitte pleaded.

"Why should I?" she demanded tartly. The look grew more pronounced as she walked through the door, Madame Lafitte followed her into the drawing room unable to still the disquiet agitating her bosom.

Lady Eleanore was seated on a divan before the fireplace looking regal and composed in a morning dress of grey silk, her only ornament a ruby brooch at her throat. She seemed all ice and steel to the girl coming to greet her.

"Cousin Eleanore," Nicole kissed the proffered cheek and decided on direct attack. "Have you written to the Viscount concerning my desire to see him before wedding plans go forth?"

"So you have not changed your mind?" Lady Eleanore questioned reprovingly.

"I regret that my wishes do not meet with your approval, Cousin, but I must insist. It does not seem improper to me to want to become acquainted with my prospective bridegroom."

"I daresay it does not. I *suppose* one must make allowances considering your unfortunate upbringing." The Viscountess was prepared to be equally direct.

Nicole's quick temper flared, and this time she did not bite back her retort. The obvious slur on her background was too much to bear. "My upbringing as a French girl of gentle birth was the equal of any, I dare say. As a matter of fact, there are those who feel that true culture stops this side of the English Channel, dear Cousin. I believe England has been aptly described as 'a nation of shop-keepers,' has it not?"

Lady Eleanore's prolonged gasp echoed ominously about the room. Cold with fury she drew herself up to the full limits of her imposing height. "You *dare* to speak to me that way?"

Nicole merely stared in return.

"You may be sure Ardsmore shall receive a full accounting of the quality of person, or should I say *lack* of quality of the person with whom it is his misfortune to be forced to ally himself."

"I am sure my quality or lack of it will be sufficiently compensated for by the price tag I bear."

"I find your manner common and vulgar."

"And do you find the subject of money also common and vulgar?"

"You are insulting as well."

"The wedding can always be called off," Nicole stated quietly.

"Do not try to threaten me, you wicked girl. How would you like to return to Beauvais and enjoy the luxuries of French culture that you could afford should you reject the Viscount?"

"There are worse conditions than poverty."

"Really? And what are they, pray tell?"

"I suggest you consider a loveless union with a fortune-hunting rake," Nicole retorted heatedly.

"Nicole, Nicole, *taisez-vous*." Madame Lafitte inter-

24

vened, no longer able to suppress her concern. *"Composez-vous.* This is not to be countenanced. Lady Eleanore is soon to be your mama-in-law. Only think what you are saying. You must apologize and control your tongue."

Madame Lafitte's outburst provided the necessary break in hostilities. Nicole visibly wilted as waves of shame washed over her. How could she have spoken with such disregard for the proprieties? What was wrong with her?

The Viscountess seemed to recover a semblance of her lost dignity. "I think, perhaps, enough has been said. I shall write Ardsmore at once and let him take matters into his own hands. It is regrettable that you choose to think of the Viscount in such unflattering terms. There are young ladies of *breeding* among the English *ton* who would not find your prospects so distasteful." And having the last word, she flounced through the doors leaving behind a stricken Nicole.

What devil had prompted her to lash out so wildly? Nicole no more thought of Valentin as a fortune hunter than as a country peasant. With characteristic French practicality, Nicole accepted the contract set up by Aunt Sophie as a mutually beneficial pact. She found nothing distasteful in the fact that both she and the Viscount were in need of the fortune thus supplied. In fact, it created a condition of equality between them. It was Lady Eleanore that she could not abide. But why, oh, why, had she lost her temper? What would Valentin say when he heard about her shocking behavior? She did not wish to offend him, but fear and pride warred within her. What if he reacted to her as his family had done toward her mother? Could she bear it—loving him the way she did?

As the days passed, the atmosphere remained tense between Nicole and Lady Eleanore. Each refrained from causing further rift in the uneasy alliance necessary between them. Almost docilely Nicole submitted to Lady Eleanore's carefully worded advice about her new wardrobe, and when the Viscountess suggested a series of small dinner parties to introduce Nicole to members of society, Nicole acquiesced without demur.

Nevertheless, it was not without some trepidation that she approached her initial presentation which was to be a dinner party for twelve. Lady Eleanore had prepared well, and the dining room at the Hotel Belmontaine was sumptuously decorated for the occasion. Everywhere were gilt-framed mirrors reflecting a myriad of candles in golden sconces; lavish paintings of ladies in silks and satins disporting themselves amid the shrubberies of luxurious gardens lined the walls. The long dining table was hung with a figured damask cloth bordered by heavy Belgian lace. Dainty pink roses on the gleaming china were complemented by tiny nosegays of fresh roses at each place setting. Lady Eleanore was a true Harcourt when it came to spending money, and she was no less adept at the consumption of fortunes than were her improvident husband, the late Viscount Ardsmore, Harrison Harcourt, and his now-penniless heir, Valentin.

Lord Harrison had been something of a scandal in his day, squandering great quantities of his inheritance in the usual high-born pursuits of gaming and wenching. His credentials of birth and rank were impeccable, and he used them to accommodate his aristocratic pleasures without the slightest nod to propriety. The more outrageously he flaunted decorum, the more society fawned upon him. His wife, Lady Eleanore, a person of great style and rank in her own right, accepted the code of her husband without a qualm and pursued her own pastimes of lavish parties and extravagant intrigues that were equally costly and shocking. However, no outrage was deemed improper as long as it was performed with style.

And now here was Lady Eleanore marshalling all her considerable talents to ram through this marriage with a French nobody. Well, she would do it—gritted teeth or no. The dinner tonight was step one in her campaign. It must provide the seal of approval for Nicole's candidacy; hence, the guest list was drawn from the ranks of the elderly and respectable. The guests included family friends of the Harcourts lately arrived from England. Among them were two pompous couples, the Montgomerys and the Wexfords. The Montgomerys were so advanced in years that Nicole wondered at their daring to travel from England to Paris during the chill of winter. Roger Montgomery's every breath was an audible wheeze, and his gaunt-faced wife appeared consumptive. Nicole reasoned, however, that the discomforts of travel notwithstanding, Paris must still be a more pleasant milieu than dreary London with its fog and continual damp. Her recent visits to the houses of Parisian couture had convinced her that half of England's aristocracy must have fled to Paris since Napoleon was safely removed from the scene. One heard more English than French in the streets these days.

The Wexfords were a contrast to the lean stringiness of the Montgomerys. Both were short and rotund, and Morley Wexford seemed a likely candidate for apoplexy. The Wexfords' daughter, Karen, who accompanied them, did little to add youthfulness to the gathering with her prissy airs and prim features set in a look of haughty disapproval.

The Envoy Extraordinaire to the British Embassy, Lord Wolsey, an elderly gentleman with a long white mustache, was accompanied by two youthful attachés, Charles Humphrey and Gerold Apley. Whatever natural high spirits they possessed were overshadowed by the presence of their superior.

The gayest member of the party was a snowy haired antiquarian, the Marquis de Crécy, whose distant relation to the Harcourt family entitled him to the familiar address of "Uncle." The Marquis de Crécy exuded an elegant, if doddering, charm. His old-world manner could still bring sighs of pleasure from feminine lips. He found Nicole to be a visual delight and lost no opportunity of telling her. *Ravissante* and *charmante* were but a few of the lavish terms he applied to her, and Nicole, for the first time since her arrival in Paris, relaxed and blossomed under his approving eye.

If the company was dull, the food was superb, and the menu provided by an excellent French chef was delicious and ample. There were multiple courses including poached turbot, dressed Cornish hens, Boeuf Bordelaise and veal fillets in cream. Countless dishes of savory vegetables and relishes accompanied each course along with a sparkling Burgundy and white Bordeaux. The dessert course was replete with crème tarts, jellies, fresh fruits, fragrant cheeses and a superb meringue glacée.

It was Nicole's good fortune to have the Marquis de Crécy seated on her right and Charles Humphrey on her left. Between them she was able to conduct a pleasant conversation on the entertainments to be found in a Paris recently emerged from the shadows of war.

The Marquis questioned Nicole about the social diversions of Paris while dessert was being served.

"I have not had much opportunity to avail myself of Parisian entertainments, *Monsieur le Marquis*. As you know, I have spent most of my youth in the village of Beauvais where life is quite simple."

"Ah, then you have many delights in store for you."

"I am looking forward to the entertainments of the Parisian *beau monde* with much anticipation."

"Oh I say, Miss Harcourt," broke in Charles Humphrey. "I had the good fortune of hearing la Catalani at the Somerset soirée the other evening. What a voice. That is a treat you must give yourself one of these days."

"I do enjoy the music of the opera greatly, Mr. Humphrey, but I confess that my first love has always been the ballet." Nicole looked defiantly down the table into the shocked eyes of Lady Eleanore.

"Nicole, dear child," Lady Eleanore spoke hastily. "Perhaps you would enjoy some of this *mousse au chocolate*. I do not believe you have tasted it yet."

"You are very kind, Cousin Eleanore, but I could not swallow another morsel of this divine assortment," Nicole replied sweetly and turned back to the Marquis. *"Monsieur le Marquis . . ."*

"You must cease this formality, child. I am, after all, a member of the family, however distant. Please call me Uncle Maurice like everyone else."

"Very well . . . Uncle Maurice," she smiled shyly. "Do you ever attend the ballet?" She returned to the forbidden topic, unable to resist the temptation to taunt Lady Eleanore.

"Frequently, *ma chère*. You must allow me to escort you to a performance of the Opéra de Paris in the near future. They have a new company recently formed that does a very creditable job."

"The Opéra de Paris! Why that is the same company my . . ."

"Ladies," Lady Eleanore rose from the table almost knocking over her chair and diverting attention from Nicole. "I believe it is time we left the gentlemen to their port." And without further pause she led the ladies from the dining room into the drawing room. She made certain that Nicole was given no further opportunity to pursue the subject of the ballet. For that evening, at least, Lady Eleanore held sway and squelched the imp of mischief that Nicole had foolishly courted at dinner.

Chapter III

During wedding preparations an unexpected ally for Nicole arrived at the Hotel Belmontaine. Peregrine Harcourt, the Viscount's younger brother and family scapegrace, barged in on a morning conference. Since he had just arrived on the Continent, Lady Eleanore had no advance warning and was not altogether pleased at this appearance.

"Perry! Good gracious, what *are* you doing here?"

"Just had to come, mother dear." He grinned mischievously. "This is where all the excitement is." He bent to kiss his mother's cheek. "Couldn't stay away, now could I, if Val is going to be hog-tied?"

"Don't be vulgar," his mother retorted impatiently. Turning to Nicole she announced, "You two have never met. Nicole, my younger son, Perry. Perry, your cousin Nicole."

"So this is my future sister-in-law! What a lucky dog Val is." He smiled broadly and bowed over Nicole's hand.

"Perry," his mother snapped. "Do you always have to make a display of yourself?"

"But mother, I am only admiring true beauty. Ain't we lucky to have her a member of the family?" He winked at Nicole.

Nicole found his boyish charm irresistible.

Lady Eleanore ignored his question and commanded, "Sit down, and stop this foolish posturing. Have you been thrown out of school again?"

"Not exactly."

"And *what,* pray, is that supposed to mean?"

"I was sent down for the remainder of this term."

"Oh, Perry, Perry, whatever am I to do with you?"

"Don't fret yourself, mama. I can take care of myself."

"If only the Viscount were here," Lady Eleanore moaned.

"Well he ain't. Besides, Val will be too busy with his own life to worry about mine. Don't you agree, cousin Nicole?"

"I am sure he will always have time for the family."

"She is not only beautiful but a diplomat as well. I bet old Cecily's eating her heart out."

"That will be enough from you, sir! You have brought on one of my headaches," Lady Eleanore complained.

"I am sorry, mama." He did not sound very contrite to Nicole. "Can I get you something?"

"No, no. I shall just retire to my room for a while. You two have a nice chat, and I will send Cecily down to you."

Perry closed the door behind his mother. "I hope you

have not let mama upset you unduly. She can be a bit high in the stirrups at times, but eventually she comes around. However," he whispered conspiratorially and came to sit beside Nicole, "Cecily is a different matter. That little viper has venom in her bite."

Nicole was delighted by his candor, and a quick sympathy was established between them.

"Now quickly before Cecily joins us, let me make arrangements to take you riding in the park tomorrow."

"That would be lovely." Nicole smiled happily.

And true to his word, Perry took her riding; nevertheless, after a few whirlwind visits to Belmontaine, he was not to be seen most days. The young Harcourt kept rooms with friends in a less affluent section of Paris, where the *bonhomie* was more to his liking and his movements under less surveillance. It was not to subject himself to days of duty under mama's watchful eye that he had crossed the Channel, but to plunder the wicked delights of a Paris now wide open to the young and the reckless.

The days were too busy for Nicole to miss Perry. There were innumerable trips to the dressmakers for fittings and social events in the evenings that she was expected to attend. And always present was the strain of avoiding verbal battle with Lady Eleanore. Fortunately the necessity for meek acquiescence came to an unexpected pause when Lady Eleanore accepted an invitation for a weekend in the country with her friends, the Wexfords.

"I cannot understand your reluctance to join us this weekend, Nicole," Lady Eleanore was saying with some asperity.

"It is just that I am fatigued to death and would enjoy a quiet weekend. I have had so little time to myself."

"But what shall my friends think?"

Nicole perceived that actually Lady Eleanore was tempted to be free of her.

"I think my lady has forgotten Madame DuPlessis is to begin work tomorrow on Nicole's headdress for the wedding," Madame Lafitte reminded.

Nicole turned a relieved face to her friend. "You are absolutely right, Fifi."

"So," Lady Eleanore fumed, not liking to have the initiative taken away from her. "It will be as you wish, Nicole. But I will make the final decision on all wedding apparel."

"I am perfectly capable of choosing an appropriate headdress."

"Are you, Nicole?" It was Cecily who as usual grasped every opportunity to sneer. "How many weddings of the *beau monde* have *you* attended lately?"

"Cecily, that will be *quite* enough." Lady Eleanore intervened before insults could be exchanged. "Nicole will have her quiet weekend. I dare say it will do us all some good to be apart for a time. We shall return Sunday evening. Until then, Madame Lafitte, I leave you in charge."

"*Oui,* my lady. Nicole is a good girl. She will be no trouble."

It was late Friday afternoon when Nicole and Madame Lafitte returned from the DuPlessis establishment and Nicole impulsively hugged Madame Lafitte. "Oh, Fifi, a whole weekend free from sour faces and unkind words! I could kiss you for remembering Madame DuPlessis." She whirled happily about the room.

"*Ma foi,* I too feel the happiness. It is a weight lifted, *n'est-ce pas?*"

"Now, what shall we do first?"

Madame Lafitte turned from the window. "Me, I shall rest. But you, I think, already have a visitor. It is the brother of your betrothed."

"Perry? What perfect timing." Blowing Madame Lafitte a kiss, she hurried from the room.

Perry persuaded Nicole to go riding with him even though it was a cold blustery day, and they rode along the Champs Elysées toward the Tuileries Gardens. The brisk November weather had driven most people indoors and the park and gardens were nearly empty. Nicole stared at the palace that had once housed Louis XVI and Marie Antoinette and still later the Emperor Napoleon. Today, however, British uniforms were guarding the building deserted by the French nobility.

It had been a difficult time for Nicole in this country, mad for Napoleon Bonaparte and his war against England. Her half-English nationality had plagued her often enough during those years at St. Agnes's private school for girls where she was sometimes referred to as "the English spy." But her earlier childhood in England had not been much better with the constant moving about and bitter quarreling between her parents. Even later as a young woman, her mother's self-pity and complaints against fate and the Harcourts had played havoc with Nicole's peace of mind. Would she ever find contentment, Nicole wondered—especially at the hands of a "Harcourt"?

"Cousin Nicole," Perry chided. "I have been trying to attract your attention for the last five minutes."

"I am sorry, Perry. What is it?"

"I wondered if you wished to take a brief stroll through the gardens."

"Yes, I would like that very much." As they alighted from their carriage Nicole noted, "We seem to be the only adventuresome souls about today. Oh look, there are still a few valiant roses holding on."

"You ain't going to turn sentimental on me, are you?" Perry teased. "I didn't think you were the type."

"Heavens no." She bent to smell the roses.

"I say, look who's coming. If this don't beat all."

Nicole looked up to see Perry slapping a tall, slim gentleman on the back.

"Well, well, Perry. What brings you to Paris at this time of the year?" The gentleman regarded Perry with a touch of humor in his fine grey eyes.

"Come to see my brother get hitched, naturally."

"So the rumors are true."

"Cousin Nicole, please forgive my manners. This is Gordon Danforth, a friend of Val's."

"I am honored, ma'am." Mr. Danforth bowed and removed his hat from his head. The wind whipped at his neat brown hair.

"This is Val's future bride, Gordon, Miss Harcourt."

"Then I am twice honored."

"I am happy to meet you, Mr. Danforth. Are you in Paris for long?" She surveyed the rather austere looking young man before her, guessing his age to be somewhere around thirty.

"That is difficult to say, ma'am. I am with the diplomatic corps and orders can change overnight." He smiled warmly. "And may I offer my best wishes."

"Why yes, of course," she smiled but with some constraint.

"Where are you staying, Perry?" Danforth turned to her escort.

"Oh, around. I have a friend across the river," Perry answered vaguely. "But most days you can find me at the Hotel Belmontaine where Nicole and my mother are staying."

"If I may, Miss Harcourt, I shall give myself the pleasure of calling one afternoon this week to pay my respects to you and Lady Ardsmore."

"I am sure Lady Ardsmore will be as delighted as I to receive you," Nicole replied courteously.

"Then I shall see you both soon." He tipped his hat once more before moving on.

"Perry!" Nicole stormed as they turned back to their carriage. "I thought you understood that matters have not been completely settled between your brother and me."

"Oh, sure, I understand."

"Then why did you blurt out about the marriage?"

"But Nicole, all the wedding preparations are going on and besides," he hesitated then plunged on, "I don't see you gainsaying Val. I never knew a woman yet who could."

"Oh really!" She froze with indignation.

"Please don't be angry with me," Perry begged. When Nicole did not answer he added, "You and Val are going to make a smashing couple. I know it." He clasped her hand.

"Do—do you really think so, Perry?" she asked hopefully.

"Sure I do. Wait until you meet him. Val is terrific, even if I say so myself. I can't wait until he sets eyes on you. Is he in for a surprise!"

That evening Nicole and Madame Lafitte had an early supper followed by a cozy chat before the fire in the drawing room.

"It is like old times, Fifi. Just you and me."

"*Oui,* only it can never be the same again. I think I am developing a permanent headache."

"Oh Fifi." Nicole laughed and hugged her.

"You laugh, but it is true. Each evening I crawl into

bed shaking with tension. I worry about you, *mon petit chou.*"

"Fifi, why? I am perfectly capable of taking care of myself."

"This is what I pray each night."

"Dear, dear, Fifi, do not fret so." She paused, regarding her friend. "Come, I have an idea. Tonight I shall tuck you in."

"Non, non, chérie . . ."

"Mais oui, I insist. You shall have a cup of chocolate before retiring, as we used to do. And I shall borrow a few drops of Lady Eleanore's laudanum to ensure you a good night's rest."

"But it is I who must see to you."

"You always have, but tonight you shall let me indulge you. Please Fifi."

"You are a sweet child, Nicole."

"And you are my dear friend. Come along, Fifi. I shall order the chocolate."

With a helpless little gesture, Madame Lafitte gave in to Nicole.

Some time later Nicole left her old friend drowsing comfortably in bed. Once in her own room, Nicole dismissed her maid and changed into her night clothes. Then she sat before her dressing table administering the required hundred strokes to her lustrous black hair before retiring for the night.

The tranquility of the evening was suddenly interrupted by a muffled pounding at the front door. There followed an incoherent clamor of voices and then a hasty knocking at Nicole's bedroom door. She opened it to be confronted by a much agitated servant in nightdress informing her that his lordship, Viscount Ardsmore, had arrived and was insisting upon an audience with the mistress immediately. The shock of this news nearly overcame Nicole. She turned pale with fright but answered the servant with as much calm as she could muster.

"Please inform his lordship that I have retired for the evening and will be happy to receive him tomorrow morning at his convenience."

Within moments a roar from below assailed her startled ears. "At my convenience, is it? NOW is my convenience!" The words were followed by a pounding on the stairs, and suddenly he appeared in her doorway. VALENTIN. His unruly blond hair was tumbling over his forehead and his eyes were blazing with cold blue fire.

Nicole stood frozen in the center of the room, her violet eyes dark stains of fear and her mouth trembling with unspoken words. She clutched at the wrapper covering her quivering body as the sight of Valentin blazed itself into her consciousness. He was more awesome in reality than her dreams could ever imagine. His powerful figure loomed arrogantly before her, seeming to fill the room with his vibrant presence as an undisguised masculinity comprised of a lithe animal grace and reckless daring assaulted her reeling senses. The chiseled angles of his lean face were thrown into prominence by the flickering candlelight, and his firm mouth was curved in a derisive grin.

Valentin remained standing in the doorway, surveying the quaking Nicole with insolent disdain. His cape and Hessians were dirty and mud-spattered. His whole attire gave evidence of much hard travel and wear, and yet he looked every inch the magnificent god of war that he was. At last he stepped forward and swept Nicole an elegant bow.

"Lord Ardsmore, special aide to the Duke of Wellington, at your service, mademoiselle."

"You cannot come in here," Nicole whispered trying to gather her scattered wits.

"It would seem I already *am* in here, ma'am."

"Why do you intrude yourself at such an untimely hour, sir?"

"Because I am just now arrived, ma'am."

"Could you not wait till the morning?" Nicole was beginning to recover from the shock of his unexpected arrival.

Valentin raised his eyebrows in mock question and replied with ill-concealed anger, "But I was given to understand that you *insisted* upon my presence, ma'am."

"Not so . . . so . . ."

"Yes?"

"So unexpectedly. This is quite improper."

"But what did you expect from a 'fortune-hunting rake', my dear?" Nicole's former rash words were flung in her face with quiet contempt. "If I understand my mother correctly, it seems your tender French sensibilities have been distressed by the mercenary proclivities of your English relations."

"You forget that I am half English myself, sir."

"The better half, I hope."

"What do you mean by that?" Nicole was stung into anger by thoughts of insult to her mother.

"I merely refer to the conflict of loyalties that might arise considering the recent hostilities between our countries."

"I do not believe you, and I wish you to leave my room at once," Nicole demanded haughtily, her eyes blazing with indignation.

Valentin regarded her coolly before replying. "A little firebrand, eh? Nothing I like better than a show of spirit." He started toward Nicole.

She backed from him thrusting out a hand as if to ward him off, but he flung off his cape and grabbed for the outstretched hand and pulled her toward him.

"What are you doing?" Nicole was having difficulty breathing.

"Getting acquainted, my dear, as you so charmingly requested of my mother."

"This is neither the time nor the place." Nicole could barely speak.

"I beg to differ. This is the *only* time and the *only* place for acquaintance such as I intend to make of you."

"What . . . what do you mean?"

"What do you think I mean?"

"You would not dare!"

"Oh, but I would dare. What better way have I to settle matters and ensure our forthcoming nuptials? I mean to force your hand, my dear."

"I would never marry you then, you beast," she gasped in horror; her bright eyes had turned the color of crushed violets and glistened with unshed tears.

He lessened his hold on Nicole, studying her upturned face as if really seeing her for the first time. The beauty of her delicately molded features flushed by the intensity of strong emotions arrested his attention. Her soft, full lips were parted slightly as she breathed in shallow gasps. Valentin stared into her fear-darkened eyes, noting their violet depths, and felt his purpose falter. Her wrapper had fallen open revealing an expanse of heaving ivory bosom. His eyes traveled the length of her white-clad form and back to her face. She did not flinch from his gaze, but stood before him stiff with pride despite her inner fears. His expression softened as he released his hold, then took the wrapper with both hands and closed it around her, taking her hand and placing it at her breast to hold it closed.

"You must forgive me, my dear . . . if you can find it in you. I had mistaken the situation. I shall wait on you in the morning, with all the propriety and remorse your person requires." He smiled tenderly and turned to retrieve his cape.

Unconsciously, Nicole began rubbing the wrist that he had held in his steel grip, too much overcome by his sudden shift in behavior to think what to say. Her fear had dissolved in that one sweet smile. He came toward her again and took the wrist she was rubbing and examined the angry red marks on it. "It seems I have hurt you." He raised the wrist and placed a lingering kiss on the bruised flesh. Nicole watched him wonderingly, her eyes soft and tender.

"It is nothing."

"Will you forgive me?" he asked softly.

"Of course," Nicole replied. He lifted a lock of her unbound hair, kissed it and left the room, leaving a bewildered and bewitched Nicole.

True to his word, the Viscount appeared promptly at ten the next morning, all propriety and contrition. Nicole was stricken with indecision wondering how she should conduct herself after his appalling performance of the night before. His behavior had been scandalous in the extreme, and yet tender too. Nevertheless Valentin was actually here, seeking to woo her despite the strong overtones of seduction and conquest. She decided to conduct the interview with Madame Lafitte in obvious attendance.

The ladies entered the drawing room together. Nicole caught her breath sharply at the disturbing sight of Valentin's elegantly clad form standing straight and confident before the fireplace. That the Viscount also caught his breath at the sight of Nicole she did not discern. He appeared awesomely powerful and self-assured to her inexperienced eyes. The Viscount came forward with great dignity and bowed solemnly over her hand.

"Your servant, ma'am." As he bowed, he bestowed a

disarming smile upon the chaperone and immediately won himself an ally. Madame Lafitte discreetly betook herself to a corner and seated herself unobtrusively.

"I trust you enjoyed an untroubled rest after last night's unfortunate episode." The Viscount was not one to dodge an issue. Nicole's face colored. Valentin was studying her with a look of apparent concern on his handsome face.

"I slept very well, thank you, my lord. May I offer you some refreshments? A glass of wine, perhaps?" She wished desperately to divert him from the subject of last night.

"Not at the moment."

"Shall I ring for . . ."

"Forget the amenities, Cousin Nicole. I have a few comments to make regarding last night." He sounded stern, as if he were about to read her a lecture. "First, I must offer my profound apologies for behavior unbecoming a gentleman and more importantly, for subjecting you, my future wife, to such indignities."

"Please, speak no more of it. It is past and forgotten," Nicole implored. Besides, he was ahead of her in his assumption that the marriage matter was all settled.

"But I cannot pass over it lightly. It is of deep concern to me that you have no male protector to demand satisfaction of me."

Nicole looked up in startled surprise. "But, my lord, it is yourself against whom you are seeking satisfaction. If I am willing to overlook what . . ."

"That is precisely the matter," the Viscount interrupted her impatiently. "It is not a matter for you to overlook."

The absurdity of the situation struck Nicole forcefully, and she began to laugh a little hysterically.

The Viscount stiffened visibly. "My dear girl, I fail to see . . ."

"But, my lord, it is over," she interrupted him, striving to interject a note of lightness into his heavy-handed interview.

Valentin did not respond to her effort. "Last night I believed I had grievously offended the innocence of a girl of gentle breeding," he claimed in tones of deadly quiet.

There was a sudden stillness before Nicole replied. "And today?"

"Today, I wonder if my original approach would not have proven more suitable."

There was an audible gasp from Madame Lafitte.

"How dare you!" Nicole retorted, outraged.

"Do you still ask me how I dare?" he returned cuttingly.

"You insufferable . . ."

"Fortune hunter?"

"Get out!" Nicole demanded.

"You forget, my dear, I have as much right as you to be here."

"We are not married yet."

"But we will be."

"Never."

"In less than three weeks."

"You will have to shoot me first."

"Oh no. I have infinitely better plans for you." His eyes roved over her insultingly.

Nicole turned on her heel to flee the room, but the Viscount caught hold of her arm and jerked her roughly to him. Their eyes blazed at each other, and then he deliberately clamped his mouth to hers while tangling his hands in her hair. Her gleaming tresses tumbled from the pins that fastened them. There was a flutter of distress from the distant corner, but Valentin held Nicole's head captive, and she could not move as his ardor increased. A shocked squeal of alarm from Madame Lafitte stopped him from further transgressions and he dropped his hands from Nicole.

"And now there will be no further question of the marriage taking place. Remember, my dear, in a little while you will be mine." And he was gone.

Nicole pressed trembling hands to her flaming cheeks as Madame Lafitté came running to her side.

"Mon Dieu, mon Dieu. Quel sauvage! Mais si beau, si magnifique," the little lady exclaimed, torn between outrage and admiration.

"Yes, he is rather a beautiful savage, isn't he?" Nicole too was torn between outrage and admiration.

"What is to become of you and this *Anglais,* I tremble to think. Nicole, *mon enfant,* never did I dream to witness such a scene before my eyes. Have a care, *chérie,* this affair with your English relatives will come out all wrong if you do not resolve the contention between you." Madame Lafitte's prediction struck fear in Nicole's heart, as if she already recognized its truth. She had already recognized the power of his kiss . . .

Chapter IV

Lady Eleanore and Cecily returned late Sunday night after Nicole and Madame Lafitte had retired. The following morning Nicole hurried downstairs toward the breakfast room, anxiously wondering what Lady Eleanore's reaction to the news of the Viscount's arrival would be. Nicole became aware of conversation emanating from the room beyond, and she hesitated at the threshold upon hearing Valentin's name mentioned.

"So Ardsmore is here," Lady Eleanore was saying as she folded the note her son had left for her.

"Here!" Cecily squealed. "Oh how wonderful!"

"Cecily, remember his *reason* for being here."

"Is it really settled then? Is Val truly going to marry that . . . that . . . person?" Cecily's voice quivered as if on the verge of tears.

"If I am to believe this note, Valentin has already spoken to Nicole and has settled the matter to his satisfaction."

Nicole bristled with indignation and almost stepped forth but hesitated once more as Cecily continued her lament.

"I could cry for Val. Imagine being stuck with that odious creature."

"Cecily, it is not your place to speak so. She is to be my son's wife. I know what we both had hoped, my dear. But since it cannot be, I think you must accept John Tilford. It will be arranged when we return to England."

"But I do not wish to marry John!"

"Of course you do!" commanded Lady Eleanore in exasperation. "Will you not help me make the best of this difficult situation?"

Before Cecily had time to reply, Nicole entered the room.

"Ah, Nicole," Lady Eleanore cooed. "We were just talking about you."

"So I heard!" Nicole snapped, glaring from one woman to the other.

"Please Nicole, you must not take offense. Cecily has known my son all her life . . ."

"Yes, and it seems she had plans for him too."

"And why shouldn't I?" Cecily asked testily. "He would have been mine if it had not been for that old interfering woman Aunt Sophie. I always loved Val and I always will and . . . and I shall always hate you. Do you hear me—hate you! What right do you have to him, you . . . nobody." Cecily burst into tears and fled from the room.

Both women were silent for some moments before Lady Eleanore recovered and soothed, "It was *most* unfortunate that Cecily forgot herself, but," she sighed, "I suppose I should have expected it. She has loved him for so long. I should not have brought her with me."

Nicole was no longer angry with Cecily. She understood what it meant to love Valentin. Perhaps she was wrong to come between lovers.

"Your ladyship." Violet eyes met solemn grey eyes. "Does the Viscount reciprocate Cecily's feelings?"

"Good heavens, girl, what are you thinking? My son has always treated Cecily with the respect due a young lady living under my protection."

"But . . . if he loves her," she faltered. "It is still not too late to cancel the wedding."

"Cancel the wedding! Don't be absurd. *Naturally,* I had always hoped for a match between the two of them. But Ardsmore has never showed anything but brotherly regard for Cecily."

Nicole breathed a sigh of relief.

"Besides, we are *quite* aware of what has to be done."

"Oh yes, I almost forgot the monetary situation which will benefit us all."

"That subject is closed," Lady Eleanore replied with a finality that brooked no contradiction.

Attending to pressing business on behalf of the Duke of Wellington, the Viscount did not make an appearance at the Hotel Belmontaine for some time. Nicole had little time to consider his lack of courtship while her days were filled with wedding preparations—a whirlwind of faces, voices and duties. Besides the hours spent in fittings and social affairs, there were endless consultations with a dizzying array of merchants, cooks, servants, florists, bakers and caterers, all clamoring for their share of the monies flowing lavishly from the Hotel Belmontaine.

Nicole was sleeping poorly and eating almost nothing as the approaching wedding loomed closer. She began to wonder where the Viscount was and could not shake a sense of foreboding. Why did he keep away? Buried deep beneath the surface stress of wedding preparations was a nameless fear of her marriage to Valentin. What kind of husband would he make? And more importantly, what kind of wife would she make for him?

The real fear she could not find the words to express was her fear of Valentin's demanding masculinity. The picture of him the night he had stormed into her bedroom lay buried beneath all other thoughts. It lay waiting like forbidden fruit to tempt her to dark desires she was unaware she possessed.

She would collapse into bed at night and give herself over to the ministrations of Madame Lafitte, willing herself into an oblivion of sleep that was fitful and insufficient. This state of affairs could not last. Valentin had to make an appearance sooner or later, and when he came, Nicole was unprepared for him.

On a wintry morning shortly before the wedding, Nicole heard the clatter of horses' hooves in the courtyard below and suddenly she was clutched by an unreasoning fear. Her head was splitting from the incessant demands made on her diminishing energies, and she felt unable to cope. She could not face him!

Voices in the corridor were coming nearer and she heard her name called, but was unable to respond, awaiting her inevitable discovery. At last there was a knock on the door, and the sound snapped her to her senses even though her nerves were still strung tight.

The door opened and Lady Eleanore entered accompanied by the Viscount, resplendent in his military garb.

"Nicole, look who has *finally* made an appearance! Naughty boy, staying away all this time." Lady Eleanore took her son's arm possessively and drew him a step toward Nicole.

"It could not be helped, ma'am."

Nicole forced herself to meet Valentin's eyes. There was no mockery in his steady gaze when he took Nicole's frozen hand in his, smiled brilliantly and kissed it.

"You are looking very beautiful, my dear. That shade of blue suits you admirably."

Nicole realized he was trying to put her at her ease, and she returned his smile and curtsied. "We had looked for you sooner—"

The door flew open cutting off Nicole in mid-sentence.

"Oh Val! I did not know you had arrived." Cecily stood tall and elegant in the doorway before crossing to him and offering her cheek.

"Cecily," he smiled kissing her lightly. "Are you enjoying your stay in Paris?"

"I dare say it shall improve while you are here." She smiled sweetly in return.

"I am sorry to disappoint you, my dear, but I shan't be about much."

"Why?" she paused and turned her glittering eyes onto Nicole. "Oh, you mean the honeymoon. But you won't be gone that long. You don't want to miss all the excitement of Christmas in Paris, do you?" She clung to his arm looking up beseechingly at him.

"This is not the time to be discussing Christmas, Cecily," Lady Eleanore suggested. "Madame Dupré has prepared a cold luncheon. I am sure my son must be famished."

In the dining room where a light collation of cold chicken and fruit salad was being served, the Viscount was brought up to date on the wedding plans. It had been decided that the ceremony would be performed at noon at the embassy. Valentin informed them that Wellington would not be able to attend since state affairs called him elsewhere. They also discussed the reception which would be held at the Hotel Belmontaine for those members of English society presently residing in Paris.

The Viscount commented little, accepting his mother's lead in all matters of social proprieties. However, when Lady Eleanore mentioned the honeymoon, he interrupted her.

"I think you had best leave that to me, ma'am," he drawled.

"Very well, Ardsmore. I suppose you and Nicole have matters you wish to discuss privately. Come, Cecily. We shall see you later my dears."

Reluctantly, Cecily followed in the wake of Lady Eleanore.

Valentin and Nicole remained seated at the table in silence a few moments. Finally he asked, "Shall we take a walk in the conservatory, Nicole?"

"As you wish, my lord."

He offered his arm and led her down the hall to the conservatory in the south wing of the house where the winter sunlight filtered softly through the glass onto the hanging ferns and pots of trailing fuchsias overhead. There was a marble bench surrounded by hot-house roses toward which the Viscount guided Nicole who shivered involuntarily as Valentin drew her shawl solicitously about her shoulders. Drawing her down on the bench beside him he kept his arm about her while she looked up at him for the first time and their eyes met in silent communication. Nicole was spellbound by his hypnotic blue gaze and feeling his breath on her cheek, she wished him to kiss her.

"Nicole," he whispered. Then almost abruptly he moved away from her and stood up leaning against a pillar. "You shouldn't look at a man that way, Nicole. No telling what could happen." He folded his arms across his chest.

"What way, my lord?"

52

"Never mind. I will tell you after we are married." He smiled mysteriously and her cheeks grew pink. "So let us talk about you and me and become acquainted with one another."

"As you wish, my lord."

Valentin gave a quick laugh and sat beside her taking her hand. "You mustn't keep calling me 'my lord' if we are to be husband and wife, must you?"

"No, I suppose not."

"Good." He smiled comfortably. "Now how long ago was it that we last met . . . the other evening notwithstanding."

"It was eleven years ago. The day of my father's funeral, my lor—I mean—"

"Yes? Go ahead—it's not so difficult to say my name, is it, Nicole?"

"Of course not . . . Valentin."

He regarded her warmly. "Enchanting."

Disconcerted by his gaze, Nicole spoke hastily. "I was thirteen at the time and you called me 'that ballet dancer's daughter'."

"Oh Lord," he chuckled. "You must forgive a young man his folly, Nicole; I was only nineteen at the time myself." He paused, looking at her intently. "Who would have thought eleven years would bring such changes."

"You mean in our positions?"

"That among other things."

"What other things?" she questioned innocently.

He raised his eyebrows mockingly. "The family fortunes, for one."

"Is it true that much of it was gambled away?"

"More or less. Aunt Sophie's fortune is rather timely. The inheritance solves a lot of tiresome problems."

His complacency annoyed Nicole unreasonably. "I must say you don't sound very contrite, my lord."

53

"Should I?" There was a warning gleam in his eye.

"Shouldn't you?"

Tension sparked between them as he regarded her silently. "Perhaps so," he conceded reluctantly. "But gambling is one of the Harcourt traits, as you well know," he replied pointedly.

"One I am happy to say I did not inherit," she answered tartly.

"But I recall your father indulged himself heavily."

"Are you criticizing my father?" Nicole bristled.

"Not at all. We Harcourts have all indulged our whims, and your father was no exception. Good Lord, Nicole, you must see that. He even . . ." He stopped abruptly.

"Go ahead. Say it. Even to the wife he chose!"

"Now I wasn't going to say that."

"Yes you were." She jumped up from the bench.

"Good God, don't fly into a rage." He pulled her down beside him. "It seems you have the Harcourt temper, my dear." Valentin smiled placatingly.

Nicole shuddered, attempting to control herself. They were going to quarrel again. She could feel it.

"If you will excuse me, my lord."

"No, I will not, Nicole. We are going to be married soon, and we must come to an understanding."

"I am already resigned to my fate," she replied foolishly.

"Well, that's just fine. So I'm your fate, am I? Like some bitter pill? I'm too much of a Harcourt to resign myself to fate. And furthermore, I do not relish insults from anyone, especially my future wife," he snapped.

"I—I did not mean to insult you."

"Yes you did, now admit it."

"No . . . I mean . . . it was not intentional . . ."

"Well, that at least is a start. Perhaps I will be able to change your mind in time about resigning yourself to fate." He lifted her chin with his finger and forced her to look into his penetrating blue eyes while he stroked her chin with his thumb. Once again Nicole felt drawn to him as he lowered his head to hers.

"My lord." It was Pierre. "Excuse me, but there are some gentlemen waiting to see you. They say it is important."

The Viscount swore to himself. "Very well, Pierre. I shall be along directly." He stood up. "It seems I am needed elsewhere, so I will take my leave of you now, Nicole." He kissed her hand perfunctorily and left.

Nicole sat staring disconsolately after his departing figure. She had wanted him to kiss her. How could he just walk out in such a cavalier manner, leaving her hanging mid-way between fear and desire? It was humiliating to realize that he could manipulate her feelings so easily. She struggled with herself for several minutes before regaining her composure and retracing her steps down the hallway. The sound of agitated voices reached her from the open library door.

"Hell and damnation, Danforth. Couldn't you have done something to ward off this young fool?"

"I am afraid not, Ardsmore. Your brother had no choice but to challenge him to a duel."

"Of all the blundering maneuvers . . ."

" 'Pon my soul, Val. What was I to do? Stand around and let him insult the family about that ballet dancer?"

"Quiet!" The Viscount warned, closing the library door and shutting off the sound of their voices.

Ballet dancer! Those words reverberated sickeningly in Nicole's brain. Did they refer to her mother? She clenched her hands convulsively to her sides. Who else could they mean? It must be her mother. Cheeks flaming with humiliation and rage, she crossed the hallway and fled to her room where she paced the floor restlessly. Was she never to be free of her mother's past? Her mind was a chaotic turmoil as she tried to recall just what she had heard. What was that about a duel? Was Perry to fight a duel? Oh, she could not stand this half-knowing. She must have the complete truth. She would seek out the Viscount now and confront him. But first she must calm herself. Valentin must be made to speak honestly with her, and this matter of her mother must be settled once and for all.

She reached the Viscount just as he was seeing Perry and Danforth out the door.

"My lord, I must speak to you."

He turned to her, a brief frown creasing his features as he ushered her silently into a small salon and closed the door firmly behind them.

"What is it you wish to say, Nicole?"

"I must be frank with you, my lord." She paused searching for the appropriate words. "I overheard part of the conversation between you and your brother . . ."

"That is unfortunate."

Ignoring his remark, she continued. "And I . . . I think it concerned my mother, did it not?"

"Nicole, I feel it would be best if this matter were not discussed between us at this time."

"But there was talk of a duel, was there not?" she persisted.

"Nicole . . ."

"But Perry would be foolish to acknowledge the intended insult."

"My sentiments exactly—except that the young fool called him out."

"You . . . you must stop him!"

"I quite agree with you."

"But what will you do?"

"My dear Nicole, that is *my* business."

"And mine."

"No! I do not think so. I shall handle the situation. It need not concern you further."

"But . . ."

"Please let me handle the affairs of this family. I especially do not want my mother to hear of this."

"Surely you can tell me what you intend doing."

"No, I will not . . . and furthermore, in the future you will oblige me by having confidence in my judgment."

"How can I?" She hesitated before going on. "You must be the first to admit that the Harcourts are not known for prudent judgment."

"*Touché,*" he laughed scornfully. "But you will have to trust me. After all, I am to be your husband. Perhaps this leopard can change his spots. Now you will have to excuse me. I have a most pressing appointment."

Nicole watched in frustration as her fiancé walked out the door.

Chapter V

According to their arrangement Danforth met the Viscount at the *Chat Noir* late in the afternoon because it was at this particular gaming hell that Lord Crawley spent most of his time since his arrival in Paris. Valentin and Gordon mounted the stairs to the second floor and unobtrusively entered the gaming rooms; the Viscount noted with satisfaction that few players were as yet in evidence. A scant handful were seated at round tables where they were quietly engrossed in faro or deep basset, and the muffled sounds echoing from the next room indicated that the roulette tables were also in use. However, it was the card table at the far end of the room that commanded the Viscount's attention. Seated at this table was the imposing figure of Lord Joseph Crawley, Valentin's target for the evening. Crawley was a swarthy man with heavy features that bore a look of perpetual cynicism but not un-attractive withal.

Nodding to various acquaintances and passing a comment with one or two others, Gordon and Valentin walked across the room until they reached the game being played by Crawley and his three comrades. Noticing the glazed look in the gambler's dark eyes, Danforth issued a quiet warning to Valentin. "Careful, Crawley's been drinking." To which Valentin remarked, "All the more fitting."

When the play was momentarily broken by one of the players' withdrawal from the game, the Viscount immediately assumed the vacated chair at the table.

"If you don't mind?" Valentin smiled smoothly.

"Ardsmore." Crawley eyed the Viscount suspiciously. "I didn't think your game was faro."

"My skill has never been questioned, but if you have some objection . . ." He left the remark unfinished.

"None! None!" Crawley claimed through tight lips. "The stakes are high, however," he taunted.

"That suits me." Valentin leaned back in his chair and reached for his money pouch.

"Pound points then?" Crawley sneered, his hard eyes daring the Viscount to accept.

Valentin nodded curtly as Crawley broke a pack of cards. The waiter poured fresh brandy into the glasses and play was resumed.

Valentin had observed his opponent at play several times before. He knew him to be a showy player who often took risks; he himself was a cool but daring game-ster. Within the hour it was apparent that luck was running in Crawley's favor, although Valentin had been able to hold his own. Toward early evening the other players began dropping out, claiming engagements elsewhere until only the Viscount and his antagonist were left.

Valentin shuffled the cards, the sapphire on his small finger flashing in the glowing candlelight. Crawley called for a refill of brandy and studied the contents of his glass. Then gulping a mouthful, he turned his full attention to the Viscount. Some decision seemed pending.

"Well, Ardsmore, it is just you and me now." A meaningful sneer had crept into his voice.

"As it was meant to be." The Viscount's rejoinder was low and ominous.

"Do you think you can afford to continue, my lord Ardsmore?" He scooped up the cards with a slight flourish.

"I'll manage, Crawley." Valentin's eyes never left Crawley's face.

"Will you? And on what resources? Or do you play with your future bride's prospects in mind?"

Finally the opening had come. "Perhaps you would like to explain yourself, Crawley," Valentin questioned quietly.

"I merely remark on your coming nuptials," he replied smugly.

"As you did yesterday for my brother's benefit?"

"Your brother is an impudent cub who interfered in a private conversation."

"And you are an unprincipled scoundrel for accepting the challenge of a mere boy!"

Crawley pushed back his chair, knocking it to the floor as he jumped up. "No one calls me names!" he hissed.

"I just did. You are a coward as well as a scoundrel," Valentin taunted deliberately.

"Coward? Scoundrel?" Crawley ejaculated. "You'll pay with your life for those words!"

Picking up his glass, Crawley dashed the contents into

61

Valentin's face. There was an audible gasp from the few remaining occupants of the salon. But the Viscount only smiled contemptuously as he wiped the liquid from his face.

"I believe the choice of time and weapons is mine," he spoke drily.

"It is!" Crawley spat at him.

"Then tonight. The Field House at ten, with swords."

"Tonight? Impossible. I am meeting your brother in the morning."

"Either accept or be known for the coward you are."

"Ah, so that's your game? Very well, Ardsmore. I'll finish you tonight and your brother in the morning. You think you've outfoxed me, but you haven't. I've waited for this a long time," he growled angrily.

"So have I." Valentin's voice was cold with contempt.

Danforth stepped between them, fearing the blazing hatred would engulf them on the spot. "Gentlemen, until tonight." Danforth managed to get Valentin across the room and down the stairs to the foyer.

"You've accomplished the first part of your plan," he murmured as they donned their greatcoats and walked out of the *Chat Noir*.

Valentin nodded, still caught in a fever of hatred. However, once outside in the evening air his anger cooled, and he spoke matter-of-factly.

"I have to cripple that right arm of his so he can't use it in the morning against Perry."

"Crawley will be out for more than just the drawing of a little blood, Val. That man had murder on his mind."

Comprehension flickered briefly in Valentin's blue eyes. Then he shrugged. "His enmity is nothing new. Sometimes it amazes me that Crawley still harbors a grudge that neither he nor I began, and one that should have passed on with our fathers. But since he chooses not to, some day it will end in death for him or me."

Let us pray it is not yours, Danforth thought gloomily.

"Come, my friend, don't look so downhearted," Valentin cajoled. Then, changing the subject he asked, "Tell me, how is Miss Rutherford?"

Danforth shrugged. "I have not seen her for some time, but we are expecting to settle matters between us shortly after the New Year."

"Then you too will be entering the bonds of matrimony. Ah, what the indolent gentleman is forced to do because of finances," he mocked himself.

"I think the beauty of your fair maid will ease the pain," Danforth said roguishly.

"*Touché*," Valentin agreed. And for the moment both men were diverted from their encounter with Crawley.

That evening at the Hotel Belmontaine, Pierre scurried into the drawing room and whispered to the Viscountess. Her eyes flew open and she cast a worried glance at Nicole. Then rising stiffly from her chair, she issued a curt order to both Nicole and Cecily who were watching her. "Wait here. I shall return momentarily." Lady Eleanore preceded Pierre out of the room.

Eyeing each other expectantly, Cecily rose and tiptoed to the door, opening it a fraction. Nicole could not resist the temptation to follow Cecily's lead. Peering through the crack, Cecily gasped as Nicole reached her side. "It's Tessa Von Hoffman!"

Over Cecily's shoulder, Nicole glimpsed a rather tall dark-haired woman whose rich attire and haughty manner exuded an aura of glamor. She was gesticulating vigorously with one hand, but her voice was low and tremulous and her words were indistinct. Her tirade was apparently halted by Lady Eleanore, for the visitor was seen to pout haughtily and draw herself up with disdain.

Cecily eased the door shut and leaned against it eyeing Nicole slyly. Crossing to the fireplace before speaking, Nicole turned her steady gaze onto Cecily and asked, "Who is Tessa Von Hoffman?"

"Gracious, all these weeks and you still haven't heard of the beautiful widow?"

Nicole hesitated before replying. Cecily's desire to have Nicole question her about the woman was transparent. Nicole forced herself to respond calmly as she seated herself in a wing-backed chair beside the fireplace. "No, so why don't you tell me since you seem to be so well informed."

"Perhaps I should not." Cecily contemplated the nails of her right hand and eyed Nicole stealthily under downcast lids.

"Then do not," Nicole retorted with some resolution. Intuition warned her she would be better off not knowing.

Still Cecily baited her. "Well, I suppose I ought to tell you. I mean—you really should know. After all, it does concern you directly."

Nicole clasped her hands together before insisting with some impatience.

"Either get to the point, Cecily, or don't bother telling me."

"Well," said Cecily, enjoying herself, "Karen Wexford, who knows just about everybody, says that Tessa Von Hoffman has been seen everywhere with Valentin."

Nicole would not be drawn in. Shrugging her shoulders and holding Cecily's gaze she asked, "So?"

Aggravated by Nicole's indifferent manner, Cecily gave up the cat-and-mouse game and cried, "It's common knowledge that she came back from Vienna with him."

Except for her tightly clasped hands, Nicole remained outwardly calm. This is what she had suspected. "Rumors don't concern me, Cecily. There is always gossip."

Cecily cut in, "Oh for heaven's sake, Nicole. Must I really spell it out for you?" Cecily came to stand over Nicole.

"I do not wish to hear any more," Nicole protested, trying to rise, but Cecily placed a firm hand on her shoulder as she sneered, "Well, you're going to." And taking her hand off Nicole's shoulder, she let the bitter, jeering words drop into the silence that had sprung up between them. "Tessa Von Hoffman is Valentin's mistress!"

Nicole bit her lower lip to keep it from quivering and stared determinedly up into Cecily's gloating face.

"Does it really shock you, my dear? You've grown quite pale. I don't see why it should. After all, you and the Viscount are hardly a love match. It's only a marriage of convenience," Cecily taunted viciously.

Stung beyond endurance, Nicole retorted through bloodless lips, "That's right. That's all it is." She continued to meet Cecily's malicious glare steadily.

Still trying to inflict pain, Cecily cried, "Then you surely don't expect him to remain faithful to you?"

Nicole refused to respond to any further venomous taunts. Already tormented by jealousy, she would never let Cecily know how hurt she was.

Her moment of triumph rapidly fading, Cecily withdrew to the window and stared moodily outside. Baiting Nicole was rather useless. Impossible to believe, but Nicole seemed to care nothing for Valentin. It was she, Cecily Fairfax, who agonized over his affairs. How she hated Nicole and her apparent indifference!

The muffled rattle of wheels and horses' hooves brought Cecily out of her reflections. "She's leaving. Aunt Eleanore certainly made short work of her."

Nicole's wilting body snapped to attention as the Viscountess entered the room. She had never seen the lady look so haggard. The usually taut facial muscles sagged, revealing the tell-tale lines of age about her mouth and eyes. What had taken place between her and Tessa Von Hoffman? Nicole felt a surprising rush of pity for the older woman. Yet she waited in strained silence for her to speak. However, even after seating herself before the fire, Lady Eleanore did not satisfy their curiosity.

But Cecily could bear it no longer and blurted out, "What did she want?"

"Be still!" Lady Eleanore's voice cracked with exasperation.

"Aunt, everyone knows about Valentin and the merry widow."

"*Cecily!*" Lady Eleanore hissed and turned an anxious glance to Nicole.

Having recovered her composure by this time, Nicole commented quietly, "You need not fear my reaction. I am well aware of the circumstances surrounding this marriage."

Flustered only momentarily, the Viscountess replied, "Yes, well, it is a wise woman who does not plague a man for his past indiscretions. I am certain that the Viscount knows nothing about this . . . intrusion. It was a most unfortunate incident. Nevertheless, it is the future that must concern you. Once you are married to Ardsmore I'm sure you and he will handle the matter to everyone's satisfaction." The lady sighed wearily.

Never would Nicole accept with resignation another woman in Valentin's life. Even if he were discreet, and it was accepted behavior by the *beau monde*. But she held her tongue, too disturbed by the knowledge of Tessa Von Hoffman to argue.

A rap on the door brought all three women to attention. However, they all relaxed at the sight of Madame Lafitte.

"Excuse me," she said softly. "It grows late and I was wondering whether I was needed any more this evening." She looked anxiously at Nicole.

"We were just about to retire, madame. Perhaps Nicole wishes something." Lady Eleanore was once more in command of herself and the situation.

Cecily's voice called across the room. "But you haven't told us why that woman had the nerve to come here!"

Lady Eleanore hesitated before answering Cecily's insistent demand. "It . . . has all been taken care of."

"You had best tell us, Lady Eleanore, for none of us shall be able to rest until you do," Nicole demanded in turn.

The Viscountess paused and looked agitated once more. "Oh, very well, my son . . . Valentin, at this very moment is about to engage in a duel."

"Oh, God," Nicole cried—all forgotten but Valentin's safety.

"And Madame Von Hoffman wished me to stop it."

"You? Incredible. How?" They all spoke at once.

"Exactly! To think I would interfere in a matter of honor."

"But why is Val involved in a duel?" Cecily questioned anxiously.

"It is all Perry's fault," Lady Eleanore stated.

"No, that is not true," Nicole whispered almost inaudibly. The three ladies stared at her. "I am the cause."

"You! But how?" Lady Eleanore demanded.

"The past still haunts us, Cousin Eleanore." Nicole's voice cracked.

"The past?" Lady Eleanore paused, then shook her head as comprehension dawned. "You mean . . ."

"Yes, yes, Sylvie Harcourt, my mother. The poor lady still cannot rest in peace," Nicole cried in anguish.

"Hush child, don't become hysterical."

"Your son might be killed over a scandal that should have died years ago. Oh dear Lord, what is the use? It shall never work." Nicole closed her eyes and hung her head dejectedly.

"Now stop that talk, Nicole!" Lady Eleanore stormed. She crossed the room to sit beside the girl, a bright, brittle smile on her face. "Everything will be all right. Why, I have the greatest confidence in Ardsmore. Lord Crawley," she snapped her fingers, "is no match for him. You shall see." Mentally she shook off her own fears for the Viscount's safety. "Believe me, I know my son." She clasped Nicole's hand with one of her own.

Startled, Nicole did not know how to respond. To accept it as a genuine gesture of comfort would be reassuring, but how could she trust this woman who so coldly planned the marriage of her son to a woman he did not love?

Before Nicole could decide what to do, Cecily broke in. "But how can we just wait and not know . . ." Cecily did not need to complete her question.

"I have already sent Pierre to the *Chat Noir* for the information we seek. Until then we must wait," the Viscountess stated firmly. "Madame Lafitte, if you will read to us, I think the time will pass more quickly."

The flickering torchlight and the wintry moon cast long eerie shadows across the freshly fallen snow and lent a disquieting effect to the restless figures gathering in the courtyard of the Field House.

At ten minutes past ten Joseph Crawley arrived with his second and a surgeon. Nodding curtly to the silent group, he eyed his tall, slim adversary. In a few minutes this arrogant Ardsmore would feel the steel of his blade.

That would wipe the imperious smile off his face. Crawley's lips curved in a cruel smirk.

"Well, sir," Valentine taunted his formidable enemy, "Shall we get this affair over quickly? I have better things to do with my time."

"It will be my pleasure, Ardsmore. I can hardly wait for the joy of running you through."

"Gentlemen," Danforth called, "this is a duel of honor. Let us hold to the rules. It is my duty to ask each of you to settle this matter peacefully according to . . ."

"Save your breath, Danforth. I have no intention of drawing off even if Crawley were to beg my forgiveness," the Viscount added scornfully.

Turning a fiery red, his lordship shouted, "Insolent dog! I will beg your forgiveness when hell freezes over."

There was a clash of swords as the two men swept into sudden action. Time after time their blades hissed against each others' as they parried backward and forward over the crunching snow. Their blades flashing in the moonlight, each antagonist sought an opening or an advantage. Murderously Crawley drove his point against the Viscount's only to find it artfully blocked. Each time he thrust, Valentin skillfully outmaneuvered Crawley's bold strokes.

The Viscount's eyes danced with delight as he parried still another of Crawley viciously aimed assaults. Crawley fought with furious intent, desire for Ardsmore's death driving him almost to recklessness. Valentin, on the other hand, fought dispassionately. Knowing his own mastery of the weapon, he deftly controlled the execution of each stroke. He did not wish to inflict a mortal wound. His aim was a disabling strike to his enemy's right arm, rendering it useless and thereby guaranteeing Perry's safety.

Finally, the Viscount's chance came. Feinting a thrust,

he forced his adversary off balance. With a swift, darting movement the point of his sword drove into Crawley's upper arm. Valentin stepped back breathing hard as the Crawley's sword sagged but steadied within seconds. Disbelief flickered in Crawley's eyes momentarily as Ardsmore saluted him. The recovering man lashed out driving Valentin into temporary retreat. Valentin widened the distance between them, allowing his infuriated opponent to chase him halfway across the courtyard. Then the Viscount halted as his panting adversary closed the gap between them. Now he waited somewhat impatiently for his next opening. He was certain it would come soon enough. The Viscount leapt aside and chuckled mischievously as Crawley lunged forward once more. Valentin gave him no time to recover before his blade made straight for Crawley's heart, stopping short of piercing the flesh. Crawley gasped audibly as he envisioned death at the hands of his deadly enemy, whose cold blue eyes glittered with contempt. Next he felt a cold draft as his shirt was ripped open and Ardsmore mockingly stepped aside. Enraged by this humiliation, Crawley lashed out wildly. Passing below his opponent's hacking weapon, Valentin struck once more squarely through the right wrist. Crawley's blade dropped as blood flowed freely over his hand. His second immediately hustled him off to the waiting surgeon.

Danforth smiled wanly and went to Valentin's side. "There is no need to worry now, Val. Lord Crawley won't use that arm for quite some time. Perry is safe."

"Yes, until he opens his mouth again. Thank God it all turned out right." A brief smile lighted his weary face.

One of Crawley's men approached. "The surgeon has informed his lordship he will not be able to use his right arm for several weeks."

"You may inform Lord Crawley that the Harcourt honor is satisfied on both accounts, and if he wishes to withdraw from tomorrow morning's duel of pistols, the incident will be forgotten."

"That is most generous of you, my lord. Undoubtedly his lordship will accept your proposal."

"Undoubtedly," Valentin nodded. "But reluctantly," he added to Danforth. He shrugged into his greatcoat. "Let's find Perry and ease his mind."

The grandfather clock had just finished chiming the half hour. Twelve thirty and still no word. The women huddled deeper into their shawls as dying embers spurted fitfully on the hearth. Madame Lafitte's voice droned on, a murmur floating against their tired brains. They struggled to maintain an air of dignity and calm against the increasingly gloomy thoughts swirling about in their minds. At last the sound of a horse clattering across the cobblestones of the courtyard aroused them from their lethargy. With a start they were on their feet, but an imperious wave of Lady Eleanore's hand kept them from bounding into the corridor.

"We will receive whatever news with dignity," she managed to say steadily just before a shout of "Mama!" greeted their ears and the door swung open.

"Good Lord!" Valentin exclaimed with some consternation as he surveyed the distraught expressions on the faces before him. They continued to stare at his ruffled hair and sparkling eyes.

"It is only me." He began to chuckle. "You look as if you have seen a ghost. Weren't you expecting me? Pierre's message said you were."

"Don't you laugh, sir, or I shall box your ears. How could you be so reckless and risk a duel so close to your wedding day?" Lady Eleanore's relief turned into anger.

"A duel? Who told you anything about a duel?" His eyes narrowed and sought out Nicole.

"Never you mind. Just tell us what happened."

He grinned once more. "Lord Crawley is at this moment nursing a wounded arm."

"And you?"

"As you can see, I am all in one piece, and extremely pleased with the results of tonight's work." He crossed the room to kiss his mother's cheek.

Somewhat soothed, she said, "I never doubted your skill for a moment, my son."

"My ability with the sword is seldom questioned, ma'am. I wish the same could be said of my authority." Once again his eyes swept Nicole.

He suspects me of informing on him, she thought incredulously. The fool! As if I would tell his mother even if I did know what he was planning. She threw back her head defiantly and met the challenge in those piercing blue eyes. I should tell him it was his mistress who flouted all convention by coming here.

Lady Eleanore, intercepting the clash of eyes, placed herself between them and announced, "This affair has upset us all and kept us up unnecessarily late, so bid the ladies goodnight, Ardsmore, and be on your way."

"Might I have a word alone with my fiancée?" he asked.

"No, no, the girl is exhausted. Besides, you are promised to us for the weekend. There will be plenty of time to chat then. Come, I will see you to the door."

"There is no need, ma'am."

"There is every need," she informed him emphatically.

Noting the determined tilt of her head, Valentin acquiesced, saying, "Well, ladies, it seems I am dismissed. Until tomorrow, goodnight." He saluted smartly and escorted his mother from the room.

It was sometime later before Lady Eleanore returned to usher them all to bed. As Madame Lafitte helped Nicole prepare for bed, she listened to the girl's vehement outburst against the morals of the Viscount. Sighing heavily, madame cajoled persuasively, *"Ma chérie,* it would not be wise to reproach him for the *faux pas* committed by that . . . woman." She waved aside Nicole's protest and continued, "She has much gall, that one, but remember you are not his wife yet. You would only anger his pride and jeopardize your chances for winning his heart."

"But, Fifi, it was his mistress who dared come here, insulting all of us."

"And do you think to gain his love by storming at him of insults? No, *chérie,* a jealous rage now would only force him to defend his position. And the wedding only a few days away. Wait. Bide your time. Once you have his love you will not suffer the burden of such women. So promise me, little one, to say nothing of this Von Hoffman woman."

Nicole flounced upon the bed and pursed her lips. "Fifi, he thinks I informed on him. I saw the accusation in his eyes. How can I just ignore it?"

"Be assured Lady Eleanore has already straightened him out on that matter. Why do you think she accompanied him to the door? The Viscount does not lack for sense, I think. The Von Hoffman woman will not intrude here again. Unless I am sadly mistaken, she will be so informed shortly."

Madame Lafitte could not have been more correct, for at that very moment the Viscount was mounting the stairs two at a time to Tessa Von Hoffman's boudoir. Without knocking he flung open the door and strode into the room. A startled cry sprang from the flimsily clad woman reclining on the settee. She rose to a sitting position, clutching the diaphanous garment about her.

"Valentin, thank God! I thought you might be dead."

73

"Damn you, Tessa," he lashed out at her and crossed the room.

"What?" Her head flew back to meet the angry blue eyes. "I am frantic with worry for you, *mein Herz,* and you come storming in here to 'damn' me!"

"How dare you go to my mother?" he roared.

"How dare I?" She rose from the settee, allowing her dark tresses to fall over her silken shoulders. "Do you think I am some common tart from the streets that you speak to me so? You insult me!" She turned her back to him.

Reaching out and grasping one of those tawny shoulders, he swung her around to face him. Annoyance was still visible in his set features. "My future wife resides there."

"You led me to believe *I* would be the future Viscountess," she snapped.

"Never!" he denied emphatically. "You knew from the beginning what our relationship would be. You never wanted or expected anything more."

"I could kill you for such indifference," she stormed. What he claimed was once true, but no longer. She wanted him for her own.

He chuckled softly. "Could you, love? Well, I could have almost killed you for upsetting my family tonight." Encircling her slender throat, he added half in jest, "Don't ever put me in a spot like that again."

Catching his change of mood, she playfully simpered, "Created something of a stir, did I?"

"Heed my warning, you minx," he said ominously, but laughter was in his eyes.

"And if I don't?" she taunted.

"Don't tempt me too far."

She moved closer to him, pressing her body against his and smiling temptingly up at him. The heat of her flesh aroused his own sensual appetites. Crushing his lips to hers, he groaned, "You witch, it's too bad I still want you."

"Ah, Ardsmore, we both know what we want. You want my body, but I . . . I want all of you."

"Liar," he said softly and refused to listen to any further protests as he carried her to the bed.

Much later, as Tessa casually stroked his muscular chest, she asked in what she hoped was a nonchalant tone, "This girl, the one you are to marry, what is she like?"

Sitting up abruptly, he answered curtly, "She is what she ought to be." He rose from the bed and began to don his clothes.

"That could mean many things. I wish to meet her," she stated flatly.

Before she realized what was happening, he was towering over her clasping one of her thin wrists cruelly.

"I wasn't joking when I told you earlier to stay away from my family . . . especially her," he threatened.

"Darling," she cajoled, "you know I only wish to please you."

"Let's keep it that way." He increased the pressure on her wrist.

"Valentin, you hurt me," she cried.

His fingers relaxed. "Sorry, my pet, but let that be a reminder to you that I mean business."

"You are terribly ferocious about this one, *mein Schatz.* Why? What does she have, I wonder?"

"Just leave her out of our discussion."

"Ah, you are cruel. I fear this girl already has some hold on you. Perhaps she is the one to capture that elusive heart of yours, eh?" There was a melancholy note in her voice, as if she were becoming aware of the fleeting hold she had on his affections.

75

"No woman will ever own that," he joked. "But enough of this. I must be on my way."

She clung to him. *"Liebchen,* do not go yet."

"But I must." He removed her clinging arms from about his neck. "Now be a good girl," he murmured.

"Will I see you soon?" she asked, sadly realizing their relationship was nearing its end.

He hesitated, then spoke rather sharply. "I doubt it. Certainly not before Vienna. The wedding is in a matter of days, as you know." Grasping his discarded coat, he bent quickly and kissed her cheek. For a moment he paused and regarded her fondly, but the next second he straightened and crossed to the door. He turned to look at her and said quietly, "Take care, Tessa, my love." And he was gone.

Sleep did not come easily to Nicole that night. Thoughts of her impending marriage harried her remorselessly. Could she honestly convince herself that she would be able to overcome the odds pointing to the failure of this union? Wasn't it foolhardy believing it would all work out the way she wanted it to? Throwing back the bed-covers, she got up and crossed to the window to stare at the glow of moonlight on silvery snow. It was so peaceful and calm as a few flakes floated gently earthward. Would she ever achieve such harmony in her life? Especially marrying a Harcourt? But whatever Valentin brought her, she knew she wanted him with all her heart.

Chapter VI

Having left Tessa shortly before dawn, it seemed to Valentin that he had just fallen asleep when his valet was waking him. Disgruntled, he crawled from bed and prepared himself for the day. Disquieting thoughts pursued him all the way to his mother's home. Damn, he couldn't help it if he had thought Nicole guilty of revealing his whereabouts to his mother. She was the logical choice. Hadn't she questioned him yesterday morning about what he was going to do? But that was not what was really bothering him, and he finally admitted it to himself just as he reached the house. It was Tessa! The way his mother had taken him over the coals for Tessa's scandalous behavior still made him shudder. He should have foreseen the problem and set Tessa straight, yet what had he done after being in her company for less than ten minutes! He had succumbed to her blandishments as usual.

Hell, wasn't a man entitled to some relief, especially after the night he had put in? Nevertheless, it was Nicole's knowledge of Tessa that he could not accept. Most men had mistresses, but the wise man didn't flaunt them before his family. He would not repeat his father's error.

A very defensive Viscount presented himself to the ladies a few moments later. He surveyed the trio before him with appreciation. His mother was splendid in her morning dress of plum silk, and Cecily was charming in a blue frock, but it was Nicole, appearing almost angelic in a soft pink muslin, that caused the catch in his throat. Every time I see her, he thought, she is more beautiful. Tessa had asked him what Nicole had. Wouldn't she have laughed if he had replied, "Innocence." But God, it was there—that purity and womanliness at the same time. He felt his brow grow damp and cursed himself for a fool.

"You see, madame, you said ten o'clock, and I am here," he announced.

"Then we can be off. We do not want to keep your Uncle Maurice waiting. He has planned this weekend at his chateau for some time. Here is Perry now. We are all ready."

Escorting them to the waiting coach, Valentin decided to repair the damage done to his relationship with Nicole, and holding her back, he took her arm solicitously, remarking, "I hope the ride will not prove tedious for you. The chateau is not too far from Versailles and well worth visiting." He turned on one of his most engaging smiles and immediately Nicole found herself forgiving him.

"I am looking forward to the weekend very much."

"I hope one of the reasons is the time we will be able to share there together."

Flustered, she answered faintly, "Of course, my lord."

78

"Nicole," he chided softly, "I thought we had agreed to first names."

"Yes, yes, certainly . . . Val," she blushed prettily.

"Come on you two," Perry called. "There'll be time for that later."

Valentin assisted Nicole into the coach, then mounted his horse and turned to Perry beside him. "Clod! Will you never learn to keep that mouth of yours closed?"

"What did I do now, Val?"

"Never mind," his brother sighed in exasperation. "Just learn when to speak, will you?" and the Viscount spurred his horse on its way.

Upon their arrival the Marquis escorted them into his resplendent state dining room. It was reminiscent of the now untenanted palace of Versailles. Ornate golden paper decorated the walls and tawny satin draperies covered the long narrow window embrasures which flanked one side of the room. The opposite wall was dominated by a magnificent sculptured fireplace containing a blazing fire. On the ceiling paintings of nymphs and cherubs floating among clouds of muted pinks and golds created an airy impression of heavenly realms.

Awestruck, Nicole sat back in a velvet chair and pondered the fate of the king and queen who had dined some twenty-three years ago at this very table so elegantly set with its embossed china and deep-cut crystal. Poor Marie and Louis! Poor Marquis! So much of his world had been swept away and only some of the outer trappings remained. Strange that Valentin's next comment should echo her own thoughts.

"We have been transported to the past, *Monsieur le Marquis*. It is quite an honor to be wined and dined as if we were royalty."

"Good food and drink are a few of the pleasures that I can enjoy these days. At least when my gout is not acting up. Besides, I wish to treat this lovely young lady to the joys of the *ancien régime* before it passes away with me."

"Oh, Uncle Maurice," Nicole protested as he took her hand and kissed it.

"We did not dine in the white salon, *mignonne,* because it is much more intimate, so I wanted to save that pleasure for you and this young rascal to enjoy on your honeymoon."

The color mounted in Nicole's cheeks. "That is very kind of you," she managed to stammer.

"What about your museum?" Valentin interjected trying to smooth over Nicole's confusion.

"That's a must, Nicole," cried Perry. "You could spend a month in there and still not discover all Uncle Maurice's monstrosities."

"You could spend a year in there and never discover its meaning, you young buffoon," stormed the Marquis. "Come, let us retire to the drawing room. Later we will look over my treasure trove. Right now I wish for a game of cards. What do you say, my dear?" he addressed Lady Eleanore. "Cecily and Perry against you and me." Perry was about to protest when he caught the Marquis's eye and changed his mind. The Marquis turned to Valentin and Nicole. "You two may explore some of the chateau." With that peremptory remark he escorted the others to the drawing room.

"In his own inimitable way, Uncle Maurice has given us the opportunity to be alone," Valentin chuckled.

"Yes, so I noticed," Nicole returned his lightheartedness with a smile.

They wandered down the main hallway which was lined with armor and pieces of sculpture. "The wedding plans are just about completed?" Valentin queried, striving to make conversation.

"Oh yes. Your mama has performed miracles."

"Never let it be said that my mother does not rise to the occasion. She is one of London's most notable hostesses, as you will undoubtedly find out."

"Yes, she is an amazing woman." Nicole neatly side-stepped the issue.

"I hope you don't mind my having arranged for us to spend our honeymoon here at Uncle Maurice's."

"Oh no. I shall look forward to it."

"The Marquis doesn't use the chateau much these days. He spends most of his time in Paris."

"Yes, I know."

"There are some fabulous rooms if I remember correctly." He opened a door and ushered her into a huge chamber. She gasped and turned wide violet eyes on him.

"This is what is known as the museum room. I think the Marquis wanted us to wait, but to be the first to capture that expression on your face is worth it." Taking her hand, the Viscount led her forward. "Maurice was able to save most of these antiques during the Revolution by having them hidden. Some others were left behind. Fortunately, the marshal who occupied this chateau saw the value of these treasures as well as the rest of the chateau and did not allow them to be destroyed."

"I have never seen a collection like this before." Nicole began to wander among the valuables gathered from many ages. There were tapestries and shields from the Middle Ages lining the walls, and marble statues and vases were crowded carelessly into corners. Egyptian bowls and Grecian urns were scattered upon long trestle tables, and priceless treasures were strewn on the floors. It was as if a giant treasure chest had been emptied thoughtlessly without regard for order, or concern for value.

81

"It makes me giddy," Nicole laughed. "I don't know where to look first." She glanced over her shoulder at Valentin as he strolled behind her. "It would take weeks, perhaps months to go through it all."

"I think we can spare some time on our honeymoon for sorting through it. But I can't guarantee how much," he grinned.

Trembling inwardly she looked away and reached for the nearest object. Valentin leaned over her and extracted the goblet from her fingers while placing a restraining hand on her shoulder. His sudden nearness, and the strength of his warm fingers on her shoulder were causing her heart to flutter wildly. The man truly was a devil. One minute heartlessly cool, the next charmingly sweet.

"This goblet," he was saying quite innocently, "is from Vienna, where we shall go following our honeymoon to join the British delegation."

"The Duke is already there?" she asked softly.

"No, but he will be soon."

"I have heard that Vienna is a very gay city."

"It is. And I shall be only too happy to show you the sights, my sweet." His hand glided from her shoulder to her chin, sending a series of thrilling tremors along its way. "I have hired rooms for us on Lothmann Strasse which is quite fashionable."

"Will . . . will we be expected to do much entertaining?" She forced herself to ask nonchalantly while his fingers lightly caressed her cheek.

"Some. Does it frighten you?"

"No—no, I was just wondering."

"Don't let it concern you. I think it more likely we shall be entertained. I have a feeling everyone will want to meet the lovely young Viscountess," he said slipping his other arm about her waist.

"My lord," she pleaded, afraid of her own feelings, "Val—I think we should be getting back to the others." She placed both hands on his chest trying to extricate herself from his embrace.

"Not just yet," he murmured persuasively. "I want to show you something unusual." He released her from his light embrace and walked over to one of the chests and knelt beside it extracting what appeared to be a mask. "This has always intrigued me." He stood up as Nicole came to his side. "It looks like a part of a jack-o-lantern, yet I'm sure it is much older."

"Oh, do let me see," she exclaimed reaching for the object.

"It seems to be made of a light wood or possibly a type of linen," he commented as he handed it to her.

"It appears to be a mask of some kind. See the hooked nose and the turned-down mouth."

"Unfortunately, only a portion remains, making it difficult to decide what it actually is," Valentin's face was close to Nicole's as he ostensibly examined the artifact. "Maurice should get an expert to start sorting this stuff."

"Oh, but look," Nicole deftly maneuvered away from his disturbing nearness and held it up to her face, "see how it covers the face?"

He started to laugh. "Beauty and the beast. Would a kiss break the enchantment, I wonder?"

"You make fun of my theory, sir?" Nicole demurred.

"No, no, my love, I quite agree. It's probably from the Commedia dell'arte. Perhaps Harlequin."

"Oh, no, not Harlequin—he was never as grotesque as this creature, I am sure."

"Well, one of them, then."

"I think not."

"Oh?" A note of surprise crept into his voice.

Nicole grew cautious. "Perhaps, Val . . . do you think it possible to have come from an even earlier period of the theatre?"

"Such as?" He became faintly interested.

"Greece."

"Greece? Good heavens girl, I have never heard of anything so fragile surviving that era of the theatre."

"Don't laugh. Perhaps this is a first." Nicole was a little offended at his superior tone.

Valentin noticed and proceeded jokingly, "So you would disagree with my judgment?"

"I would."

"Look at her," he addressed the ghosts of the past. "Defiant and stubborn. I think I shall have to teach the lady proper respect for her future husband."

Responding to the jocular note in his voice, she retorted laughing, "So it is a master-slave relationship you are expecting, my lord."

"What's this? Mockery too? I'll 'lord and master' you," he said reaching for her, but she slipped out of reach. "Come here!" he demanded.

Nicole shook her head no, backing away playfully.

Valentin began to advance toward her, but she moved behind one of the tables.

"Do not forget, lord and master, these are priceless antiques."

"And she dares to lecture me as well. Hmm. Shall we see how daring she is after I turn her over my knee?"

Suddenly Nicole was not sure if he were playing. "You wouldn't!"

Valentin shouted with laughter and Nicole relaxed perceptibly. With lightning speed he crossed to her and imprisoned her in his arms.

"You tricked me!"

"Of course. Remember that in the future. I am notorious for pursuing my prey until I have won," he teased, "and to the victor go the spoils."

"And what do you wish from the vanquished?" She looked up at him impishly, perceiving the answer and willing to concede.

"Nicole," he whispered placing his mouth to hers. Surprisingly gentle, his kiss expressed a deep yearning and she responded warmly. Valentin lifted his lips and murmured in her ear, "My sweet," kissed it and then let his lips travel up to her cheek and to her eyes. It was bliss to feel his arms tightening around her and to give herself up to the moment. She slipped her arms around his neck and returned his kiss eagerly. The gentleness deepened to passion and his caressing hand slipped to her breast. She stiffened slightly and stepped back.

Immediately his hold slackened, but he did not let her go as he said, "I did not mean to frighten you, but you will be my wife in a few days."

"Yes, I know." She looked up to him with troubled eyes. "It is just that . . ."

"I know," he smiled endearingly, "you don't have to explain." Then he kissed her lightly upon the forehead.

"Oh, here you two are." Cecily stood in the doorway.

Nicole jumped, but Valentin held on to her hand.

"That's right, Cecily," he said. "Here we are," and he winked at Nicole.

Could she ever love him more than at that moment? Nicole smiled contentedly up into his handsome face.

Other guests arrived for the evening meal and later a musicale was held in the drawing room. Nicole did not have another moment alone with Valentin until early the following afternoon when they joined Cecily and Perry for some ice skating.

Hurrying Nicole over the ice, Valentin managed to leave the others behind.

"Don't you think we should have waited?" she questioned breathlessly.

"No, I don't, my love. We haven't had a moment alone since yesterday and aren't likely to again until after the wedding. And I can't wait that long."

Pleased by his eagerness, she sped along beside him enjoying the strong movements of his body beside hers. Looking down at her, he caught Nicole's appreciative glance and pulled her closer against him not noticing a twig jutting through the ice. One moment they were skating smoothly along, and the next the two of them were sprawled across the ice.

"Nicole!" he called pulling himself to his feet and racing to her assistance. "Are you all right?"

"Yes, yes," she laughed brightly. "I have not taken such a tumble since I was a child."

"Here, let me help you to the embankment. It was my fault." He seated her on a log at the edge of the lake. "You are sure you are all right?" he inquired anxiously.

"Oh yes. And you?"

"I am fine just as long as you are. I don't want to lose you, my love." Valentin pulled an unresisting Nicole into his arms and began kissing her. Then moving her against the embankment of soft snow, he rested his lean masculine body next to hers and pressed his knee intimately against hers. Deep within Nicole a rising desire wrestled with a growing sense of panic. His sexuality frightened her, but she could not deny his kisses as he imprisoned her more firmly beneath himself.

Valentin heard his name being called from a distance and rose abruptly. "Until our wedding night, my darling," he whispered as the others came into sight.

Chapter VII

Danforth puffed on his pipe and leaned back in his chair as he watched his tall friend pace back and forth between two windows stopping at each to stare at the street below.

"Still snowing?" Danforth questioned.

"What?" Valentin turned to him.

"Is it still snowing?" He raised his eyebrows.

"Oh, yes. It may hold up the wedding party."

"Never fear, old friend, they will be here on time." Danforth laughed, enjoying the Viscount's agitation.

Pulling the watch from his dress uniform, Valentin commented, "Almost noon."

"Join me in a glass of sherry?"

The Viscount absentmindedly accepted the glass.

"To your marriage."

Valentin eyed him briefly before he drank.

"I envy you, my friend. She is a beautiful girl."

"Yes, I believe the Harcourt luck has held after all." He finished his wine. "I can tell you when I first heard the conditions of Aunt Sophie's will, I was mad enough to go into battle without my sword." He laughed.

"I'm glad common sense prevailed as well as good fortune." Danforth smiled in return. "You won the prize, I would say."

"Indeed I have." The Viscount adjusted his sword hilt and pulled on his white gloves just as Charles Humphrey poked his head through the door announcing the arrival of the wedding party.

Percy Pembroke, the civil magistrate, was already standing in front of the fireplace which was adorned with garlands of red and green. Lord Wolsey was greeting some of the guests at the doorway. The main room to the registry was large and sparsely furnished except for a few gilt chairs. On a table before the fireplace lay the registry book which would be signed by Nicole and Viscount Ardsmore at the end of the ceremony. Chairs for those in attendance had been set up on either side of a narrow red carpet that ran the length of the room.

Lady Eleanore entered on the arm of Reginald Glenville, Envoy Extraordinary to the British Embassy. She was followed by Cecily who was accompanied by Perry. Lady Eleanore was looking very elegant in a deep purple gown of softly draped velvet trimmed with ermine cuffs. She wore a headdress of matching velvet and ermine. Cecily's costume in teal blue and cream satin was no less elegant. The remaining guests were mostly male, being made up of embassy staff members and military officers of the Viscount's command.

When everyone was seated, the Marquis de Crécy escorted Nicole into the hushed room. Her wedding gown was all she could have hoped it to be, and every detail served to enhance her own natural beauty. Lady Eleanore had wisely chosen a heavy ivory satin that seemed to intensify the warm ivory of Nicole's own coloring. Ignoring the favored Empire line, Madame DuPlessis had suggested a medieval line that softly molded Nicole's willowy figure to the hipline and fell in gleaming folds to the floor. The high-necked bodice was overlaid with Valenciennes lace in a deeper shade of ivory and richly studded with hand-sewn crystals that gave the appearance of crushed diamonds. The long sleeves fit her arms tightly and ended in points at the wrists. The headdress was a diamond tiara to which were attached clouds of tulle that descended to the floor. A lesser beauty would have been overpowered, but for Nicole the sumptuous costume was a fitting background to her own dark beauty. Her glowing face and shining violet eyes subdued the richness of her raiment into a proper setting.

Nicole saw no one but Valentin, standing tall and magnificent before the fireplace.

Uncle Maurice brushed her cheek with his fingers before pressing her forward to the Viscount, and placing her cold hand into her bridegroom's warm one, he took his place beside Lady Eleanore.

The civil ceremony was brief, and the formalties were completed with the signing of the registry. Lord Pembroke concluded by saying, "You may now kiss the bride, my lord." Nicole raised tremulous lips to the man who took her in his arms and lowered his face tenderly to hers. The ritual kiss was over all too soon, and Lord Wolsey was offering a champagne toast before they returned to the Hotel Belmontaine for the reception.

The reception proved the test of endurance Nicole had anticipated. Her new husband stood protectively at her side throughout the tedious receiving line, and cued her unobtrusively in matters of names and identities of the personages presented. She did little more than smile and murmur appropriate rejoinders as the Viscount deftly carried the burden of small talk and pleasantries necessary. Later she was led by an unflagging Valentin through the demure bridal waltz under the watchful gaze of admiring gentlemen and envious ladies. Valentin was all the male strength and gallantry any bride could desire.

"You dance superbly, my dear," Valentin spoke softly into Nicole's ear.

"The least one could expect from a ballet dancer's daughter, my lord," she rejoined impishly.

The Viscount regarded Nicole thoughtfully for a moment. "Do you still chafe under that old grievance, my love? There is no need. Have done with the past, sweetheart." He spoke so seriously that Nicole caught her breath and looked carefully into his eyes, reading deep sincerity there.

Striving to express her response, she added, "If I dance well, my lord, it is only that you lead so well."

Valentin paused in their dancing and lifted her hand, placing a fervent kiss upon its fingers before the watching eyes of the assembled guests. Nicole felt herself transported with joy at his gallant salute. Here was her knight come to claim her before all the world.

Much later, after consuming copious quantities of champagne, Valentin assisted Nicole in cutting the cake and tossing the bouquet. The time had arrived for the exhausted couple to make their departure. The Viscount led the way to the flower-strewn coach waiting to transport them to the Marquis's chateau. Nicole's final look at the group surrounding the carriage was a brief glimpse of Madame Lafitte, her old friend and mentor, who was leaving in the morning for her sister's home in St. Rémy. Next, her glance rested on Lady Eleanore who forced a bright smile to her lips before reaching for Maurice's arm; and finally Nicole noted Cecily's taut form at the edge of the crowd. There was open hatred in her gaze, and Nicole averted her eyes.

"Cold, my dear? Here, let me adjust this rug." Valentin tucked her in carefully.

"Thank you," she murmured as the carriage pulled out of the courtyard.

An uncomfortable silence enveloped both of them. What did one say at a time like this?

"I sent your maid and my valet on ahead. They should have everything in hand by the time we arrive." Valentin spoke first.

"That was thoughtful of you," Nicole replied.

They lapsed into silence again.

"I . . . I did not expect so many people," Nicole tried to bridge the gap in conversation, "even though your mother indicated that it would be a large gathering."

"Most of the guests were relatives or friends who were already in Paris." He yawned and stretched himself. "Lord, but my head is splitting. I shouldn't have stayed out so late last night."

"You were celebrating last night?"

"Danforth had quite a send-off for me. It was a rousing good time . . . but then that is not for a lady's ears."

She shot him a searching glance that stopped him from further confidences. "Never mind that, however . . . this is our wedding night." He slipped his arm through hers. His touch had an incredible effect on her, yet her fears of the night ahead made her uneasy and her apprehension increased as the distance to the chateau lessened.

"At last," he sighed as they arrived at their destination.

It was a relief to him to have this awkward journey come to an end. He assisted her from the coach, and as they reached the doorway, he swept her into his arms.

"What . . . what are you doing?"

"I believe that it is customary," he said stepping through the doorway.

"But . . . that is on entering one's own home for the first time."

"Oh, you see I am not up on such things, but I shall remember for later. Where do we dine, Henri?" Valentin questioned the waiting butler.

"In the white salon, your lordship."

"Put me down," Nicole whispered.

"Why? I rather fancy you in my arms." He proceeded to carry her up the stairs.

"The servants will think you are drunk."

"Not much, madame." And he kept her in his arms until he placed her on her feet in the white salon. "Well, look about you, my dear; I would say Uncle Maurice has outdone himself."

The high-ceilinged room was a mass of white flowers, and the mingled fragrance of roses and lilacs wafted gently through the soft light of descending dusk. A branch of glowing candles lighted a small table laid with shimmering silver and crystal. The white satin draperies at the long casement windows were embroidered in silver thread, and the whole scene was one of quiet luxury. It followed well after the hectic crush of the wedding celebrations.

"Champagne?" Valentin offered.

Nicole refused.

"You must join me in a toast." He poured two glasses and came to stand beside her. "Here, my love." He handed her the glass, then led her toward the table laid with a light supper of cold chicken and lobster. "To our future."

Nicole smiled at him uncertainly.

"Don't look so dubious," Valentin laughed. "Remember what I told you once before. We are not resigned to our fate; we Harcourts make it." He touched his glass to hers and drank deeply. Nicole sipped hers lightly.

Henri appeared at that moment to serve supper. Valentin continued to fill his glass until Nicole found herself saying, "Valentin, don't you think you have had enough?"

"Never fear, madame, I still retain my faculties." He paused considering her. "Would you care to retire now?"

The question startled her.

"I shall come to you shortly." He rose.

There seemed to be no alternative but to follow his lead. He held the door open for her as she passed through it.

In her room the maid chattered lightly about the wedding as she helped Nicole out of her traveling suit and into her nightgown of flowing white satin. She brushed Nicole's silky dark hair straight down her back and tied a pink ribbon through it.

"Thank you, Margot, you may go."

"Yes madame, and may I . . ."

"No, no, please say nothing." Nicole's agitation was increasing by the minute. She took a few turns about the room, mumbling to herself incoherently and then threw off her peignoir and slipped into the waiting large bed. It seemed an eternity, but finally she heard footsteps advancing down the corridor and the door to the outer chamber clicked open. She heard the Hessians fall to the floor, and then he was standing in the doorway, his jacket unfastened. He seemed to sway a little as he advanced across the room, and seated himself on the edge of the bed. She could not look at him but kept her eyes downcast. He was studying her as his fingers touched her hair and released the ribbon holding it. Slowly his hand slid down her shoulder and slipped off the straps of her nightgown. She stiffened slightly.

"Beautiful," he murmured clasping her to himself. "Relax, my sweet." Finding her lips he kissed her slowly, moving himself the length of her body.

She tried to relax, but as his kisses became more insistent, she began to pull away. He pinned her down with the full weight of his body, and now she began to struggle. He continued to murmur endearments, but his hands and body became more demanding. "You go too fast, my lord," she whispered frantically. He restrained himself with a shudder and raised his head to gaze searchingly into her eyes. In moments he divested himself of his clothing and extinguished the candle.

"Give yourself to me, Nicole. Don't be frightened, I will show you the way. There is no going back now." And with a groan he clamped his mouth to hers again.

Finally the storm of his passion subsided, and she lay quietly in his arms. He had hurt her, but she did not care since he had sealed her as his own in the white heat of his passion, and she was glad. She now belonged to him completely. Her own ardor had not broken the bonds of maidenly training, but she was not troubled by this for she had yet to discover the depths of her own passion.

Gradually Valentin's breath grew even and she lay quietly in the crook of his arm, his lips resting on her hair. "Darling," he whispered, "my sweet." A rush of love welled up in her so powerfully Nicole felt she must drown in the rapture of it. A little more and Valentin's deep breathing showed that he was sleeping peacefully. She moved to adjust herself to him, and he stirred and mumbled, "Tessa."

Nicole stiffened. *Tessa!* She felt herself choked with dismay. Had Valentin been too drunk to realize he was making love to her and not Tessa? He had called her Nicole during his lovemaking, but now, in his sleep, he called for his mistress. Oh God, and she had thought he loved her, when all along it was Tessa who held the secret place in his heart. What a fool she was. It was all pretense. What did a man of the world want with an inexperienced girl? Fool! Fool! Fool! And she had cherished a dream of him all these years when really she was nothing to him.

Once again he mumbled an endearment caressing her and letting his head fall upon her shoulder. Nicole could have cried out with anguish in her need to get away from him. In a while his arm relaxed its hold on her, and she slid carefully out of the bed. She shivered and searched in the darkness for her peignoir. Stumbling blindly until she found the divan, she threw herself onto it in a miserable huddle of grief and despair to wait the coming of dawn. In the first faint light of the emerging day, she struggled into her clothes and left the room.

The Viscount woke to find the bed empty. Remorse overcame him. Damn! Why had he drunk so much last night? His indistinct recollection was of Nicole's timid response to his passion, and Valentin was filled with a yearning tenderness for her. He hoped he had not frightened her unduly by being too forceful. He had better go to find her at once. Perhaps he should apologize for his lack of control.

Valentin found Nicole seated at the breakfast table, an empty coffee cup before her. The dark look she gave him did not augur well, but he plunged ahead.

"Good morning, my love, I see you are an early riser."

She did not answer him.

He hesitated, then continued, "Nicole, sweetheart, look at me."

Still she was silent.

"If I ... last night ... if I offended you, I ..."

She didn't give him a chance to finish. She was certain he was going to mention his mistress's name again, and that she could not bear.

"There is no need for pretense, my lord. We are neither of us children. We are both aware that this is not a love match but a marriage of convenience."

Her words caught him off guard. What point was she making with this talk of a marriage of convenience?

"I fail to follow your words, Nicole. What is this talk of convenience?"

"Surely you will agree that honesty will save us both unnecessary pain," Nicole responded in a voice empty of feeling. He would never know the depth of her suffering. Never!

"I am as desirous as yourself that the truth be maintained between us. Your words suggest that I have something to hide." The Viscount strove to sound calm.

"Whatever you desire, my lord, you may be sure there is nothing hidden."

"Nicole! Say it out and have done with this hinting. What is it that you hold against me?" Valentin demanded, his exasperation getting the better of him.

But again she would not speak.

"If it was my want of proper conduct last night, I am all apologies. I admit I drank too much."

She cut him off. "Say no more, I beg you," she claimed in a strangled voice. "What is done, is done."

His face grew stricken. What had he done? "Good God, Nicole, what is it? What have I done?" He reached to take both her hands in his, but she snatched them back as if burned.

"No, don't!" she whispered and jumped up and fled from the room.

Valentin stood watching as she ran from him, the blood

96

frozen in his veins. What had he done to cause such a reaction?

Nicole remained barricaded in her room for the remainder of the day, and a much cowed Viscount prowled restlessly about the chateau alternately raging against himself, Nicole, his mother, Aunt Sophie and the whole Harcourt clan. But beneath it all was a secret fear lest he should have inflicted some wound on Nicole too painful to be faced. Reckless and abandoned he may have been in his countless amours, but never had he violated the code of a gentleman by brutal conduct toward the gentler sex. Had the strain of this godforsaken marriage caused some hidden warp in his nature to suddenly surface?

By God, he would have the truth from Nicole. He stood outside her door ready to batter it down should she refuse him entry, but he hesitated before knocking and was lost. Once again fear of what he might have done overwhelmed him and he turned on his heel and sought refuge in the library, drinking himself into a blind stupor of oblivion. They saw no more of each other that day.

The following morning hunger drove Nicole to the breakfast room. There was no sign of the Viscount, and a much bewildered household staff served breakfast with quiet restraint. As Nicole applied butter to a croissant, Valentin entered and seated himself across the table from her. She kept her eyes downcast, unable to eat. There was no sound of movement from the other side, and she could not resist a brief glance in that direction. The haggard face across from her shocked her into wide-eyed wonder.

"Valentin!"

"So, you condescend to speak to me, madame?" He took refuge behind a front of disdain. Somewhere in the alcoholic excesses of the preceding night, Valentin's self-esteem, no longer able to bear the weight of an unnamed guilt, had magically emerged as the injured party. This unfortunate tactic of self-preservation kindled an immediate like response in Nicole and cast the unhappy pair into a condition of stalemate.

"It is only that you do not look yourself, my lord," she shrugged, as if commenting on the inanities of the weather.

"Do not trouble yourself on my account," Valentin returned in an equally bored fashion.

"I do not, my lord."

"That is well, *my lady.*"

A bleak two days of stiff formalities passed before Valentin's sense of the ridiculous asserted itself. Besides, his determination to leave Nicole alone began to pale. What had he done to offend her so? He must get it out into the open once and for all. He still retained the impression that Nicole had responded to him on their wedding night. Her present behavior was a contradiction.

Twilight was descending around the enclosed summerhouse where Nicole sat reading when she became aware of Valentin's presence in the room. He was leaning against the door jamb observing her.

"What . . . what are you doing here?"

He sat down next to her on the divan. "Now that is a foolish question."

"I thought we settled everything the other day."

"We settled nothing the other day."

"I beg to differ. We made ourselves perfectly clear. We understand each other very well."

"No, I'm afraid *I* don't understand. Perhaps you had better explain what changed your mind so quickly from wedding night to morning. I felt you respond to me."

"I . . . I did not."

"I don't believe you."

"Do I offend your prowess as a lover? Perhaps you should go to Tessa Von Hoffman for solace."

"Tessa? Why do you bring up Tessa at this time?" he demanded in sudden anger.

"She is your mistress, is she not?"

"She *was* my mistress!"

"You still love her," Nicole accused.

"How do you know whether I still love Tessa or not?" He sprang up and paced the floor indignantly. "If the truth were known, I never loved Tessa. She was an enchanting diversion. Nothing more."

"How can you say that when . . . when . . ."

"When what?" Valentin demanded. He stopped his pacing and stood over her.

Nicole looked up at him with reproachful eyes.

"What has Tessa to do with any of this, Nicole? She's nothing to me. What I want to know is why you turned against me after our wedding night."

Some of Valentin's bewilderment communicated itself to Nicole. Could she have been wrong? Did Tessa truly mean nothing to him?

"But you spoke her name."

"When did I speak her name?"

"After you . . . after we . . . after . . ."

"After I made love to you?" Valentin finished with a look of growing wonder on his face. "You mean I spoke her name that night?"

"Yes." Nicole answered quietly.

"What else did I say?" Valentin demanded.

"Nothing." A mere whisper.

"Nothing!" Valentin was incredulous. "You mean these days and nights of torture were caused by nothing more than my speaking Tessa's name?" He grabbed the flinching Nicole by the shoulders.

"Nothing more? What *more* was necessary?" Nicole challenged.

"You *are* serious," Valentin replied, both wonder and laughter struggling to come to the surface. "You're truly serious." And with that he began to laugh.

It was fatal. Nicole felt her cheeks burn with humiliation. She struggled for some dignity. "I do not feel it to be a laughing matter."

"I dare say not. Humor is *definitely* not one of your strong points, m'dear." And he continued to laugh with increasing enjoyment.

Seeking blindly to wound, Nicole lashed out, "I would rather lack a sense of humor than a sense of honor."

"Honor? Now how does honor enter into your pretty scheme of values, Nicole? I can hardly wait to hear it."

"Well, I did not mean exactly honor. I meant . . ."

"Yes, yes, I'm all ears."

Valentin's apparent enjoyment of her confusion goaded Nicole to further foolishness. "I meant . . . 'Manliness.' "

"Oh?" Valentin stopped laughing abruptly. "Manliness? I don't quite draw the connection." He smiled dangerously.

"It was our wedding night."

"Indeed it was."

"And it was your lack of . . ." she hesitated.

"My lack of what?" he prodded.

"It was your blunder, not mine."

"So I blundered did I? Perhaps we should play out the scene again?" Without warning Valentin dragged her off the divan onto the Persian rug and flung himself on top of her, crushing her mouth to his in a bruising kiss. Struggling like a tigress, Nicole freed one arm and swung at his face, but he grabbed the arm and pinned it beneath her with the other one. This demon lover swept aside all resistance. He would have his way with her, and she was carried along on a fierce tide of passion. In the deepening shadows of dusk he held her captive and she surrendered.

"Val," she whispered submissively next to his cheek.

Suddenly he was up and staring down at her insolently. Confused and bewildered, Nicole lay motionless, throbbing in every nerve.

"Any complaints this time?" he taunted, then walked away to stare moodily out of the window.

Nicole stumbled to her feet, seated herself on the divan, and unconsciously began to smooth her tumbled hair and wrinkled clothing. She had surrendered, and all he could do was mock her. "I despise you," she cried in humiliation.

"You don't mean that," he taunted again.

"Oh, but I do! Lord, how I loathe you and all the Harcourts! Why don't you go away and leave me alone?"

"Stop this nonsense, Nicole!" Valentin came toward her.

"When will your insufferable pride accept the fact that I don't want or need you!" She remained vehement.

Stunned, the Viscount hesitated, then shrugged his shoulders with resignation. "Very well, if that's the way you feel, I shall oblige you. I have had enough of this temperament." Without another word he stalked out of the summerhouse slamming the door behind him.

Some time later Nicole stirred from the cramped position in which she had sat since her husband had walked out on her. Returning to the chateau, she saw that the place was a blaze of lights and that the door stood open. Valentin's curricle was drawn up in front of the portico and his valet was strapping a valise to it. Trying to control her chaotic thoughts, she crossed to the entrance just as Valentin, dressed for riding, emerged.

"Val?" she faltered. "Where, where are you going?"

"As you suggested, away . . . to Vienna." He pulled her

out of hearing distance of the servants. "That should effectively remove me from your world."

Merciful heavens, what was he saying? She had to stop him, but he was still speaking.

"After all a *marriage of convenience* such as ours doesn't necessitate our living together. You may journey to London with my mother. And furthermore your self-righteous attitude is becoming a bore."

Nicole's lips quivered and her eyes filled with tears. All the things she most feared were falling from his lips, but her stiff pride refused to allow her to protest.

"Damn you, don't cry about it," he hissed. "These are your own wishes, aren't they?" He paused. "Well, aren't they?"

"Yes, yes! I can't wait until you are out of my life for good!" How could she be saying these things? What perversity drove her?

"That can be easily arranged," he drawled and sprang into the waiting curricle. Wielding his whip to the horses, they leapt and plunged ahead spraying stones and gravel as they gathered speed and carried him out of her life.

She watched thunderstruck until Pierre, who had been hovering nearby, placed an envelope into her hand saying, "From his lordship, my lady."

In a daze Nicole made her way to her room where she read a list of instructions from the Viscount. The last was the most devastating—he would not interfere in her life as long as she remained discreet. Oh God, what had she done? Flinging herself across the bed, she cried until she slept as in a nightmare. Visions of Valentin as he scorned her haunted her tortured sleep.

She awoke to a household buzzing with the fact that his lordship had departed leaving his wife behind. She refused to leave her room, hoping against hope for the return of her bridegroom, but he did not come.

When Nicole finally left her room, it was under the surreptitious surveillance of the servants who watched the girl wander aimlessly about the silent chateau.

In the back rooms of the villa rumors were rife about the departed bridegroom and his forsaken bride. Snatches of past conversation were repeated, exaggerated and expanded during the course of the retelling. The Viscount's sudden departure; Nicole's weeping into the night; her silence for over twenty-four hours; no word from him; no action from her. What could it mean? But the bride remained oblivious to their speculations.

Late the next afternoon, Nicole wandered into the museum room. The tirades of recrimination and self-pity which had consumed her were now over, leaving her in a state of numbed apathy. There was only a dull insistent ache around her heart. Absentmindedly she stared at Uncle Maurice's treasures. Lifting one object after another and viewing them with unseeing eyes, she let them slip through her fingers. Silent tears began to course down her face as she retrieved the broken mask from the trunk on the floor and remembered that happy playful moment with Valentin in this very room. This mask which had once hidden unnamed players' faces and feelings could not provide her with the same anonymity. She must wear the face of grief before the mocking world. Her swollen red eyes stared back at her from a gilded mirror on the wall. There was no disguising what had happened to her.

If only she could call back those words and change the consequences of their last scene together. It was a scene that replayed itself cruelly over and over in her mind. His claim that he had never loved Tessa. His bewilderment at her reaction to his having spoken Tessa's name. Perhaps she had made too much of it. But why had he tried to belittle her? Why hadn't he made her go to Vienna with him? Did he really want to be free of her? She couldn't think about it any more. She must escape her own plaguing thoughts.

Running out of the museum room along the corridor to the terrace doors, she flung them open and fled into the cold winter air. Heedlessly she raced toward the lake stopping abruptly to stare at its frozen banks. Even here memories assailed her.

"Oh Val," she cried to the icy wind.

But she couldn't go on like this, torturing herself. She must take hold of her shattered life. While the brisk breeze cut across her tear-stained face, causing her to catch her breath in deep gulps, she sighed and began to summon her courage. She wasn't defeated yet. She would consult Uncle Maurice. Maybe it wasn't too late. Perhaps a letter to Val? Determinedly she strode back to the chateau.

That very day Nicole wrote three notes and dispatched them by messenger to Paris. Anxiously she waited the replies. First came the reply from the Marquis expressing his concern and the desire to be of service. Next came Madame Lafitte's assurance that she would join Nicole at the Marquis's home as soon as possible. The last was a devastating response from Lady Eleanore castigating Nicole's actions. Nicole immediately crushed it in her hand and flung it into the fire. All her resentment toward Lady Eleanore flared forth again.

A few days later Nicole arrived at the Hotel de Crécy where she was met by a grim Uncle Maurice. She had never seen the old gentleman look more severe or forbidding and there was no welcoming kiss of the hand or cheek as on previous occasions. He beckoned her into the drawing room rather curtly as a sense of panic seized her fading spirits. His first remarks did little to lessen her fears.

"Well, my dear, it seems you and Ardsmore are continuing the fine Harcourt traditions of scandalous behavior."

Nicole shrugged, unable to meet his eyes.

"Would you like to tell me about it?" Maurice queried.

"There is nothing to tell."

"That is not what the gossip mongers are whispering. The servant grapevine has already spread tales," he added vehemently.

"I see," she said stiffly.

"No, I don't think you do."

It had been wrong to come here. The Marquis took sides with the Harcourts and there would be no help from him. It had been a false step.

"I think you had better be prepared for the worst."

"The worst?"

"Yes."

"What do you mean?"

Relentlessly the Marquis went on, "Before returning to Vienna, Ardsmore came to Paris to see Tessa Von Hoffman."

"Oh." She grew deathly pale and turned abruptly from the Marquis. "It was to be expected." So there was to be no reconciliation. She would never forgive him for turning to Tessa. Never!

"I see. Then perhaps you are better prepared for the future you have carved out for yourself than I expected," he asserted angrily.

Straightening her back in response to his outburst, Nicole turned to face him. "I ask nothing from anyone. I am quite capable of handling my own affairs. It was a mistake to come here and I shall leave at once." She started toward the door, but his voice arrested her.

"Foolish child! Do you think that I too intend to desert you?" he shouted at her.

Nicole's lips quivered, but she refused to give in to her

emotions. Noticing her effort, Maurice softened. "Come here." He opened his arms. "We shall plan the future together if you will accept the advice of an old man."

Trembling with relief and exhaustion, Nicole flung herself into his arms. Minutes passed with neither speaking; however, the interlude of comfort was brief. Distant chimes rang and Nicole questioned, "Are you expecting company?"

He shook his head negatively just as his butler announced Lady Eleanore. She burst into the room, a dignified but determined figure.

"So, Maurice, you have chosen to support this *malcontent!*"

Maurice forced Nicole into a chair before addressing the dowager Viscountess. *"Ma chère* Eleanore, won't you please be seated while I ring for some refreshments?"

"I do not want refreshments, Maurice! I want an explanation of this fiasco. I should have known this girl would cause a scandal and follow her mother's example, and I want to know what she intends to do about this shocking breach of duty." Lady Eleanore pointed a quivering finger at Nicole.

"It was your son who walked out on me! Perhaps you had best ask him." Nicole rose hastily to defend herself.

"I have already received a communiqué from him informing me that I must take you to London with me."

"You need not bother yourself. I have no intention of returning to London."

"You what?"

"I am going to remain right here. After all, Paris is my home, and now that I am independently wealthy, there is no reason why I should go where I am not wanted."

"If you . . . if you choose to remain here *unescorted* . . ."

"Uncle Maurice has graciously consented to be my

chaperon. And Madame Lafitte will be returning quite soon from her sister's."

"Maurice, you are not going to support her in this . . . this act of defiance!"

Forced into the role of mediator, Maurice attempted to control the rising tide of emotions. "Eleanore, I think it best at present for Nicole to remain here."

Both women began to speak at once.

"Nicole! Eleanore! Enough! This caterwauling will desist immediately!" he demanded frantically. They grew silent. "That is better. Now it is quite evident that you and Nicole are no better suited to live together in your present frame of minds than were Ardsmore and Nicole! This marriage happened too quickly." He peered hopefully from one woman to the other. "Perhaps in time . . ." He saw the warring look on Nicole's face and added, "But we shall have to wait and see, eh? In the meantime I shall acquaint Nicole with Parisian society."

"But everyone will be talking about Valentin and me."

"She is right," Lady Eleanore agreed.

"Eleanore, you know better than anyone the time to hold your head highest is at the moment the heat is hottest. Let them gossip. What can they prove if the Harcourts close ranks? All anyone need know is that Ardsmore is completing his assignment for the Duke of Wellington in Vienna."

"I still think she should return to London with me."

"Well, I won't!"

"Then I am washing my hands of you, my girl. Your mother took the same defiant attitude. It is a nightmare repeating itself." She rose instantly. "Maurice, I pity you your burden." She glared at Nicole. "But I accept your gallant offer to help the Harcourts out of this . . . this disastrous situation. As for you, Nicole, I hope in time you come to your senses."

Maurice kept Nicole from replying with a beseeching look. "I shall escort you to the door, Eleanore." He took her by the elbow and firmly closed the door behind them.

Eleanore stared up at him. "Did she tell you what went wrong?"

"No."

"Oh, I could box both their ears."

"The damage is done. Now it must be repaired. I shall see to Nicole for the present."

"I hope you . . . we do not regret this, Maurice," Eleanore cried in an anguished whisper.

"Well, well . . . we must play for time, my dear. A reconciliation might be managed in the future. Let us take one day at a time."

"Perhaps you are right, but I am most uneasy about the distance between them."

"Think how lucky you are that it is happening on the Continent. When you are in London, it will be easier to pooh-pooh the rumors," he chuckled.

"If only you are right."

"When do you return to London?"

"Very soon."

"*Bien,* I think it is best. If you are not here, there will be no need to explain why Nicole is not staying with you. She simply decided to wait in Paris for Ardsmore to complete his work in Vienna, eh?"

"Yes, his commission is up in a few months."

"By then we will hope for a change."

They had reached the entrance. "*Au revoir,* Eleanore. God speed."

"Good-bye, Maurice, and God bless." Briefly she clung to him as he kissed her cheek.

Upon returning to the drawing room, Maurice encountered a stormy Nicole.

"Did you pacify her?"

"Now, now, *mon enfant*. Did I not try to comfort you? Could I do less for a woman I have known for thirty years?" he grumbled.

"I am sorry, Uncle Maurice. It is just that everything has become so confusing."

He laughed. "To say the least, my child. To say the least."

She smiled tentatively and relaxed.

Chapter VIII

Lord Ardsmore arrived at his headquarters in Vienna one bitter winter night during a heavy snowstorm. His rooms overlooking the Danube were damp and sparsely furnished, doing little to relieve the gloomy thoughts filling his mind about life in general and women in particular.

In the days following his arrival he threw himself into his work preparing for the Duke of Wellington to replace Lord Castlereagh at the Congress of Vienna. It was a difficult job requiring the arts of diplomacy as well as the social graces. The major negotiations of the Congress were conducted at balls and receptions and in secret committees rather than in formal sessions. The atmosphere of social gaiety masking the diplomatic intrigues in which the

fate of nations was decided by an uneasy alliance of the
Great Powers demanded constant attention from the Viscount. It afforded him little time for his own problems.

However, on returning to quarters one night he found a
letter from Lady Eleanore that was all complaints about
Nicole. The thoughts about his marriage which he had
pushed to a corner of his mind came forth to plague him.
Why hadn't Nicole gone to London with his mother so he
could have some peace of mind? The girl was being deliberately unpredictable and obstinate, making the breach
between them worse than it was. She was a fool!

But he had washed his hands of her, hadn't he? She
could go to blazes and he was well rid of her. Or was he?
Could he really push Nicole out of his life so easily? The
memory of those violet eyes shimmering with unshed
tears cut his heart to the core. Damn it all, he was in love
with Nicole and she hated him! Hell, what was the use of
torturing himself? Nicole was in Paris and he was in Vienna. He would have to close the door on that problem
for the time being.

Among those stationed with the Viscount in the Aus-
trian capital were several of his comrades from his Penin-
sular campaigning. It was a seasoned corps from the best
families of the English aristocracy that the Duke of
Wellington had gathered about himself. They were a fine
blend of hardy manhood and cultured breeding, and
they addressed themselves to the duties of military diplomacy with a charm and skill that made them the envy
of less polished contingents from other countries.

The Viscount spent whatever free time he had in the
rooms of one or another of these gentlemen playing card
games and enjoying the friendly raillery of his comrades.
But cards no longer supplied the excitement they once
did and now that money was not an urgency for him, he

found the spice of gambling losing its savor. He was not sure this was an altogether agreeable consequence of his sudden change in fortune.

An even less desirable change he began to perceive in himself was in his regard for the ladies. Vienna was overflowing with exotic lovelies from many nations, yet it was a rather detached view he took of the fairer sex lately, and many a fetching smile was rewarded by a distant gaze from the Viscount.

It was thoughts about this very change in himself that interrupted his card game in Major Ainsley's rooms one night. The Viscount was losing steadily but could not rouse himself enough to really care, which made him wonder if the rewards of a beautiful wife and a ready purse were indeed so rewarding after all. God keep him from turning into a sober figure of propriety! He laughed aloud at the absurdity of such a thought.

"Well, Ardsmore, it's a deuced queer sort who laughs when his blunt is spent on hands such as you have held this evening," Major Ainsley commented with a note of disapproval tinging his words.

"It's a strange circumstance, I'll agree, Ainsley. But it was not exactly the turn of the cards that stirred my humor," the Viscount replied lazily.

"And it was not the wine, I'll wager. This Rhenish will do when there is nothing else, but it cannot compare with a hearty claret or Burgundy if you ask me," interjected Captain Wentworth.

"And who asked you?" Ainsley jeered good-naturedly. "What I want is the Viscount's explanation for that cursed laugh that rattled my play just moments ago. Come, now, Ardsmore, out with it. The Congress taking its toll of the old brain box, eh?"

"I must admit I would rather fight my wars on a battlefield than in the ballroom, but it's not the Congress that piqued my fancy just now," Valentin replied.

Andrew Van Stratton, a new member of the Duke's staff, took up the discussion. "Well, if it's not old Hookey and the Congress, then it must be a female. Nothing like the fairer sex for cutting up a man's peace. Who is it these days, old man?"

Ainsley, noting the sudden dark look on the Viscount's face, sought to cover Van Stratton's blunder. "Put a damper on it will you, Andy. Don't you know his lordship is a respectably married man these days? Hear that wife of yours is a real beauty, Ardsmore."

If anything, the Viscount's face grew darker, and there was a sudden tension in the air. No one spoke, fearing to add to the offense—whatever it was. Realizing his ill humor was spoiling the game, the Viscount relaxed and spoke jestingly. "Beauty though my wife may be, she will never cast the cloak of respectability over these shoulders. God prevent it until I am dead and buried."

"Here, here!" shouted Wentworth.

The others quickly took up the cry and turned to their cards with a sigh of relief. Their good friend had been acting deuced queer lately.

The time was passing with equal strain for the new Viscountess. As she sat alone before a dying fire one evening, Nicole was suddenly startled by a tall blond figure standing in the doorway.

"Val!" she cried jumping to her feet only to realize her mistake.

"Sorry to have startled you like that, Nicole." Perry hesitated, uncertain of his welcome.

"Just for a moment I thought . . . well never mind . . ." she stammered. "Do come in. I am so glad to see you."

Perry came forward and clasped her hand in his. "Come sit beside me and tell me what you have been doing since the . . . wedding." Embarrassed, she lowered her gaze from his.

"Gee, Nicole," he sympathized. "I don't know what has got into that numbskull of a brother . . ."

"Perry, please," she pleaded tightening her grasp on his fingers. "Let's not talk about it. No serious discussions right now."

"As you wish," he smiled reassuringly. An awkward silence reigned briefly until Perry jumped to his feet and reached for the bell cord announcing, "Let's get one of those lazy servants to bring us a bottle of Burgundy. If you were a man, Nicole, I would suggest our getting foxed together."

"That's all I would need to complete my ruination," she frowned.

"Believe me, I wouldn't tell," he smiled mischievously and turned to the servant who was entering the room. "Ah, Jacques, a bottle of the Marquis's finest Burgandy, if you please."

Within minutes Perry was pouring two glasses brimful of the sparkling liquid and, handing one glass to Nicole he said, "I shall now propose a toast. To my freedom!"

"Your freedom?" Nicole questioned.

"Yes, Mother and Cecily are leaving in the morning and I shall be entirely on my own."

"But are you not to accompany them?"

"Heaven forbid!"

"Perry, you are incorrigible!" she laughed.

"Quite! And shameless too. A true Harcourt. Live for today and forget about tomorrow!"

Sobering immediately Nicole asked, "Is that the trouble with the Harcourts?"

"Hey, no serious conversations. You so decreed upon my entry. Remember?"

"Yes, so I did."

"Then no sullens. All right."

"You're right, Perry, no sullens. Let's drink to this moment and our friendship."

"I like that. To us!" He took a hardy gulp. "Since I am sticking around a while—at least until I return to school—will you let me be your escort?"

"That is kind of you, Perry, but I am afraid I shall not be going anywhere."

Perry nodded in agreement but asked anyway, "Have you done your Christmas shopping?"

"Why, no. I have not given it much thought."

"You mean you haven't considered what you'll give your favorite brother-in-law for Christmas?" She laughed at his banter. "Then tomorrow, my lady," he bowed. "I shall escort you to the finest boutiques along the Rue de la Paix and Rue de Rivoli. There you may shop until your heart is content. Will you come?"

"How could I refuse? Yes, I should love to come with you."

"And where do you plan on taking her?" came an angry voice from the doorway.

"Oh, Uncle Maurice, I didn't know you had returned." Nicole hurried to his side and took his arm, leading him across the room.

"It is a good thing I came home early or this rascal would deplete my wine cellar." The Marquis picked up the decanter and studied its contents.

"Unfair, Uncle! I have ordered but one bottle," cried Perry.

"Of my best, nephew." The Marquis scowled as he scrutinized the label. "You chose well."

"Won't you join us?" Perry asked warily.

The Marquis snorted and accepted the glass Perry handed him, then seated himself beside Nicole. "And where do you propose to go tomorrow?"

"Christmas shopping."

"Ah, yes, the time grows near. One tends to forget at my age." He nodded his head reflectively. "Very well, nephew, you may escort her on the condition you behave like a gentleman."

"Uncle," Perry claimed in mock sadness, his hands over his heart. "You wound me."

"Ha! That would be impossible, you young scapegrace."

"*Monsieur le Marquis,* again I protest. What kind of impression will you be giving my sister-in-law?" Perry was beginning to bristle at the insults.

Before the Marquis could reply, Nicole intervened, "Gentlemen! Not another word on the subject or I shall retire immediately."

"You see, nephew, you have managed to upset the lady."

"I? That's not so . . ."

"Are you contradicting me?"

"Why you cantankerous . . ." Perry fumed.

Nicole jumped to her feet and, as she marched to the door the quarreling pair ceased their wrangling and apologized simultaneously.

"That's better. Let us enjoy the remainder of the evening in peace."

Reluctantly they seated themselves on either side of her and applied themselves to the remaining wine and to entertaining Nicole.

"Hang on!" Perry shouted to Nicole over the noise of the busy shoppers. They were maneuvering along the crowded boulevard among the jostling throngs darting in and out of the festively decorated shops. Perry and Nicole entered a couturier's where Nicole searched for a suitable gift for Madame Lafitte. She decided on a silk scarf in peacock blue and continued to the perfumers and jewelers under Perry's guidance.

"Isn't it exciting? I just adore the Christmas bustle."

"Exciting?" Perry stared at her in bewilderment.

"Everyone seems so happy today and just a few months ago the French people were so desperate. It's like a miracle. There's a feeling of hope again, and Christmas is such a glorious holiday. We must celebrate it fully." Nicole chatted happily. "Do you think you might get us a Yule log?"

"The wassail punch is more my style."

"That too. And I will decorate the mantle with ferns."

"Sure seems like a lot of fuss," Perry grumbled.

"Oh, Perry, where's your Christmas spirit?" she asked but did not wait for a reply. A jeweler's window display caught her eye. "Over here, Perry. I think I have found just the gift for Uncle Maurice."

He pushed his way to her side and looked at the blue and gold cloisonné snuff box Nicole was pointing to. "What do you think?"

Perry shrugged, but Nicole was already entering the shop. In her haste she almost collided with a gentleman who was about to leave.

It was Perry who recognized him. "I say, Danforth, do you make it a habit of following us, or is it coincidence that you keep popping up when I have the pleasure of accompanying my sister-in-law?"

"A most happy coincidence I can assure you." Gordon Danforth smiled fleetingly and bowed to Nicole who had turned to face him. "Lady Ardsmore, my pleasure."

"Mr. Danforth, how nice to see you again."

"Thank you. Are you doing your Christmas shopping?"

"Yes, and you?"

"The same."

She did not like his scrutiny and turned abruptly to the clerk to order the snuff box.

"Would you have time to join me for an aperitif before . . ."

"Oh, I do not think we will have time." Nicole interrupted him before Perry could reply.

Undaunted by his sister-in-law's denial, however, Perry contradicted her. "Sure we do, Nicole. We have the whole day, and my feet are killing me!"

"There is a splendid restaurant at the end of the arcade. Quite exclusive. Shall we say about four?" Danforth seemed as determined as Perry that she would concede to their wish. Nicole hesitated between good manners and a rude refusal. She could murder Perry for forcing her to associate with this man whom her husband considered his closest friend.

"Very well," she acquiesced rather ungraciously.

"Until four," Danforth bowed solemnly and retreated.

"Nicole, why didn't you want to meet him? Gordon Danforth is a perfect gentleman and . . ."

"And a spying friend of your brother's!" she spat at him. Perry opened his mouth to protest but Nicole silenced him, "I do not wish to discuss it! Let us finish our Christmas shopping."

Nicole fumed inwardly through the next half hour as Perry hovered nearby in his own black mood. Finally she asked, "Don't you have any shopping of your own to do?"

"As a matter of fact I do!"

"Well, then, go do it!"

Color suffused his face as Perry jammed his hat on his head, whirled on his heels and stalked away. Realizing she had hurt him unjustly, Nicole's anger turned against herself. She had been unkind to one who had treated her only with consideration. It was her infernal Harcourt temper. She must apologize to Perry and find an appropriate gift to accompany that apology. Returning to the jeweler's, she selected a silver stick pin for her brother-in-law and had it wrapped in holiday paper. As she turned to leave, her attention was caught by another piece of jewelry. It was an emerald and sapphire stick-pin cunningly fashioned as a mask of tragedy. It was the perfect gift for Valentin. She stared transfixed by the desire to buy it. The temptation was too powerful to resist. "I'll take it," she heard herself saying, and gathering her purchases she left the shop to meet Perry in the arcade.

They met Danforth in a small café on the Rue de la Paix. Although Nicole tried to cover her agitation from Valentin's polite well-mannered friend, conversation was strained. She could not relax in Gordon Danforth's presence. For Nicole, his loyalty to the Viscount was an obstacle impeding the natural flow of friendship between them. She was seeking a means of early retreat when she heard her name being called. She turned to see a fair-haired girl in a faded blue gown making her way toward the table.

"Nicole, is it really you?"

"Geneviève!" Nicole exclaimed rising to embrace the girl joyfully. Geneviève Lumière and Nicole Harcourt had been inseparable friends at St. Agnes's School but had not seen each other in recent years.

"*Ma chère* Nicole, how wonderful to find you like this." Mademoiselle Lumière smiled and looked at Nicole's two companions whom Nicole introduced while inviting her to join them.

"Only for a moment. I am with *Tante* Aline," she explained as she was seated. "So, *mon amie,* you are a married woman. I . . . I am . . . happy for you."

Nicole knew the cause of Geneviève's hesitant good wishes. "I was sorry to hear about Henri, Ginny. Your brother was a dear friend to me, and I shall always remember him kindly."

Geneviève seemed to forget the others. "He had hoped to make you a member of the family one day . . ."

Casting a nervous glance at the two men, Nicole spoke hastily. "But, Ginny, you must know that could never have been."

Catching the anxiety in Nicole's voice, Mademoiselle Lumière recovered her poise and turned the conversation into less sensitive channels of school-day recollections. Danforth and Perry questioned the girls about St. Agnes's and added a few anecdotes about their own school days that amused their feminine listeners.

"Oh, but it is so good to laugh with you again, Nicole. How I have missed our cozy *tête-à-têtes.*" She paused glancing around the room. "But now I must leave you and join *Tante* Aline. She grows impatient, I fear."

"Very well, Ginny, but you must come and visit me soon. We have much to catch up on. Madame Lafitte is returning to Paris any day now and will insist on seeing you."

"I too would like to see the good woman again," Ginny claimed earnestly. "Nicole, *chérie,* we will have a long visit, *n'est-ce pas?*"

"Indeed we shall," Nicole reassured her.

"My aunt beckons . . ."

"Allow me to escort you, Mademoiselle Lumière,"

Danforth said as he rose to take her arm and she smiled up at him as they moved away.

Placing the last branch of ferns above the mantle and stepping back, Nicole observed her handiwork. "Mmm, what do you think, Jacques?"

"Very nice, madame."

"Do you think the Marquis will approve?"

"*Mais oui,* in the old days *Monseiur le Marquis* and his family celebrated the *Noël* in great style."

"You have been with him a very long time?"

"*Oui,* when he was separated from his family all those years ago, I was the only one left."

"What happened, Jacques?"

"*Monsieur le Marquis* and his family planned an escape, but the Marquis was taken ill and could not travel, so he ordered the family to go ahead without him. Unfortunately they were taken captive by the citizens of the tribunal. In the confusion the Marquis did not discover what had happened to his family until we reached England. Then it was too late." Jacques shook his head.

"I see," Nicole said quietly. "We must make this a happy time for him."

As they sat before the fire later that evening, the Marquis remarked, "I thought that young scalawag was going to join us for midnight Mass."

"I am sure he will be here presently. I do not know what is keeping him."

"Probably decided he could not take the religious service. Protestants are all alike," he grumbled.

"Uncle, perhaps you forget I fall into that category myself."

"Your mother was Catholic."

"Yes, but my father was a Protestant."

"You cannot help it if you had strange parents."

Nicole laughed, "I suppose that is one way of looking at it."

"Now, do not take offense at an old man, *enfant*."

"I love you too much to do that, Uncle Maurice." Impulsively she kissed him on the cheek. "I could not take offense at you."

Suddenly there was a loud crash outside the drawing room, and Perry exclaimed, "Damn, I told you to hold it, Jacques!"

"But, my lord, I could not do both," Jacques complained.

"What is it? What is it?" stormed the Marquis as he and Nicole rushed to the entrance. "A forest! He has brought a forest into my home! I knew it! I knew it would happen! He has finally lost his last scrap of sanity."

"I lugged this . . . this monstrous log all the way from the Left Bank and this is the thanks I get . . . recriminations!" Perry retorted.

"Oh, Perry," Nicole cried happily and ran to him. "You did not forget the Yule log."

"And the vendor told me it was big enough to last until New Year's Day."

"What?" exclaimed the Marquis.

"Well, isn't it one of your Frenchy customs?"

"Frenchy!" sputtered the Marquis. *"Sacré Bleu!"*

"He did not mean it, Uncle," Nicole interceded coming between them. "Besides, Perry is right. In Provence it is the custom."

"This is not Provence," the Marquis exploded.

"But, Uncle, Perry has gone through all this trouble just to please us and I think it was a lovely gesture. Thank you." She kissed Perry's cheek. *"Joyeux Noël,* Perry."

"Happy Christmas, Nicole," he said kissing her on the lips lightly.

The Marquis, observing the glow in Nicole's eyes, softened. "Very well, come along, boy, help Jacques and me get this thing into the fireplace so that we can go to church."

On Christmas Day Nicole and the Marquis were joined by friends for dinner. Perry, Danforth, Geneviève and her Aunt Aline, whom Nicole had invited, and Madame Chenier, an old friend of the Marquis's from the days before the Revolution, gathered in the drawing room where the Yule log blazed invitingly.

Before dinner the Marquis closeted himself with Danforth in an effort to gain some information concerning the Viscount. Danforth was the one who had informed the Marquis of his nephew's liaison with Tessa Von Hoffman following the honeymoon débacle. Although Danforth was unable to furnish the old man with further information, he agreed to keep him abreast of the news.

After a magnificent dinner which included both the French and English Christmas specialties of roast duck, peacock Strasbourg, mince pie and two puddings—black pudding and English plum pudding, Nicole and Geneviève entertained the others by playing the piano and singing.

Toward evening Perry disappeared for some three-quarters of an hour, and when he returned with Jacques, he wheeled in a large bowl of wassail punch containing hot ale, spices and toasted apples. After one glass of the strong herb punch, the merriment of the company increased. The Marquis and Madame Chenier began reminiscing about the good times at the court of Versailles. Their infectious laughter over youthful follies grew boisterous, and Perry plied them with more punch and eager questions. Gales of laughter erupted, and in the warmth and glow of the cozy room all abandoned their stiffness and formality.

As the night wore on, Gordon Danforth and Geneviève Lumière were observed to leave the group, and their absorption in one another was noted by more than one interested party.

"Your voice is enchanting, mademoiselle," Gordon was saying to her.

"Monsieur Danforth, you try to flatter me, I think." Geneviève dimpled prettily.

"No, I am in earnest."

"Then you are kindness itself, for . . ."

"I assure you I am not being kind, only truthful."

Touched by his sincerity, Geneviève gazed wonderingly into his eyes and Gordon caught his breath at the intensity of feeling this winsome creature aroused in him.

Breaking the awkward silence that stretched between them Geneviève asked, "You have enjoyed the *Noël?*"

"Immensely, for it gave me the opportunity to see you again."

"Monsieur." She blushed.

"I say, you two," Perry broke in on them. "Come and join Nicole and me in a game of whist, will you?"

"Only if you insist," Gordon replied.

"Well, if that don't beat all," Perry cried. "What about you, mademoiselle?"

Geneviève laughed gaily at Perry's chagrin. "But of course, we will join you. Will we not, Monsieur Danforth?"

"Only if I may be your partner?"

"Most certainly," she agreed taking his proffered arm.

Later when Danforth escorted the Lumières home, no one was particularly surprised and Nicole wondered if Gordon and Geneviève could be attracted to one another. Unusually intellectual for a girl, Geneviève would be drawn to a quiet, studious man such as Gordon Danforth. As for him, he would find Geneviève not only lovely but intelligent and sensitive. They would suit temperamentally very well. Yet it would not do . . . Geneviève's background and his. Perry had told Nicole that Gordon Danforth was a younger son with little money, and Geneviève was penniless. She paused in her reflections. Was it possible that Danforth was after some information about the new Viscountess through her friend, Geneviève? No! She would not let such suspicions spoil an almost perfect day. If only Valentin had been here to share the festivities.

And what was her husband doing at this moment? Was he alone in Vienna? Or was he spending his time with friends? And what friends? Another woman? She must not think it! She would force her thoughts to other things. But had Valentin spared her one thought since that fateful night?

In point of fact, Valentin was standing at a pair of opened balcony doors and looking out across the boulevard toward the Gothic spires of St. Stephen's Cathedral.

"Come back to us, my lord," came the beckoning cry of one damsel from the party inside. Not heeding her, he stepped out onto the balcony and listened to the solemn sound of the church bells striking twelve. Christmas was over. A feeling of overwhelming loneliness crept over him as he fingered the small box in his pocket. He had not sent it after all. Just as he had not sent the notes and letters he had written since his arrival in Vienna. They had met the same fate as the small jewel box in his hand. All to naught.

"Ardsmore, we are all going on to Gustav's. Are you coming?" a fellow officer asked.

"But, of course, he is coming," a low sultry voice said beside him. "There will be dancing, singing, games, and . . ." she looked up at him with dark liquid eyes. "And

126

. . . who knows what else, eh?" She laughed seductively and wound her arm through his.

For a time he stared at her. He did not feel the least desire to join them. How could one woman do this to him? It was ridiculous of Nicole—just because he muttered a woman's name in his sleep. But it was more than that. He should never have forced Nicole to yield to him and then walked out on her. What rotten behavior! If only he had held his temper and soothed her hurt pride. He sighed and dragged on his cigar. Then looking more intently at the girl beside him, he forced a wry smile, "Hell, why not? The 'what else' may prove interesting." Sauntering into the room with the woman he thought, tonight I will have a good time and be damned to Nicole!

Chapter IX

At the request of the Marquis de Crécy, Madame Lucille Chenier became the new Viscountess' companion and preceptress into the ways of the Parisian *ton*. Quick to grasp the sketchy facts placed before her about her charge, Lucille took on her duties enthusiastically. A number of strictures were imparted to the Viscountess about the *beau monde*. The solecism she must avoid at all costs was to admit that there was a breach between her and the Viscount. This was of utmost importance. In no way was she to provide the scandal mongers with food for gossip.

On the night of the Wexfords' ball, Nicole's first appearance in a society function since becoming the Viscountess Ardsmore, Madame Chenier presented her to the Marquis.

"Well, Maurice, *mon ami,* what do you think of your niece's appearance?"

The Marquis squinted at the vision in front of him. Nicole wore a gown of cream-colored satin overlaid with sheer gold netting and the Ardsmore diamonds at her throat. *"Magnifique,* child, they shall have little time to speculate on your marriage when they are confronted with your loveliness. If I were younger myself, I would fall under your spell."

"Uncle, you shall make me blush."

"Nothing but the truth, *chérie.* My nephew must have taken leave of his senses . . ."

A warning look from Madame Chenier stopped him as she covered smoothly, "Young couples often have their differences, *n'est-ce pas*? Tonight as I have already instructed Nicole, she is to gloss over the breach so that a satisfactory image can be maintained. And if Lady Eleanore instructed the Viscount as you recommended in your letter, we should contrive to squelch the gossip nicely."

"It makes my head spin."

"No, Nicole, not yet. Perhaps by the end of the evening we can permit that, but now we must go . . ."

"To meet the enemy!" concluded the Marquis, and they escorted the Viscountess to the carriage.

Flanked by Madame Chenier and the Marquis de Crécy, Nicole entered through the wide double doors into the Wexfords' ballroom. Her first impression was of a splendid, gold-tinted room filled with swirling dancers in colorful gowns and uniforms. As they advanced farther into the room, Madame Chenier and the Marquis began to greet various acquaintances, some of whom Nicole remembered from her wedding day. Nicole was subjected to undisguised scrutiny as introductions were pressed upon her, and her attention was drawn from one claimant to another.

A waltz was struck up by the orchestra, and Gordon

Danforth, emerging from the sea of unfamiliar faces, came forth to claim her hand. She gratefully accepted his arm and proceeded to the dance floor where they circled the ballroom in companionable silence until Danforth spoke.

"I hope I find you well, Lady Ardsmore."

"I am very well, thank you." Why, she wondered, could she not relax with this man?

"You are in extremely good looks this evening, and if I am any judge of society, you will be taken up and become all the rage."

"My dear sir, you will turn my head with such flattery."

"It is merely the truth as I see it. The Viscount will be proud to hear of your success."

The mention of Valentin startled Nicole. "You are in contact with my . . . my husband?"

"On occasion. Val and I are very close to one another."

His words were a thorn stinging her pride and stirring her discontent.

"Your friendship is one of long standing, is it not?"

"Indeed it is. We are like brothers."

"How charming," Nicole could not avoid a sneer creeping into her voice.

"Do I detect a note of disapproval?" Danforth seemed surprised.

"What is there to disapprove of in the loyalty of friendship?"

"It is a loyalty I willingly extend to you. I seek to be no less a friend to you, my dear Viscountess."

"Come now, sir. Surely you are not serious." Nicole's exasperation could no longer be concealed.

Danforth stiffened. "I am afraid I do not understand."

"As the Viscount's closest personal friend you must be well aware of the situation between my . . . husband and me."

"Yes, I am." He did not prevaricate.

"Well then?"

"I repeat, my lady, I would deem it a pleasure if I may ever be of any service to you," he stated formally.

Nicole bit her lip and mumbled a thank you. Actually she wanted to be on better terms with Gordon Danforth. There was no need to antagonize him. He was a link with Valentin, and too, she wanted to ask him about Geneviève Lumière. She was curious to know if an attachment were growing between them.

The music stopped, and she was immediately surrounded by supplicants for her hand for the next dance. She accepted a young officer in a Cossack uniform and was led to the dance floor.

"Well, Danforth," the Marquis pounced as Danforth walked toward him. "Any word from that damnable nephew of mine?"

"I have not heard from him of late, my lord. Besides I do not believe this is the time or the place to discuss the matter." Danforth looked over his shoulder at several interested faces, including that of Constance Burton whose chief contribution to society was her talent for scandal mongering. Danforth tried to signal the Marquis of her presence, but it was useless. The old man plowed on.

"What do you think he intends to do about this abominable situation?"

"Please, sir, if we must discuss it, I believe the room to our right is available."

The Marquis leaned on the arm of Danforth, who escorted him to a small salon off the ballroom.

"Well?" Maurice retorted once inside.

"There is little I can tell you that you do not already know. As I told you, I have received one letter from Val

132

on matters of duty. He made no reference to the Viscountess."

"I wonder if the Von Hoffman woman is with him."

"No, she is still in Paris. As a matter of fact she was seen in the company of Lord Crawley just last night."

"That cur! This whole situation will not do! It just will not do! The Harcourts! The whole pack of 'em are forever getting themselves in trouble, including that meddlesome old fool, Sophie Harcourt. She could not mind her own business—dragging that girl back into the family. Sheer folly! Sheer folly! When you write that nephew of mine, tell him I have a few words to pass on to him."

"I will, my lord."

Danforth was happy to escape from the quarrelsome old man who had decided to remain in the quiet of the small salon instead of rejoining the festivities. Danforth scowled slightly when he emerged from the room and noticed Constance Burton moving away from the door. How long had she been there? He hastened to find Nicole with Madame Chenier and joined their party just as Perry appeared.

"Ah, Gordon," Perry Harcourt grinned at him. "I would say my sister-in-law has made a hit. Devilish pretty girl, isn't she? Don't see why Val . . ." Danforth grasped his shoulder.

"One of these days, boy, you are going to wag your tongue once too often."

"All I said was . . ." The clamp tightened on his shoulder, and Perry caught the warning glance in Danforth's eyes. "Oh, I see." Perry noticed Nicole's frozen stare and blushed a fiery red.

Another partner presented himself to Nicole, and she swept away on his arm. Madame Chenier and Danforth chatted quietly as they watched Nicole's graceful form glide smoothly around the ballroom floor. Seeing no further opportunity to speak with the Viscountess, Danforth took himself to one of the card rooms.

"Well, Madame Chenier," it was Lady Wexford approaching. "Your charge is becoming the center of attention."

"*Oui,* so it seems. How lovely to be young and acclaimed."

"But think of all the problems of the young. All that emotional distress over their romantic involvements and such . . ." Her meaning implicit, Lady Wexford's voice trailed off.

So the confrontation was about to begin, thought Madame Chenier as she remarked, "Then it is best they are left in care of the young who can handle them. Ah, here is my charge. Are you enjoying yourself, my dear?"

"Immensely, Madame Chenier," Nicole replied.

"*Bien.* Lady Wexford was just remarking on your apparent success. You must be sure to report the news of your gracious reception to the Viscount in the very next letter you write to him. I am sure it would gratify him to know of your triumph."

"Indeed yes, madame," Nicole picked up her cue without a flutter and joined ranks with Madame Chenier in the developing skirmish. "It is just as my husband assured me before he returned to his duty."

"And what was that, *ma chère?*"

"Only that I would be well looked after in his absence by his family's friends and acquaintances."

Lady Wexford was hard put to conceal her annoyance at this smug exchange until Constance Burton joined their group and lent her support to the outflanked Wexford detachment.

"Lady Wexford, I was hoping to see Tessa Von Hoffman here this evening," Constance Burton murmured ingratiatingly.

"I am not certain. I believe she has been called out of town."

"Oh, no, I heard young Gordon Danforth mention that she did not leave Paris after all. You have not had the pleasure of meeting her have you, Lady Ardsmore?" Lady Burton smiled slyly.

"And I hope she never will," injected Madame Chenier before Nicole could reply. "That woman is becoming the talk of the *ton* with her exaggerated exploits. If she is not careful, she will soon find herself disbarred from polite society. Nicole, I see your Uncle Maurice beckoning to us. If you will excuse us." Madame Chenier steered Nicole away from the other women. "Pay Constance no heed. She has been spiteful ever since your mama-in-law snubbed her at Almack's a year ago. As for the Wexford's, they numbered themselves among Cecily Fairfax's friends," Madame Chenier explained.

"I cannot endure much more of these polite faces masking spite and malice," Nicole complained.

"Everyone wears a mask or two and you must not forget it, *ma chère*. Perhaps you, too, wear one, eh?" Before Nicole could reply, Madame Chenier addressed the Marquis, "Have you come to take us to supper?"

"I would be honored, ladies. I have already ordered Peregrine to secure a table for us."

It was also Perry who filled their platters and then urged Nicole to try some of the rarer delicacies which adorned her plate. "Try this canapé. It is a creation of the Wexfords' chef, and it is quite superb."

Nicole nibbled lightly at the stuffed oyster and declared it delicious.

"I consider myself an expert on fine food," Perry boasted.

"In my day I, too, was a connoisseur," stated the Marquis.

"You, Uncle!" Perry grinned mischievously.

"Do not laugh, my lad. Ask Madame Chenier if I were not."

"It is true, Perry," Madame Chenier verified. "In his younger days your uncle gave dinner parties that were unsurpassed."

"I cannot believe it, Uncle."

"You best had, my boy. Just because I do not entertain very much any more does not mean that I never did."

"Egad, Uncle Maurice, don't break a blood vessel. I believe you."

"Of course he does, Uncle Maurice," Nicole added. "How could he forget that wonderful weekend we spent with you at your chateau?" Both Nicole and Perry were relieved to have Gordon Danforth join them at that moment and divert the conversation.

When they returned to an almost deserted ballroom, Perry was hailed by a young officer and his wife who were coming off the dance floor; accordingly Nicole was introduced to the Bramwells.

"We have already met," smiled Helen Bramwell, "at your wedding. But how could you be expected to remember so many new faces? I could not remember a thing about my wedding reception, could I, Harry?"

"No, my pet, but the champagne had something to do with that, I suspect," her indulgent spouse teased.

"Horrid boy," she giggled.

"Come let us have a glass now," Harry Bramwell suggested.

"Great idea! What shall we toast?" Perry agreed enthusiastically.

"To a continuing peace. I desire no wars to interrupt our honeymoon."

"Do not even suggest it, Harry. It upsets me terribly to think of you in battle. I do wish you would resign your commission."

"I'll wager Lady Ardsmore has not made such a request of the Viscount."

Helen Bramwell looked at Nicole searchingly and cried, "And I'll wager Lady Ardsmore wishes the Viscount were here right now instead of being away on duty."

Several onlookers joined them, eagerly waiting for Nicole's reply.

"Well I . . . I would not want to see the Viscount shirk his responsibility. He has an obligation to the Duke of Wellington."

"I cannot be so noble," Helen sighed. "I can only think of Harry and me, and what it would do to us if we were separated."

"Not all marriages are love matches, however," a new voice commented from among the viewers. Nicole swung around to face the woman who had just spoken those malicious words. She was stunned by the sight of Tessa Von Hoffman.

"Besides, men are ever choosing duty over their wives. It is the lot of we poor females to wait and watch, is it not?"

Nicole merely stared coldly. She would not be drawn into a hypocritical pretense of courtesy in the face of such shameless behavior. Let Tessa get herself out of it if she could.

Madame Von Hoffman looked about her seeking support from the onlookers who were growing uncomfortable as Nicole continued to stare. Trying to recover the situation, Tessa extended her hand, "I do not believe we have been introduced. I am . . ."

"I know who you are! And we have nothing to say to one another!" Nicole cut her off, and whirling on her heel stalked out of the ballroom to the suppressed gasps of those present. A frigid silence descended on the group; no one was quite sure what to say to cover the embarrassing cut Nicole had delivered Tessa Von Hoffman. It was a *faux pas* of major proportions and the shock waves were felt all the way to Vienna.

The following morning the Marquis's household was a scene of chaos. Madame Chenier had taken to her bed after reproaching Nicole for the destruction of all her carefully laid plans. "Wretched girl," she wailed. "In two seconds you ruined us all. No lady of quality would ever betray herself by behaving like a common cit. I wash my hands of you!"

The Marquis, who had merely commented on the Harcourt temper the night before, wisely stayed out of sight.

Perry was the first to arrive with an account of the aftermath. "Don't look so blue-deviled, my girl, not everyone is down on you, even if Constance Burton allied herself with Madame Von Hoffman. Danforth put the squelch there by asking Tessa about her latest amour, Lord Crawley. Neat move, eh?"

"Honestly, Perry, one minute I am so angry I would like to scream, and the next I would like to crawl into a hole and hide."

Perry chuckled and placed a comforting arm about her shoulders.

"Cheer up, Nicole, it will blow over."

"If everyone were like you, Perry dear, I should not worry a fig, but they are not. Madame Chenier will have nothing more to do with me, and . . . and even poor Uncle Maurice is in hiding today. I am so wretched."

"Then forget it and come riding with me in the park."

"I would rather die first than face all those catty snobs,

138

never knowing who will cut me to my face. It would be too humiliating."

"We'll show 'em we Harcourts don't care what they think," he spoke defiantly.

"Perry, you are a dear, but I am afraid it would take more than you and me to face them down."

"I suppose you are right." He flung himself into a chair. "Now, mama could handle them."

"Yes," Nicole admitted reluctantly.

"Don't take it so hard, Nicole, you are bound to come round. Sure wish Val were here."

Suddenly Nicole's dejection was replaced by a surge of pure fury. "If your brother were here, this would never have happened!"

"Oh . . . I forgot . . . sorry, luv . . . I did not mean . . ." he stuttered an apology.

"I know . . . I know," Nicole became contrite. "I should not take out my wretched temper on you."

"Quite all right. I don't mind. Most everyone in the family does."

"Poor Perry," she took his hand. "Whatever shall I do without you?"

"I still have a few more days to pester you." He grinned.

"I am glad of your pestering ways," she assured him.

"Speaking of 'pestering ways' you owe me a game of piquet. How about now?"

"I don't think I could begin to concentrate . . ."

"All the better. I will get the cards." Perry hurried out of the room.

Dear Perry! She was going to miss him when he returned to London at the end of the week.

Perry was right. Not everyone had dissociated themselves from her. That very afternoon flowers arrived from the Bramwells, and Danforth called with two other friends of the Viscount as a show of support for the troubled Viscountess. And by evening the Marquis joined her for supper to discuss the possibilities of a dinner party in the near future. When she protested that no one would come, he declared that society would not dare refuse his invitation. Although Nicole was not necessarily comforted by this, she voiced no further objections.

It was at this juncture in Nicole's affairs that Madame Lafitte returned. Amidst the excited clamor of ringing doorbells and running servants there was a familiar voice claiming, *"C'est barbare."*

Nicole almost shouted, "Darling Fifi," and flung herself into her arms.

"What I suffered to come to you would make a strong man weep. But *enfin,* I am here."

Madame Lafitte did not question Nicole but made small talk while she observed her former charge. Nicole talked gaily enough and laughed at the little jokes which passed between them; however, the pale face and haunted eyes told a different story. Finally she asked, *"Ma chère,* how may I help you?"

That did it. The barrier was down. The tears flowed as the story of the Wexfords' ball tumbled out, an incoherent jumble of characters and scenes unfamiliar to Madame Lafitte.

"But this Von Hoffman woman, Nicole, was it not settled with her some weeks ago?" Madame Lafitte queried.

"She is still Valentin's mistress!"

"Still? Nicole, are you sure?"

"Sure? I have such assurance that it is breaking my heart."

"Ma pauvre enfant," Lafitte sympathized. "Tell me, what is this assurance you have?"

Nicole hesitated, searching for words to relay what

seemed to her an indelicate disclosure. "Valentin . . . on our wedding night . . . he . . . he called for her."

Madame Lafitte looked shocked. "You mean the Viscount, he sent for her on your wedding night?" Her voice was hushed with incredulity.

"No, no! Of course not."

Madame Lafitte relaxed. *"Eh bien.* But I do not understand? What do you mean he called for her?"

"In his sleep, after . . . oh, you know . . ."

"And this is what makes you so sure Tessa Von Hoffman is his mistress still?"

"Not only that! There is more, much more! Did that woman not come to the Hotel Belmontaine before the wedding?"

"Oui, and Lady Eleanore . . ."

"And Lady Eleanore as usual took charge!"

"But that was the right thing for her to do, I am sure."

"Well, I am not so sure. No! Valentin's mama has treated me all along as if I were an incompetent nobody . . ." Suddenly Nicole was remembering all her grievances against the Harcourt family. The accumulated injuries both real and imagined, began to pour forth. "She made me feel unworthy of the Ardsmore name. And Cecily never thought I was good enough for the Viscount. You know that."

"That may be true, Nicole . . ."

"How can you side with them?" Nicole demanded hotly.

"Ma chère Nicole, I do not take sides with them. We do not even discuss the Harcourts." The woman tried to soothe the distraught girl.

"Oh, yes, we do! I realize it all now. That is exactly what we are discussing. I never should have married Valentin. The Harcourts hated my mother and ruined her life, and now they are ruining mine."

"Nicole, you must not say these things. It is too late for such charges."

"You do not know the final insult in this whole foolish charade, Fifi, do you?"

Lafitte was not sure she wanted to hear the rest, but Nicole plunged ahead anyway.

"My husband left me on our honeymoon and went straight to the arms of Tessa Von Hoffman." Her outrage reached its peak. "He left me and made *me* vulnerable to the maneuvers of that unscrupulous woman! And now the whole world blames me. Oh, it is so unfair! It is insupportable! Whatever am I to do?" Nicole sobbed on Madame Lafitte's shoulder.

"Hush, hush, child, you will make yourself ill. We must think . . . *oui?*" Surely there was an answer to this puzzle. But what? The girl was desperately in love with the Viscount, and it seemed to Lafitte that he was far from indifferent to his bride. Yet these two strong-willed individuals were destroying their chance for happiness. Ah, love, thy guises cause such pain to those who wear the mask.

Chapter X

Fortunately for the pining and unhappy Nicole, the Marquis came up with the right diversion for her—a night at the ballet. A love of the ballet had been instilled in Nicole since early childhood. In her youth Sylvie Harcourt had been a member of the corps de ballet, and because of her Nicole had received more than the average young lady's training in the dance. It was considered necessary that a girl of gentle breeding acquit herself well in the various country dances and waltzes of her day. But anything beyond that was uncalled for and unthinkable. Secretly, Nicole had nurtured a yearning to perform on the stage as her mother once had done.

She vividly remembered her mother's tutelage in the art of the ballet. An empty room at the back of their house had been turned into a dance studio where her mother continued to practice faithfully every morning at the *barre* and train her young daughter in the rigors and intricacies of the dance.

Looking back on it now, Nicole realized that when Sylvie Harcourt practiced her art, the intervening years of her marriage slipped away and she was once again the beautiful ingénue of the Opéra de Paris that claimed the patronage of kings. Striking various poses and attitudes, Sylvie had floated across the room executing intricate dance patterns which she had performed. Eventually she would turn to Nicole and instruct her in the five basic positions essential to the dance. Gaily she would chatter about her career and the courtship of Rupert Harcourt while Nicole worked diligently at the *barre*. When Nicole was ready, Sylvie would sit contentedly while her daughter performed for her, and a faraway look would creep into her eyes as she would recall her own youth. The spell would be abruptly broken the moment Nicole made a mistake and the recriminations would start. The Harcourt blood would prevent Nicole from ever attaining the true spontaneity of a dancer, her mother would charge with dismay.

Desperately wanting to please her mother, Nicole would steal back into the room and practice long hours hoping to undo her mother's disfavor and prove her wrong about her skill as a dancer. Nevertheless, this period in her life was short-lived, for she was soon sent to the convent school and the years passed quickly. Nicole was a young woman when her mother died, and she always regretted never having been able to win her approval.

Naturally, when the Marquis suggested an evening at the ballet, Nicole accepted the invitation with alacrity.

The fiasco at the Wexfords' ball was the last time she had mingled in society, and Nicole looked forward to the

evening despite some apprehension. Her gown for the affair was a dark blue silk in the high-waisted Empire style.
The hem, sleeves, and neckline were embroidered with
brilliants and tiny seed pearls, and she wore a matching
headress. Elbow-length white satin gloves and a dainty
painted fan completed her outfit.

As the Marquis slipped a blue silk cape about her
shoulders, he complimented her, "As always, you are
magnifique."

"Do you think I shall pass inspection?"

"But of course, my child, do not fret. We shall come
around." He patted her arm reassuringly. There was a
definite twinkle in his eyes. Nicole was certain he looked
forward to the confrontation, and his attitude gave her
confidence.

As Nicole stepped into the foyer of the theater on the
Marquis's arm, a number of interested faces focused on
their arrival. With a pounding heart, she walked slowly
through the crowd of people with her head held high.
Jeweled heads turned speculatively in their direction.
Some stared rudely while others smiled encouragingly and
greeted them. There were noisy whispers and some
friendly nods. Clearly it was a mixed victory. She was not
going to be cut—certainly not in the company of the Marquis. However, her reception was a cautious one. A dis-
tinct formality cloaked most of their polite exchanges as
they wended their way toward the grand staircase.

"*Monsieur le Marquis!*" A loud voice arrested them
midway up the staircase.

The Marquis barely turned his head to acknowledge
the man who called. "Sir." He nodded curtly and continued to escort Nicole toward their box.

"This is a pleasant surprise," Lord Crawley said as he
followed closely on their heels.

"What are you doing here, Crawley? I thought by now you would have fleeced enough pockets at the tables to return to England," the Marquis spoke contemptuously.

Crawley laughed, "Don't be such a quarrelsome old devil, Maurice. Will you not introduce me to your charming companion?"

"Damned if I will. I never liked you and neither do any of the Harcourt family!" With that, the Marquis steered Nicole into their box.

Nicole's interest was aroused. This was the man Valentin had wounded in the duel, and she longed to question the Marquis, but his set profile discouraged any inquiry about Lord Crawley.

When the curtain rose, the performers captured her attention completely and she forgot all about Lord Crawley. Seeming to ignore the law of gravity, the dancers glided and spun across the floor in fairylike motions. The beauty of their movements during the *pas de deux* surpassed her expectations. Blissfully transported by the performers' grace and charm, Nicole sat spellbound, overwhelmed by a strong desire to be a part of this enchanting beauty. To experience and share in the dancers' magical world would be sheer delight. Her mother must have felt this need and grievously missed performing in those last years with her father. A sharp pain of regret for her mother's lost world smote Nicole's heart. How deeply Sylvie must have loved Rupert Harcourt to give up such joy. Surely she had not married him just for position and money, as the cruel Harcourt family insinuated. Yet their love had failed and Nicole could not forget her mother's bitter charges against Rupert and his family.

The applause at the end of the first act abruptly drew Nicole back to the present. The Marquis asked her if she were enjoying the ballet, and she pleased him with her enthusiastic praise.

During the intermission several acquaintances joined them in their box including Gordon Danforth who offered to escort Nicole to the refreshment salon. She accepted graciously seeing it as an opportunity to question him on a matter she had been wondering about.

"My dear Mr. Danforth, I have been hoping to ask you about Mademoiselle Lumière." She noted the hot color that flushed his cheeks as he replied. "I have not had the pleasure of seeing her for several days, Lady Ardsmore."

"You must not think me forward, sir, but I could not help noticing the easy sympathy that seemed to grow between the two of you at our Christmas party."

"Not at all, my lady. Mademoiselle Lumière and I have become . . . good friends."

"Geneviève is the best of people, Mr. Danforth. Her friendship is to be greatly valued."

"I am very much aware of the lady's fine qualities . . ."

"Of course. You must forgive me if I sound critical. I am so very fond of Geneviève."

"I understand, and I share your concern for Gene . . . Mademoiselle Lumière. You see I . . . Mademoiselle Lumière . . . that is . . ." Gordon Danforth was stammering uncomfortably when he was interrupted.

"So Gordon, I see you have the good fortune of knowing the Viscountess. Would you be so kind as to introduce us?" Lord Crawley had come up behind them. Danforth scowled but made the unavoidable introductions.

"My dear Lady Ardsmore, if you only knew how desirous I have been of making your acquaintance," Lord Crawley murmured silkily.

"How kind, my lord, but I cannot imagine why you should particularly wish my acquaintance." She knew she should not encourage his attention, but the flicker of danger she felt in his presence was a temptation to her. Nicole studied the heavy features of Lord Crawley's face trying to read the character of the man who was her husband's enemy. Despite a certain predatory manner, there was an attractiveness about his swarthy skin and dark eyes.

"Perhaps you will let me tell you sometime." He was deliberately suggesting something, she felt sure.

"Perhaps I shall," she replied provocatively.

Danforth moved to end the interview by asking pointedly, "Shall we continue to the refreshment salon, Lady Ardsmore?"

But not to be outmaneuvered, Crawley intervened. "It is such a crush in there. I am sure the Viscountess would prefer to wait out here while you secure her refreshment. I will be only too glad to look after her."

Before Danforth could reply, Nicole responded, "Would you be so kind, Gordon?" It was the first time she had ever used his first name. The demands of courtesy left Danforth no recourse, so he bowed stiffly and withdrew.

"Are you enjoying the ballet, Lady Ardsmore?"

"Very much, I find their technical skill amazing."

"I take it you have a knowledge of the dance?"

Nicole hesitated. Was this a sly attempt at a slur, or was he genuinely interested? She decided to proceed on the latter assumption for the present. "Yes, it is one of my favorite art forms."

"It is also one of mine," he smiled broadly. "Do you come to the theater often?"

"This is my first time here, but I hope to see this company in performance again soon. They dance beautifully."

"Indeed they do. I am immensely pleased that you appreciate their excellence."

"Why would that be, Lord Crawley?"

"I am a patron of this troupe, and it is gratifying to find them appreciated by so lovely a lady."

She smiled, accepting the compliment without demur. "It is so good of you to support them. I understand they are fairly new in Paris."

He had managed to capture her interest at last. "This year is their début and being a young company, they are in need of all the backing they can receive. Right now they are having quite a struggle establishing themselves."

"I certainly hope they are able to continue to bring pleasure to so many," Nicole added thoughtfully.

"Including yourself, I trust."

"Why yes." Nicole stiffened slightly, sensing that he was trying to lead her to some point.

"I wonder," he hesitated a moment. "Would I be too bold in suggesting that you yourself might be interested in becoming a patron?"

"Me? A patron? This is rather sudden, my lord; I have never considered myself in such a role."

"If the idea were appealing to you, I could arrange for you to meet the director and his artists," he suggested warily.

Nicole felt herself tempted. "That would be very exciting. But you must give me time to think it over."

"Naturally."

"Excuse me," Danforth appeared with the refreshments. "I believe it is time I was returning Lady Ardsmore to the Marquis."

"Why yes, the intermission must be nearly over. So nice to meet you, my lord. I will think over your suggestion."

"You are too kind, dear lady. Until we meet again." Lord Crawley caught Danforth's eye and smiled before turning smartly on his heel and departing.

Danforth continued to stare after the gentleman's retreating figure.

"He seems a congenial man. Why do the Harcourts detest him so much?"

"That is not for me to discuss, my lady," Danforth said at his most formal. "But believe me, the Viscount would not wish you to become friendly with Crawley."

"Oh, really?" She spoke curtly and turned from him thinking she might enjoy encouraging a man the Viscount held in such contempt.

Danforth grasped her hand and said urgently, "Nicole . . . I may call you Nicole, mayn't I?" She nodded. "Once before I pledged my loyalty to you. Will you let me speak as a friend?"

"No, I would rather you did not!" Nicole pleaded and tried to withdraw her hand; however, he held it more firmly.

"Then may I offer one word of advice?"

"It seems I am obliged to listen since you insist."

"I am afraid I must, Nicole! Lord Crawley is a bad companion for anyone—especially the Harcourts and those who number themselves among Valentin's friends."

"That may be, but I consider myself an exception. I personally have no reason to reject Lord Crawley's friendship. You must let me lead my own life, Gordon. That was understood by the Viscount when he . . . left me."

"Certainly he did not mean for you to ruin your life!" he retorted in exasperation.

Stunned, Nicole stared at him. Then she laughed, "Oh, come sir, you are much too melodramatic. Now, do let us hurry or I shall miss the opening of the second act."

Reluctantly Danforth followed her back to the Marquis's box. Before taking his leave, he mentioned that business compelled him to travel to England for a brief time. However, he hoped to see her within a fortnight.

Rather absentmindedly she attended to the second half of the ballet. Danforth's unexpected departure surprised her since she had hoped to question him further about his courtship of Geneviève. He was about to confide something to her when Lord Crawley had intruded upon them during intermission. And Lord Crawley? He had surprised her too. Could he possibly be the villain everyone depicted? In the name of loyalty she should have nothing to do with him, considering that the original cause of that duel was Crawley's insult to her mother. Perry had taken him up on it, and Valentin had finished it, yet she was sure there was more than that insult causing the hatred between the Harcourts and Crawley. If only Perry were still in town, she could ask him, but he was not, and she was curious about Lord Crawley. Besides he had promised to introduce her to the dancers, and she wanted to meet them. What harm could there be in that?

Flowers arrived from Lord Crawley in the morning with a note requesting the presence of the Viscountess at a party which was to be given for the patrons of the Opéra de Paris. She hesitated, recalling the reactions of both Uncle Maurice and Gordon Danforth toward him. But she decided the problem between the Harcourts and Crawley was not her problem. Refusing to worry about it, Nicole dispatched a note to Crawley. If innuendoes about her and Crawley reached Valentin, all the better. If nothing else, it would wound his pride and give her a little revenge. Yes, Crawley would be a handy diversion. Paris was threatening to be dull, and Nicole had no intention of letting time hang heavy any longer.

The Marquis came into the salon shortly after she had sent off the message and immediately spied the large bouquet of flowers.

"What is this?" He approached the table on which the bouquet rested. "Who is your admirer, Nicole?" A hint of sternness had crept into his voice.

Hesitantly she replied, "Lord Crawley."

"What?" he shouted angrily. "The insolence of the man!"

"Uncle Maurice, it is only a bouquet of flowers."

"*Sacré bleu!*" he stormed, turning a fiery red and flinging his hands in the air. "You do not understand!"

"I understand that Lord Crawley has been kind to me where many others have not."

"Nicole *ma chère*," he shook his head angrily. "Crawley, is someone no man or lady can completely trust. He is a gamester with an unsavory reputation. Besides, he has no love of the Harcourt family. Tread softly, my dear."

"Uncle Maurice," she laughed nervously. "You make him sound sinister, and I am intrigued." Seeing his distress, she added hastily, "However, I shall remember your warning."

"That is all I ask, my child. Come, we should have breakfasted an hour ago."

Unhappily, Nicole followed, remembering the invitation she had just accepted. How was she to break this to the Marquis?

When Nicole finally approached the subject of attending the dinner party at Crawley's, she found the Marquis reluctant but acquiescent. He realized his instinct to shout at her would only stir her to rebellion. The Marquis was beginning to feel that Nicole was becoming too much for him to handle.

Nicole's curiosity about Geneviève Lumière and Gordon Danforth was satisfied the next day when her old friend came to visit. Within minutes of her arrival Geneviève was revealing the concerns of her heart to Nicole.

"Ginny, how serious is it between you and Gordon?"

"I . . . I have never felt this way before in my life."

"And Gordon?"

"I believe it is the same with him. But Nicole . . . his family . . . there is no . . . money . . ." her lips quivered. "And there is this girl . . . to whom he is practically betrothed."

"Oh, dear," Nicole met her friend's anguished eyes. "She has money?"

Geneviève nodded in the affirmative.

"Has there been a formal announcement made?"

"No . . . but there is an understanding."

"I see," Nicole whispered.

"He . . . he has gone home to see . . . if there is a chance . . . to alter the situation. But I fear it is hopeless."

"Oh, Ginny, I am sorry. If only there were something I could do."

"There is nothing." She fought the tears that threatened. "He shall do the honorable thing."

"But what of you? You said he would try to alter things."

"I know, I know, but Gordon must do what is right. And so must I."

Seeing her distress, Nicole tried to soothe her. "I should not have upset you. The power of money to control one's life is so unjust." Nicole was thinking of her own marriage as well as the plight of her friend. "There must be some way to resolve this problem for you and Gordon, Ginny dear. Do not despair; he may yet come up with a solution."

"I can't think what it could be," Geneviève answered hopelessly.

They parted shortly afterward, each saddened by the circumstances of fate over which they had no control and which contrived to make two lovely young women terribly unhappy.

A Madame Coupé was sent by Lord Crawley to chaperone Nicole the night of his party. Both Madame Lafitte and the Marquis stifled their protest about her companion until Nicole had gone. Then the Marquis stomped his cane on the floor and exploded vehemently, "Should have known Crawley would provide a chaperone of dubious character!"

"It is too bad of him to send one such as that to accompany the child. I told her I did not like this venture, but she would not listen," Madame Lafitte agreed.

"It is that damn Harcourt obstinacy! If it were not for this gout . . ." he let his voice trail off as he sagged helplessly back in his chair, his bandaged foot resting on a footstool.

"Do not worry, *Monsieur le Marquis,*" Madame Lafitte consoled, "Nicole, she is headstrong, but she is a good girl."

"Let us hope she uses some common sense tonight," he growled ominously.

Nicole found the party to be a large one with many new faces. The main salon was brightly lighted with candelabra and crystal chandeliers. Its white paneled walls and cream satin draperies created an air of opulence. The ladies were dressed in revealing pastel-hued Empire gowns. Ankles were visible as the women whirled gaily about the room with their partners, who were garbed in dark frock coats, tight evening breeches and colorful vests. Nicole began to wonder about her own appearance, for she had chosen a demure evening dress of pink satin in a classical style, with a comparatively modest décolletage. Her only ornament was a diamond pendant from the Harcourt collection.

Guiding her among his guests, Joseph Crawley casually introduced her to a half dozen new people. They were too many to be remembered, but the name of one guest startled Nicole unpleasantly. "Phillippe Beauchamp!" She repeated the name stiffly, barely disguising her displeasure. Her French past was crowding back into her life at a surprising rate—first Geneviève and now Phillippe. The grinning dandy facing her was none other than her cousin whom she had long ago lost sight of, and would gladly have had it remain so. The Beauchamp family had lived on a small farm outside Beauvais and had allowed their half-English relative, Nicole, to spend a summer with them, but it had not been a happy time and in the following years the visit was not repeated.

"Ma chère cousine Nicole," he fawned over her hand.

Phillippe had been a nasty child who found pleasure in tormenting his young cousin. His simpering cries of delight on discovering her were transparently false.

Lord Crawley observed the exchange with unconcealed interest.

"Mon Dieu, you have grown into such a beauty." Phillippe leered greedily at the diamond pendant at her breast. "I am grateful to the kind fate that has brought us together like this." Nicole snatched back her hand as he continued, "We must not lose touch again. It would be a great pity, *non?"*

"I am afraid that we will have little opportunity to resume our acquaintance, cousin. Once my husband's tour of duty is completed we will be returning to England," she replied, attempting to dampen his enthusiasm.

Phillippe shrugged. "Well, you are here now and I must make the most of what little time there is. We shall dance, *oui?*" Before Nicole could protest he swung her onto the dance floor.

"That was extremely rude, Phillippe," she cried angrily.

"*Vraiment?* Then I will apologize, *chère cousine.*"

"You were rude to his lordship more than to me."

"Who? Joseph? *Au contraire!* He will understand my desire to be with you after all these years."

"There were a number of years you forgot all about my existence," she reminded him tartly.

"But, *chère* Nicole, how could I see you? I was out of the country so much of the time during our Emperor's reign."

"Doing what?"

"This and that." He laughed uneasily. "But let us not talk of the past, but of the present," Phillippe insisted.

"As I mentioned previously, I do not think we will have much opportunity . . ."

"But, of course, your marriage to the Englishman," he seemed to sneer. "Tell me, *ma chère,* why are you not in Vienna with the Viscount?"

How did he know so much about her, she wondered angrily.

"That is our affair!" Nicole replied coldly.

"*Pardonnez moi* if I intrude. It was an innocent enough question I assure you." He watched her closely.

She lowered her eyes not wishing to continue the conversation and murmured something indistinctly. They finished the dance in silence.

"*Merci,* Phillippe, but pray excuse me. I must speak to Lord Crawley." She spoke hastily walking away without allowing him to reply.

Later that evening Nicole met the aged artistic director of the Opéra de Paris, André Volent, his prima ballerina Natalya Lavronsky and her partner Rudolph Ostrosky who invited her to have supper with them. While Ostrosky went for food, Monsieur Volent complained about the plight of his troupe.

"You see, our company has been struggling for so many years. Ever since the fall of the House of Bourbon in '93, support has been meager. Since Louis XIV established the Royal Academy of Dance in the 1600s, dancers have always enjoyed royal patronage. No more, however," the grey-haired maestro explained. "This . . . new aristocracy does not understand the arts."

"But you have received public recognition."

"Recognition, perhaps, but what good is that without financial support?"

"I didn't think. I suppose your expenses were exorbitant?" Nicole questioned.

"But of course. We need to develop a new ballet, one for our times—for our audiences. What does this generation care about Greek myths!"

"I see—to capture the imagination of the young you need to develop a new style," Nicole replied enthusiastically.

"Precisely. That means new costumes, new music, new stories . . . and above all money."

"Maestro," Rudi interrupted as he placed platters of assorted appetizers on the table. "You promised, no unpleasant reminders about our debts, *n'est-ce pas?*"

"Please, André," moaned Lavronsky. "Do not spoil a pleasant evening. Order some champagne from one of those idle footmen, yes?"

"Try one of these shrimp *diable* or stuffed tomatoes," Rudi prompted the maestro.

"Very well, I will not bore the Viscountess with our financial troubles."

"But you are not," she assured him. "I want to know all about the company."

"Ah, a true angel," Rudi pressed a quick kiss to her hand. "Nevertheless, we will not talk of our problems."

"Then tell me about yourselves. How did you manage to get here from Russia during these difficult times?"

Rudi laughed, "You sweet innocent!" She blushed indignantly. "You must promise not to divulge our secret if I tell you."

"No, of course not," she promised.

"Those are our stage names. We both are French."

"Speak for yourself, Rudolph. I, at least, have a Russian grandfather," claimed Natalya.

There was much friendly bickering, and Nicole was quite diverted by the tales of their adventures in establishing their company. For the remainder of the evening they were her constant companions, and it was not long before she found herself offering them her financial support and promising to visit them at rehearsal the very next day.

Nicole left the party expressing her gratitude to Lord Crawley for having provided her with the opportunity of meeting such entertaining people. Crawley was pleased with the results of the evening. Although he had remained unobtrusively in the background, the Viscountess of Ardsmore was being drawn into his plans for her.

Vienna, too, was a scene of unfolding drama. The city was almost giddy with the constant whirl of social events acting as cover for the secrets of nation-making. All restraint was cast aside in the mood of extravagant pleasure seeking.

At a typically festive ball at the Countess Aldenberg's castle, Tessa Von Hoffman made her appearance in Vienna creating a small stir by wearing a shocking gown that did little to conceal her obvious charms. Her bosom was all but bare, and the gown so heavily damped that it clung to her limbs revealing more than it concealed. She paid little attention to the admiring male glances cast hopefully in her direction, since Tessa had a specific target in mind for that evening—the Viscount Ardsmore! He, too, was present. As soon as she discovered his burnished blond head towering above the others, she made straight across the room for him.

"Valentin, *Liebchen,* I have been searching everywhere to find you in this mad crush. Come, talk to me." She placed a soft hand on his arm.

Good God! Valentin thought with a start of guilt. What the deuce am I to do now? He had more than he could handle already. "Tessa, my dear, I am surprised to see you in Vienna." His words were cool.

"Don't you know by now that wherever you go, I am sure to follow?" She smiled provocatively. "Come, *mein Schatz,* there is a *petit salon* where we can be private."

The Viscount had no choice but to follow her. He owed her that much.

"Sit here beside me, *mon brave,*" she beckoned invitingly.

"Tessa, my dear . . ."

"Hush," she interrupted putting her arms possessively around his neck and pressing herself to him. "Kiss me first."

He complied but it was a mechanical performance, a repeat of the scene in Paris after he had left Nicole. He had sought out Tessa in a state of angry pride that night, but found, to his chagrin, that Tessa could do nothing for him. Her voluptuous charms no longer had the power to inflame him as they once had. There remained only the cold ashes of a bright flame that had burned fiercely. He did his best to conceal it from the lady at the time, but he realized now that he should have settled the matter once and for all. Madame Von Hoffman would not fade out and quietly disappear from his life.

Tessa drew back from him and observed his perplexity through veiled eyes.

With a muster of courage Valentin began to explain. "Tessa, my dear, there is something I must say to you." He looked directly into her eyes without wavering.

"No, don't," she protested, sensing the direction in which he was moving. "It is such a joy to see you again, *Liebchen*. We will have some gay times in Vienna, will we not?" she pleaded.

"Tessa, that is what I want to talk about with you," Valentin insisted. "I am in Vienna with the British delegation. My attendance at these affairs is purely a matter of duty."

"And can you not enjoy yourself as well as perform your duty?"

"I do not seek enjoyment."

"Well, then, you are a fool! I know a sense of duty does not keep your wife from enjoying herself!" she flung at him.

"We will keep my wife out of this if you please." He was unable to suppress his anger.

"Your chivalry is admirable. But do you not care that your wife flaunts the Harcourt honor and consorts with your enemy?"

"Enemy? What are you talking about?"

"It is common knowledge that she entertains Lord Crawley. Crawley and a troupe of dancers are her constant companions. She cares nothing for your feelings."

Valentin stood up abruptly and strode across the room before controlling himself enough to speak. "Tessa, don't lie to me just to create trouble. If you are . . ."

"But, I am not, *Liebchen!* She and Crawley are causing talk." Tessa went to him. "Forget her! Let us—you and I—go on as before."

The Viscount barely heard her. A black rage stirred in his heart. "We cannot, Tessa. One cannot resurrect what is finished."

She read the finality on his face, but she persisted. "Valentin, can we not . . ."

"No, I am sorry, my dear, but we cannot."

She studied him carefully, then shrugged her elegant shoulders and replied with resignation, "Very well, but do not expect me to cry for you when you come to your senses."

"I would not expect or ask it of you, Tessa my love." He smiled grimly.

"Yes, there are limits to my generosity," Tessa replied, rallying. "I think some champagne would suit us both admirably at this time, *n'est-ce pas?*"

"A splendid idea. I will see to it at once."

Still seething bitterly over Tessa's indictment of Nicole the Viscount went in search of champagne. That damn Crawley! He would kill the cur! This blasted tangle had gone too far. But one thing was certain, he would bring his wife to heel and assert his mastery! Of that he had no doubt. He clenched his fists convulsively and pushed his way through the crowded rooms. His instinct to strike out for Paris and take command of the situation was overpowering him. God help that woman when next he laid hands on her!

Chapter XI

With Danforth and Perry in England and the Marquis confined to bed because of his gout, Nicole found more and more of her time taken up by her new friends and Lord Crawley. Madame Lafitte was the only objector to Nicole's entertainments. She tried to persuade Nicole that a ballet company was a most unfortunate association for her, that Crawley was undoubtedly suspect since he and the Viscount were hostile to one another, and that it was tantamount to a rejection of society to choose such questionable company.

Lafitte's tirades were doomed from the start, however, for it was these very reasons that drove Nicole into further associations with Crawley and his companions. Madame Lafitte's pleas for greater discretion fell on deaf ears.

One afternoon as Nicole sat beside the old maestro watching the dancers work out, he exclaimed, *"Mon Dieu!* Rudi, extend the leg but do not bend the knee. It is an *arabesque* not an *attitude,* for God's sake!"

Rudi scowled.

"Sloppy, my boy, sloppy! Do it again!"

Rudi hesitated momentarily, but as the pianist struck the chords once more, he responded.

"He is very good," Nicole dared to comment.

"Good, yes, but sloppy. The boy could be great. Unfortunately he does not care enough. No dedication."

"Perhaps it is because he is young."

"Of course, he must be young. When he grows old, he will no longer dance."

"He and Natalya are a marvelous pair of dancers."

"And Natalya, she already grows old."

"Old! Oh, no, monsieur."

"Yes, it is true. She is twenty-five and her heart begins to grow weary. She begins to think of security, a home, children. That is always the trouble with women. They are not meant for careers. It is a pity. If you will excuse me, madame." He rose somewhat slowly. "Try that *chassé* again! The two of you were not together." He walked toward the stage.

Nicole sat in thoughtful silence as the maestro lectured his troupe.

"Do I break in on your reverie, my dear Viscountess?"

"My lord, Madame Coupé, I was just lost in thought about . . . about the company's future," she said quickly.

"You have been a most generous patron, madame. Your financial support will allow them to work on a whole new production." Madame Coupé tried to flatter Nicole.

"I am pleased that I could be of assistance." Nevertheless, Nicole pondered the rashness of her act. Those hastily written drafts had depleted her bank account for the entire month. Next month she would have to be more cautious.

As on previous occasions, Rudolph, Natalya, and Nicole were invited to Crawley's for afternoon tea. Several other guests joined them including Phillippe Beauchamp. Once again he tried to ingratiate himself with Nicole who did her best to avoid his cloying attentions. She allowed herself to be drawn into a game of cards with Crawley and Madame Coupé, but before they were able to begin Phillippe insinuated himself into the group and seated himself across from Nicole. Inexperienced in the nuances of cards, Nicole played poorly, and at the end of the game she discovered to her dismay that she owed a large sum of money to her cousin.

"Do not worry about it. You may pay me at your convenience."

Upset by this obligation, Nicole slipped a pair of Ardsmore heirloom earrings from her ears and, wrapping them carefully in her lace handkerchief, handed them to her cousin. "Please keep these until I am able to repay you, at the beginning of next month."

"*Ma chère cousine,* this is not at all necessary." He hesitated briefly. "Ah, but I can see you are upset, so I will hold them for you until you wish to redeem them, and I shall leave them in the care of our mutual friend, Lord Crawley."

"Excellent idea. If you will come with me, Phillippe, we will put them in my safe."

The two men excused themselves and proceeded down the hallway speaking in undertones.

"Wait till Ardsmore gets word of this!" Joseph gloated.

"Bah! You drive a sane man crazy with your talk of this vendetta. Must I remind you again there are greater matters at stake. You will keep these earrings until I tell you otherwise. Your personal revenge will be served effectively through the cause!" Beauchamp closed the subject emphatically.

Shortly thereafter Nicole left Lord Crawley's home. As the chaise bounced along the cobblestone streets to the Marquis's home, she could not allay the unbidden thoughts that assailed her. Phillippe's malicious grin as he took the earrings, and Lord Crawley's saturnine gaze throughout the transaction loomed before her inner vision. It worried her. She had been extremely foolish in not heeding the Marquis's and Madame Lafitte's warnings. Flaunting society, spending large sums of money, and now gambling —all the worst Harcourt traits. What was she trying to do, ruin her life? Danforth's very words! Suddenly very frightened, Nicole promised herself to be more prudent in the future.

"My lady." Jacques took the Viscountess's pelisse as she entered the house.

"Madame Lafitte and the Marquis have retired, Jacques?"

"*Oui,* my lady, but there is . . ."

"Not tonight, Jacques, see me in the morning," she sighed, dismissing him and entered the drawing room where the gathering dark cast long shadows.

"You might have allowed Jacques to light the candles, my dear."

Nicole stood dead still and then began to tremble, unable to control herself.

"I hope you haven't changed your mind about coming in, madame." He rose indolently, puffing on a cigar. The flickering firelight, throwing the planes of his face into shadow, gave him a satanic appearance as he loomed before her.

"Val?" she whispered incredulously. "What are you doing here?"

"A charming greeting, dear wife," he jeered.

Stunned and no longer able to support herself, she slipped into a chair. He has come back to me, she thought, and all her longings for him surged up searing her very soul. Yet mingled with that elation were doubts about this sudden appearance.

Valentin watched Nicole warily. Noting her ashen face and the troubled look in her beautiful violet eyes, he was stirred by a need to hold her in his arms.

Moments passed while neither spoke, each adjusting to the strong emotions brought to the surface by seeing one another after so many weeks of separation.

As the silence lengthened between them, Nicole struggled against a growing sense of alarm. Why had he come? What had he heard? She watched as Valentin lighted a branch of candles on the mantle and another on the table behind the sofa and then, crossing to her chair, he stood looking down at her.

Finally Nicole spoke. "Have you been here long, my lord?"

"Two hours—more perhaps." He turned and walked to the fireplace and kicked at a log, watching the sparks fly up.

"Uncle Maurice knows you are here?"

"I spoke to him before he retired."

"You have eaten?"

"Madame Lafitte saw to it."

"You have not changed from your traveling garments . . ."

"No, I was waiting for your return." He paused, reluctant to take up the matters that had forced him on this, perhaps foolhardy, hasty journey to Paris.

Nicole, too, was searching for a means of reaching out to Valentin that would circumvent the unhappy memories obstructing the pathway between them.

Valentin turned to face her once more. "It's been a long time, Nicole. It is good to see you again."

Nicole could barely keep from running to him. "I cannot tell you how happy I am to see you, too . . . Val."

Again they waited in silence.

"Vienna . . . you are very busy there?"

"Very!"

"How long do you remain in Paris?"

"I have twenty-four hours."

Her face fell. "Twenty-four hours—that is all?"

"Even that is more than I can spare."

"I see." Her voice had lost its color. "Then I take it something urgent has prompted this sudden visit."

They both felt the chill begin to settle over them as Valentin steeled himself to speak out his reasons for coming to Paris.

"Where have you been these many hours, Nicole?"

So that was it. Someone had been acting the spy. "I have been with friends."

"Which friends?" He watched Nicole's face grow pale under his unrelenting stare.

Oh God, she quailed inwardly. What have I done? How can I tell him I was with Crawley?

"Well, Nicole, I am awaiting your answer."

"Val, it grows late. Could we not take this up in the morning?" she pleaded.

"No, we cannot. I leave in the morning."

Suddenly she grew angry that he could spare her so little of his precious time. "I wonder that you bother to come at all. Obviously, our relationship is of little concern to you."

"Do not seek to divert the issue, Nicole. I asked you who you were with this evening!"

"My friends are my own affair."

168

"Not when you consort with my enemies!"

"So it is as I suspected. You refer to Lord Crawley, I suppose."

"I do, madame, indeed I do."

"Who have you had spying on me? Tessa Von Hoffman?"

He frowned. "It does not matter who my source is. It matters only whether it is true or not."

"Oh, I see, I am compelled to answer your inquiries, but you need not answer mine, is that right?"

"That is exactly right, madame wife. You have been with Crawley this night have you not?"

"What if I have?"

At that moment Valentin could have struck her. That she could betray him so flagrantly was unbearable. "Madame, you do not know what you tamper with when you encourage that blackguard."

"His lordship has shown me only kindness."

"Have you ever wondered what might motivate his kindness to you, you little fool?"

"Your quarrel is not mine, sir."

"Little you know about that!"

"You imply much. Why don't you explain your insinuations?"

"It isn't necessary. The matter of Crawley concerns past family indiscretions that are best left undisturbed."

"I don't enjoy riddles."

"And I don't enjoy betrayal! Were you alone with him?"

"Certainly not! There were others present."

"What others?"

Nicole quaked once more. "There are some artists that I have chosen to sponsor . . ."

"Artists? Painters, you mean?"

"No . . . I . . ." she could not look at him.

"Well." He came up to her and took hold of her chin. "Look at me."

She raised her eyes to his. "They are dancers—ballet dancers from the Opéra de Paris."

"Ballet dancers!" He was incredulous. "Not even *you* could be so foolish as to take up with ballet dancers!"

"You speak as if they are lepers."

"For you they might as well be."

"How can you say that to me, when my own mother was a dancer!"

"Precisely, my dear. You are not so dull-witted as to fail to comprehend the full significance of what I mean."

"Yes, yes I *am* that dull-witted. Spell it out for me, my lord. I want to hear you say the truth to me once and for all."

Valentin considered retreating before this determined onslaught from Nicole, sensing instinctively the damage to be done by complete honesty.

"Well." It was Nicole's turn to command. "I'm waiting, my lord husband!"

"Very well, Nicole, just remember you insisted on this. Ballet dancers are members of the lower class, and one in our position does not ally himself with these people. We are forever separated."

"My mother married into the upper class."

"And ruined your father."

"What a monstrous thing to say! My mother was a beautiful, accomplished woman." Nicole's voice was full of anguish.

"That is beside the point, my dear." Valentin spoke gently, but relentlessly. "She could not be accepted into society and your father cut himself off from the Harcourts as a consequence."

"The Harcourts were cruel and heartless. They destroyed my parents."

"They destroyed themselves."

"You are just as cruel and heartless to say such a thing."

"You demanded the truth."

"Well, then, let us have the full truth, my lord. I am the offspring of one of this lower class, so why should it shock you when I consort with my own kind?"

"Because you are also the offspring of a Harcourt, and as such, society accepts you as a gently-bred lady of quality."

"Society will never forget my origins."

"It is you who never forgets your origins! You are my wife; your position is unassailable!"

"Oh, now we come to the real issue, do we not?" Nicole charged angrily. "It's all a matter of your Harcourt pride!"

"I prefer to call it my honor. My wife will not compromise my honor, do you understand me?"

"I will never understand you, sir. We are too different. I see it all now. We can never reach an understanding. Our natures are too different!"

Valentin studied Nicole coldly for a few minutes before replying. "Perhaps you are right," he stated in deadly quiet.

Nicole rose from her seat and stared calmly at him. "It has been a dreadful mistake and we should never have married."

A breathless silence ensued—during which each struggled with a bitter pride that would not let either retrieve the situation from the stubborn impasse that was materializing before their stricken eyes.

"I think we have said all that is necessary to be said between us. If you will excuse me, my lord, I believe I will retire now."

The Viscount bowed stiffly as Nicole turned with dignity and quietly left the room.

She did not see him again before he left in the morning, and nothing was solved between them except a further deterioration of their relationship.

Nicole dragged herself through weary days of dull depression, avoiding Crawley and the ballet company, unable to decide what course to follow. She could not deny her love for Valentin, but his harsh words about her mother goaded her cruelly, and she could not shake a growing desire for revenge.

Nicole was diverted from her own problems when a few days later, Geneviève Lumière in great distress arrived at the home of the Marquis. Nicole ushered Geneviève to the privacy of her bedroom where the poor girl collapsed in tears onto the bed. Nicole offered her trembling friend a glass of sherry as she brushed back a mass of Geneviève's curls from her forehead. Slowly the girl recovered, and Nicole waited for her to speak.

"I am so sorry to have come to you like this, but I have no one else to turn to," Geneviève spoke, gulping back sobs.

"What is it, Ginny?"

"Gordon returned last night."

Nicole's intake of breath was her only reply as she waited for Geneviève to continue.

"He . . . he was in a terrible state. I never saw him so disturbed. I knew then what he was going to say to me." She straightened her sagging shoulders. "He must marry the . . . young lady his family has chosen for him."

"This is what he told you?" Nicole's lips were compressed with anger.

"No . . . he said . . . he wished me to marry him. Then! Right away."

"Danforth!?" Nicole could not help being surprised. "Then he will marry you without their consent. I applaud his courage!"

"Nicole, how could I marry him?"

"What do you mean? He has asked you, has he not? And you love one another. What more is required?"

"But do you not see? My love would destroy him."

"How could your love destroy him?" Nicole asked incredulously.

"His career. He has no money to continue it on his own."

"Then he will do something else."

"What can a gentleman of his standing do? Can you see Gordon in the army? He could not even afford the commission."

"It would be difficult, but . . . perhaps the Viscount could . . ."

"Do you think Gordon would allow the Viscount to buy a commission for him?"

"No, I suppose not," Nicole agreed reluctantly.

"His honor is at stake. He is betrothed to a girl of position, and I . . . I can offer him nothing."

"But your love," Nicole retorted.

Geneviève shook her head dejectedly. "No, it is not enough."

"But what will you do?"

"I must go away."

"Go away? Where?"

"I have a plan. You must help me, Nicole, if you will," she pleaded.

"How may I help you? Oh, Ginny, are you sure this is the answer, to run away?"

"I have thought of nothing else since Gordon left me. I

must be gone before he returns this evening for my answer."

"Where will you go?"

"I have a distant relative in the south of France who will take me in. But I will need to borrow some money to get there. Will you lend me what I need?"

Nicole turned pale. "But of course I will." Where was she to get the money? Her allowance for the month was all used up. How could she ask the Marquis to lend it to her when he knew of her ample funds?

"I could leave from here in a private coach which would take me to Orléans. From there, I could travel by stage undetected."

"Surely Gordon will follow you."

"He does not know of my cousin in Toulouse."

"But your aunt?"

"She is alone now and will accompany me. I know it is a lot to ask of you, but Nicole . . . some day I shall repay you."

"There's no question of that. Do not worry about the money. But Geneviève, are you so certain that this is the right thing to do?"

"I love him . . . I will not ruin him."

Nicole held the weeping girl and found she, too, was crying. Geneviève's unhappy love brought a rush of anguish to Nicole's heart. Love was not enough after all. Perhaps, she, too should have had the wisdom to reject marriage with Valentin.

A short time later Lord Crawley received a note from Nicole which delighted him. It was the first overture she had made to him since the card game incident. Also, since Nicole had ceased going to the theater, he was beginning to wonder if he had moved too quickly. But here was another link in the chain he was forging. A note in her handwriting! She needed money and a closed carriage. She would repay him. Little did Nicole know how she would repay him. Beauchamp would be delighted with this turn of events. In a way it was too bad that it had to be this girl. He could have liked her but for the Harcourt connection. Now he would have to destroy her along with her damnable Viscount.

Early that evening, Geneviève and her aunt pulled away in a coach from Crawley's house. He turned to Nicole saying, "She is a noble lady to be sure."

"Yes," Nicole commented abstractedly as he took her arm and led her into his drawing room.

"It was my pleasure to help her even if it was rather . . . expensive."

Nicole caught his meaning. "It was most kind of you. I will repay you in a few days. As a matter of fact, I will be able to clear all my debts including those to my cousin, Phillippe, as well."

"There is no need to concern yourself about Phillippe, for he is out of the country at present, and as for myself, you know I would honor your word at all times."

Nicole went cold inside at the disturbing look on his face, yet it was gone as fast as it had come. Did she imagine it? The day had been a trying one, perhaps her brain was beginning to play tricks. Best she return to the Marquis without delay.

However, the trials of the day were not ended with her safe return to the Marquis. A pounding at the front door followed by swift strides across the foyer startled both the Marquis and Nicole at a game of piquet. A distraught Danforth stood on the threshold. "Nicole, where is she?" he cried in anguish.

"A fine greeting, my boy," barked the Marquis.

"Please, Uncle," Nicole whispered, "leave us alone for a few moments."

Reluctantly he rose, eyeing Danforth who stood rigidly waiting. "Very well, but if he goes berserk I will not be far away." With that he left them.

"Sit down, Gordon."

"I would rather stand."

"Please, I must talk to you."

"I do not want conversation. Just tell me where she is. For God's sake, Nicole . . ."

"All right Gordon," she soothed. "She left this for you." Nicole handed him a letter. He ripped it open, reading frantically, his eyes darting across the page. Then he sat down. His face had grown deathly pale and to Nicole's dismay he burst into tears, but before she could collect her thoughts, the terrible sound died away and he stood up.

"Forgive me, Nicole. I should not have given way."

"Oh, my dear Gordon, you are only human," she cried. Then she went to him and placed her hands on his shoulders and whispered, "I know, my friend . . . it . . . it is not easy to lose the one you love."

His eyes met hers and they both understood. He gathered her gently next to him and they momentarily drew solace from one another.

Finally, Nicole led him to the divan and sat quietly beside him. He spoke barely above a whisper. "She told me not to follow her. That she valued my honor as well as her own. And that God would see us through."

"She has done what she thought was best for both of you."

"Yes, I know. If only I could have seen her one more time to tell her of my love."

"She knows, Gordon."

He sighed deeply and rose. "Forgive me if I say goodnight now. I need to walk."

"You will come again . . . soon?"

"If you will have me."

"Any time."

"Thank you." He bowed stiffly and took his leave with dignity.

Days continued to pass and between the Marquis and Gordon Danforth, Nicole's time was once again occupied by the more respectable members of society. February drew to a close and a windy rainy March descended upon them.

Nicole was seated in the drawing room with Madame Lafitte when the sound of urgent voices erupted from the hallway. The door burst open and the Marquis staggered into the room gasping, "Bonaparte!"

"What is the matter, Uncle Maurice?" Nicole cried in alarm at the Marquis's grey appearance.

"Bonaparte . . . has escaped from Elba!"

"Mon Dieu!" cried Madame Lafitte.

"That fiend will drive us all back into exile!" he raved almost incoherently.

"Uncle Maurice, please do not agitate yourself so." Nicole went to him in considerable fear.

"My beloved home . . . once again to be torn from me . . . It is too much to bear!"

"Uncle Maurice, come and sit down." She grasped his trembling hand and tried to settle him on the divan, but he would not be calmed.

"I shall . . . I shall . . ." he gasped and clutched at his chest. "Nicole," he uttered and collapsed on to the floor.

"Uncle Maurice! Uncle Maurice!" she screamed as she bent over his prostrate form while Madame Lafitte ran to the door shouting for the servants.

It was a sorrowful week for Nicole. The Marquis Maurice de Crécy had collapsed and died without regaining

177

consciousness. He was buried quietly three days later and Nicole remained in semi-seclusion.

It was Danforth's arrival that brought her into the salon. "Will the rain never cease?" she asked almost inaudibly before turning from the clouded window to face her visitor. "So, you are off to Ghent?"

"Yes." Then after a pause he said, "I do wish you would reconsider and let me arrange for you to go to London."

"You know that is impossible."

"But why, Nicole? It is Valentin's express wish that you do. He wrote me requesting that I see you safely on your way. What else can you do?"

Nicole decided not to tell him that she had already accepted Madame Chenier's invitation to join her entourage to Brussels. It would bring only further objections.

"Don't worry about me, Gordon. You have an embassy job to think about. You must go. It is your duty."

"But Nicole, how can I leave you here unprotected in Paris with Napoleon advancing on the city!"

"You forget I am French, and have lived under Napoleon Bonaparte for over ten years. Do not fear for me."

"I hope Valentin will forgive me."

"There is nothing to forgive. I have made my own decision. Good luck, Gordon, and do not worry about me. I shall be fine." She extended her hand and he kissed it.

"Until we meet again. Take care, Nicole."

"Goodbye, Gordon." She watched his departure and then drew the note from the Viscount out of her pocket. She did not have to read it, for the words were burned into her memory—the cold unfeeling words that had been his only communication to her since his lightning appearance that night. No, she would not comply with his request that she join his mother in London. If only he had come to her when she needed him so desperately. Then she would have done anything he wanted. But he had not come, and she was alone, and alone she would make her own decisions.

"So, child," Lafitte startled her as she came into the room, "everyone is deserting the city. I just heard the Wexfords and Montgomerys have left for Brussels."

"And Danforth is off to Ghent," she replied. "We shall follow with Madame Chenier in a day or two for Brussels ourselves."

"You will not change your mind about England?"

"No, I will not change my mind about England. I will not go where I am unwelcome. Besides, Fifi, everyone will be in Brussels. I shall enjoy myself there much more than in some stodgy English country house," she said closing the subject.

Madame Chenier's journey to Brussels was well planned to the last detail. She arrived accompanied by Nicole and Madame Lafitte in mid-March to a rented house located on the Rue d'Anglais. It was a commodious establishment which Madame Chenier was fortunate enough to have prepared for her in advance of her arrival. Among its many rooms was a large salon with high ceilings of carved walnut and tall windows hung with heavy damask draperies in blue and gold. It would provide a fine setting for musicales and balls, both of which Madame Chenier was fond of giving. The weary travelers, however, were in no frame of mind to explore their dwelling the first night of their arrival. Each sought her bedchamber, and after a light supper served on a tray before a cozy fire, each retired gratefully for the night.

Nicole's first few days in Brussels were spent in Madame Chenier's constant company setting up house to suit their needs and familiarizing themselves with the city. It

did not take them long to be included as part of the growing elite now circulating in Belgium and populating the
capital. As Napoleon advanced into Paris, the Duke of
Wellington's presence was anxiously awaited in Brussels.
Troops from the allied nations were crowding the city in
great numbers and amidst the green of Belgian dragoons
and the blue of Dutch infantry, was the brilliant scarlet
of the British uniforms.

Despite the undercurrent anxiety over Napoleon and
the possibility of war, Brussels, like Vienna, became the
nexus of a frenzied social whirl. Determined pleasure-
seekers tirelessly pursued a daily fare of parties and balls
in an effort to ignore their fears about the inevitable confrontation with the escaped emperor. The more frightening the reports, the more frenzied the merrymaking.

It was not surprising that Lord Crawley should be
numbered among the throngs of pleasure-seekers. He presented himself to Nicole shortly after her arrival in Brussels and was well received by her. Had Nicole not been
chafing under an acute sense of Valentin's abandonment,
she might not have fallen in with Crawley's machinations
so readily again. But the injury, real or imagined, rankled
bitterly and Nicole found Crawley's renewed pursuit to
her liking. There was an aura of danger surrounding him
and despite the fears she naturally felt, she did not dis-
courage his interest in her.

She was in a private salon reading when Lord Crawley
was announced. He lingered over her hand, kissing the
fingertips in a meaningful way until she withdrew them
rather pointedly.

"Nicole, dear lady," he murmured and looked searchingly into her anxious violet eyes. He read their indecision accurately and decided that although a little circum-
spection was required, his presence was not disagreeable
to Ardsmore's disconsolate bride.

"It is good to see you, Lord Crawley," she greeted him.

"I am happy to see you joined the exodus from Paris," he replied.

"I could not be left behind. I believe all of Parisian society must have fled to Brussels."

"It is true. Even Rudi and Natalya are here."

"Rudi and Natalya? And the maestro?"

"He remains in Paris."

"So, they have left the company."

"I am afraid so. It means they must start all over."

"Surely they will be asked to entertain in a city filled with pleasure-seekers?"

"Ah, but as always there is the problem of recognition."

"Rudi and Natalya will find many houses open and ready to sponsor them," Nicole replied.

"It is certainly to be hoped. Such talent as theirs should not go without reward. And yet . . . they lack that all too necessary opening invitation . . ." He hesitated hopefully, but Nicole did not pick up his hint, so he said, "I imagine you will be entertaining."

"Madame Chenier is quite fond of musicales. Even now she is planning one for the near future. You must be sure to attend."

"Thank you, my dear. I don't suppose . . ."

"Yes, my lord, what don't you suppose?"

"Rudi and Natalya—for the musicale . . ."

"Hmm, I wonder . . ." she paused. "Madame Chenier's plans are pretty well set . . . perhaps she might be persuaded to include our friends as part of the entertainment."

"You are too good, dear lady. It is just the kind of opening they require. Once they are seen, I have no doubt of their success."

"I am sure you are quite right. And it would give me great pleasure to be the one to launch them on the road to success."

"Again, Nicole, I can only express my admiration for your kindness." He clasped her hand fervently and would not release it though she tried.

"Lord Crawley, I beg you . . ."

"Joseph, Nicole, Joseph. Do you not feel by now that you could use my given name?"

"I . . .", she hesitated.

"Come now, after all, are we not joined as partners in this venture to promote Rudi and Natalya?"

"I suppose one could regard it as rather a business venture," Nicole equivocated.

"But, of course, my dear, that is the perfect construction to put upon it. I am sure we will find it to be a most satisfactory arrangement."

He had led her aright. She now felt comfortable with her conscience and closed the interview just as he had hoped.

"Very well . . . Joseph. I shall approach Madame Chenier this very evening."

Madame Chenier was in her boudoir preparing herself for dinner at the Barclays' when Nicole approached her.

"*Mais non,* Nicole, it is not the same as having Catalani sing for us."

"I know, madame, but Rudi and Natalya were members of the Opéra de Paris. Surely they are acceable," she coaxed.

"Two Russian dancers? I do not know, *chérie.* I shall think upon it, eh?"

"That is all I ask, madame." Nicole rose from the footstool and started for the door.

"*Mon enfant,*" Madame Chenier stopped her.

"*Oui,* madame?"

"Why is it that you champion these dancers?"

Madame Chenier observed a clouded look come into Nicole's violet eyes. "I know you will tell me of the hurt your mother suffered at the hands of your in-laws, but . . ." she held up her hands as she saw Nicole was about to protest, "let me finish, *enfant,* but did they not suffer too? And this handsome husband of yours, did he, too, humiliate your mother? Was he not merely a boy at the time?"

"You do not understand," Nicole drew in her breath.

"Is it that I do not understand, *chérie,* or is it that you are looking . . . for revenge?"

"Revenge? Oh no, madame . . ." Nicole denied vehemently, suppressing her feelings of guilts.

"I hope this is so, for you may be sacrificing your whole life over imagined slights."

Nicole hesitated, suddenly unsure of herself. Could this be true? But all those things her mother had said, and Nicole had witnessed. And what about Val's brutal condemnation of her mother? That was no mere slight! That was unforgivable! And his betrayal with Tessa . . . She shook her head negatively and said, "No, it is not my imagination, Madame Chenier."

Madame Chenier sighed, "Very well." And then added, "There is one more thing you should know."

Nicole waited for Madame Chenier to speak.

"Tessa Von Hoffman is here in Brussels." Rising, she came to Nicole. "Promise me, *ma chère,* no further confrontations with that woman."

"I shall not be so childish again, of that I can assure you!"

"*Grâce Dieu!* So now go and dress for the Barclays'."

183

Chapter XII

The confrontation between the Viscountess and the brazen Von Hoffman woman Madame Chenier dreaded did not occur until the following week. It was at a performance of Mozart's *Le Nozze di Figaro* that Nicole was put to the test concerning Tessa Von Hoffman. As she and Madame Chenier relaxed with the Barclays over refreshments during intermission, Nicole was surprised to come face to face with Tessa Von Hoffman in the company of Lord Crawley. Polite greetings were exchanged by those present, but Madame Chenier watched Nicole with anxious eyes.

"My dear Tessa," Lady Barclay was saying. "How did you find Vienna while you were there?"

"Utterly captivating. Such gaiety has never been equaled. Not even in Paris!"

"How I envy you," Lady Barclay exclaimed. "Tell me, is Metternich as dashing as they claim? Did you meet the Czar?"

"I have heard the Congress seldom meets in formal session, and very little of their work is accomplished," Lord Barclay claimed sourly. "Too much carousing, if you ask me."

"It is only the opinion of a mere woman, my lord," replied Tessa, coyly, "but I think more than carousing transpires at those gay parties. The Duke himself is often to be seen in society, and his brilliant corps of young officers never misses an event."

"Perhaps you have had the good fortune of meeting Lady Ardsmore's gallant husband on such occasions," Lord Crawley suggested blandly.

"But, of course, who could miss the handsome Viscount. He is always on the front line of duty. The Duke relies on him greatly," Tessa replied smugly.

Nicole stiffened with sudden anger. What game was Crawley playing bringing that shameless woman here to flaunt her knowledge of Valentin so brazenly for all to hear? She felt she would burst with the effort to appear calm.

"The Viscount is always one to do his duty. His devotion to the Duke is well known," Nicole stated coldly.

"It is a comfort to know that men of Wellington's caliber are working for our welfare," Madame Chenier added.

"It would be more comforting if Wellington were here in Brussels," Lady Barclay complained. "One hears such rumors regarding Napoleon."

"Do not trouble yourself, Lady Barclay," Tessa soothed. "I am quite certain we will hear of Wellington's arrival any day now. I have it on good authority." Tessa insinuated much.

Oh, the gall, Nicole fumed inwardly, violet eyes flashing.

Shortly thereafter Crawley and Tessa Von Hoffman returned to their box. They left behind a relieved Madame Chenier, but a disturbed Nicole. The appearance of Tessa Von Hoffman inflamed her desire for revenge against her husband. The need to strike at the Viscount and make him regret her existence became a driving passion. Discretion be damned! She was riding with Crawley tomorrow and would use him to get back at Valentin. Lord Crawley might be playing a dangerous game, but so could she. If Joseph Crawley thought he was using her to attack her husband, all the better, for it suited her own plans perfectly.

Events conspired to assist Nicole in her pursuit of foolish vengeance. Madame Chenier was invited to join the French court at Ghent, and the Viscountess would be her own mistress with only Madame Lafitte to act as mentor. The very day of Madame Chenier's departure, Nicole invited Joseph Crawley, Rudi Ostrosky, and Natalya Lavronsky to her home. Madame Lafitte looked askance on these arrangements but posed no immediate objection.

"Since Madame Chenier is not here, I have decided to go ahead with her plans for a party on my own. And you, Rudi, and Natalya, will provide the entertainment. What do you say to that?"

"*Chérie,* what a marvelous idea!" Natalya cried happily.

"*Merci, mon ange.*" Rudi kissed her hand, and drawing her to her feet, he whirled with her around the room. "But you are a born dancer!" he commented enthusiastically. "You should perform with us."

"Don't be absurd!" Nicole struggled to free herself from his hold.

"Think what fun you would have. You would be the envy of the *beau monde*. Maybe even start a fashion that all the society ladies would be mad to follow."

187

"Ridiculous! Ladies of quality do not perform."

"Ridiculous? Why?" drawled his lordship coming to her side. "Women of the nobility have often performed in various tableaux and pageants."

"You see! It is not so foolish as you think." Rudi seconded Crawley.

"Yes, I suppose there is something in what you say," Nicole admitted reluctantly.

"Are you afraid of what your husband might say?" Crawley taunted.

Nicole's eyes flashed dangerously. "My husband has nothing to do with it. It is simply that I am not trained as a professional dancer."

"You would not actually have to dance. Would she, Rudolph?"

"No, a small part could be arranged where you would appear briefly."

"What . . . what part could that be?"

"I know," Natalya claimed coming to them. "That part of the Egyptian princess who is about to become the bride of the pharaoh."

"That is perfect! The princess dances to please the pharaoh," Rudi explained.

"Actually all she does is introduce the other dancers," Natalya added. "That would be Rudi and me."

"Magnificent!" Lord Crawley encouraged.

"With two or three rehearsals, you will be perfect as the princess," Rudi continued eagerly.

"I do not know. What would I have to do?"

"Simply pantomine a few graceful movements at the feet of the pharaoh. Then there would be the clash of cymbals and Natalya and I would appear and do our dance."

"That is all?"

"That is all."

"It does sound simple."

"Enough, my friends, you are pressuring the lady. She must have time to consider. After all, her in-laws may not approve . . ." Crawley struck the very note to rouse Nicole at last.

"Oh, nonsense, Joseph. How could I offend society in my own home by merely introducing the dancers. I will do it!"

"Very well, if you insist." Crawley smiled triumphantly.

Nicole experienced some uneasiness as she contemplated the events set into motion by herself, Crawley, and his friends long after her guests had departed. Would she regret her rash decision? But it was the perfect opportunity to strike back at Valentin and the Harcourts. So they scorned her mother for a dancer, did they? Just wait until they heard of her performance with Rudi and Natalya! What would Valentin do? What could he do? No doubt he would come to Brussels with Wellington, and family pride would force him to seek her out. Nicole trembled with hope and fear. She was playing with fire, but she wanted a showdown between them. Perhaps fate would force them to solve their marital dilemma, and that was what she really wanted, and she knew it. Nicole whispered a prayer, "Yes, in Brussels my love, we shall see."

So Nicole continued with her plans to perform at her party. Every detail must be perfect, including her own début. She worked tirelessly with Rudi, and it seemed that destiny was conspiring to accomplish her aims. Madame Chenier extended her stay indefinitely in Ghent, and all Nicole's preparations moved ahead smoothly.

Madame Lafitte's efforts to forestall Nicole's plans to perform with the dancers at the coming reception met with stony resistance from Nicole. There was little Lafitte could do other than act the part of chaperone whenever the dancers or Lord Crawley were in the house. And they were there daily.

The lady tried to reassure herself that Nicole's plan was not as outrageous as she knew it to be. Her charge's part was little enough, consisting of a few whirls and graceful turns—but the costume was far too revealing! She shuddered, watching Nicole practice her obeisance before the reigning pharaoh.

"Lovely, my dear, Nicole. Absolutely lovely," Crawley praised her as their practice came to a close one afternoon; however, he did not see the look of black disgust Lafitte directed to the back of his head. How she would like to murder the man!

Natalya, who had been assisting as pianist during the practice sessions, began to play a lively gypsy tune with much gusto. Immediately Rudi broke into a spirited Cossack dance whirling around the room and catching Nicole by the waist, forced her to dance with him. Something primitive and wild within her responded, and soon the pair was stomping and twirling in true gypsy fashion, clapping their hands and clicking their heels in a joyous impromptu romp. They whirled madly until they collapsed in an exhausted heap on the divan.

"But you are a wild gypsy at heart, my dear Viscountess! You are wasted as the wife of a British officer. You were meant to be a dancer!" It was heady wine to hear Rudi praise her so, but in her heart of hearts all Nicole wanted was to be the adoring wife of one particular British officer.

The day of Nicole's party arrived bright and clear with unseasonably warm temperatures for early April and augured well for the turnout that evening. Nicole spent the early part of the day overseeing the final decorations of the grand salon which had been turned into a ballroom for the dancing. At the far end of the room a raised dais had been contrived as a stage for the evening's entertainment. The musicians were to assemble in a small alcove to the left, and an antechamber to the right was to be used as the backstage area for the dancers.

All day long, great baskets of flowers filled with irises, nasturtiums, lilacs, and chrysanthemums in blending hues of blues and purples arrived from the florist. They were banked in profusion about the dais and garlanded with trailing greens of ivy and fern in trellises over the French doors leading out to the terrace and gardens.

The dining room was arranged to accommodate long tables covered in heavy linen and adorned with glittering crystal and silver awaiting the sumptuous buffet now in preparation in the busy kitchens.

Nicole managed to avoid the reproachful presence of Madame Lafitte under pretext of one duty or another, and in late afternoon she took to her room with strict instructions to her maid that no one was to disturb her. She would try for an hour's rest in preparation for the evening's activities. But try as she may, sleep would not come. She was too worked up with nervous energy, and repressed misgivings over her audacious début. Giving up the pursuit of rest as useless, she rang for her maid to prepare her bath.

She was finishing her toilette when Madame Lafitte finally cornered her. As her maid adjusted the small jeweled plume in her hair, Lafitte entered her room.

"Well, Fifi, how do I look?" She rose showing off her Empire gown of pale violet silk with a net overdress sprinkled with diamantés. Gleaming amethysts accentuated the fullness of her bosom in the low-cut dress.

"Beautiful, *chérie*." A nervous hand plucked at the delicate sleeve.

"You may go," Nicole nodded to her maid who silently

191

withdrew. "Well, what is it, Fifi? I can see you will not be satisfied until I allow you to speak."

"*Chérie,* do not do this foolhardy thing."

"Fifi, there is nothing the least bit foolhardy in my plans. It has all been worked out very carefully. I am sure I will do my mother proud," Nicole answered defiantly.

"And the Viscount? Will he be proud? What of him?" Lafitte countered.

"We have been all through that, and I will not have you spoiling my evening. I am nervous as it is. Now if you will excuse me, my guests are about to arrive." Determinedly Nicole marched from the room.

Although many ladies and gentlemen of distinction were in attendance, Nicole's entrance on Lord Crawley's arm created a stir of excitement. The colors of the ballroom decor were chosen to enhance Nicole's ensemble. The entire setting was a dramatic backdrop to her own vivid beauty, and the scene was altogether one to dazzle the senses. It was a night for revelry and drama.

Between dances the floor was crowded with lovers, gossipers, and intriguers, and as the night wore on the note of gay abandon increased. It needed only the stunning news of the arrival of the Duke of Wellington in Brussels to mark the night as a momentous occasion. The news swept the ballroom like wildfire and cast the revelers into a frenzy of expectation.

Nicole moved happily among the guests until she heard the report of the Duke's arrival. For a moment she froze. To her the news meant only one thing. Valentin was in Brussels! She was seized by an unreasonable desire to flee, but she knew that if she succumbed to the feeling seeking to master her, the evening would be ruined. The only thought that came clearly through was that she must pro-

ceed with the entertainment as planned. Forcing herself
into an unnatural calm, Nicole changed into a harem skirt
of deep purple trimmed with gold and a matching bodice.
Her midriff was lightly concealed by diaphanous gauze,
and her feet were bare. A filmy cloak was clasped over
one shoulder to ensure that her attire was not completely
immodest. This had been added at Madame Lafitte's en-
treaties.

The time for her performance approached, and while
the guests were at supper, chairs were set up at one end of
the ballroom where the entertainment would take place.
Several candelabra were lighted near the stage area, and
the remainder of the room was darkened. Finally, the anticipation was over, and a clash of cymbals announced
the arrival of the pharaoh. Violins struck up the princess's
theme music. It was her cue!

Controlling a quiver, Nicole moved forward into the
light toward the pharaoh. She knelt as a supplicant at his
feet and stretched out her arms to him. Receiving a nod
from him, she rose and whirled gracefully extending her
arms toward the right. There was another clash of cymbals, and Rudi and Natalya appeared. As they reached
center stage, Nicole whirled again and sank at the pharaoh's feet. Unable to resist the impulse, she stole a quick
look at the spectators. Lounging against the wall was the
one person she feared to see. Valentin was glaring across
the room at her! Nicole closed her eyes, almost fainting
with alarm. When she opened them, he was still there in
his brilliant red uniform, his blazing eyes stabbing hers
angrily. The remainder of the performance passed in a
blur. There was music and movement, but she saw none
of it. A burst of applause and shouts of bravo greeted her
ears, breaking the trance which held her. And then a
throng of well-wishers was surrounding the performers,

laughing, and praising them. Presently there was a break in the crowd, and the tall, handsome figure of her husband faced her.

"Nicole, my dearest, I compliment you on a most amusing homecoming." The stormy eyes and strained voice belied the arched grin as he raised her hand to his lips.

Collecting her wits, Nicole replied in what she hoped was a calm voice, "I am pleased you enjoyed the entertainment, my lord."

"How could I do otherwise, when you present us with such a charming view of your accomplishments." His sarcasm was unconcealed.

Turning to the onlookers he declared, "I am sure our guests are hoping for an encore." He flung a challenge to her, daring her to go further, then eyed her smugly as she blanched.

The Harcourt devil was loose tonight!

"Encore?" She looked at him in puzzlement as several of the guests murmured encouragement. "I . . . planned . . . that is . . . none has been planned."

Through the uttered protests of disappointments, Valentin whispered next to her ear, "Thank God! At least that is one humilation I am to be spared." He squeezed her arm in a warning gesture as he led her through the crowd and ordered quietly, "Change at once."

Seized by a blinding anger, Nicole wrenched free of his grasp. He was taking charge! She would show this arrogant man once and for all that she would not take orders from him. "No, wait! I almost forgot. Rudi? Where is Rudi?"

"Here, my lady."

"Rudi, do you remember the dance you were showing me the other day?"

"The dance?" he questioned.

"Come Rudi, tell the musicians what you wish them to play."

He still hesitated, "But, madame . . ."

"Quickly, Rudi," she sighed in exasperation at his reluctance.

"Very well," he acquiesced and began speaking to the musicians.

Nicole was afraid to look at her enraged husband who had recovered enough composure to resist the impulse to drag her off the floor. The music began, and Nicole whirled around Rudi who clapped his hands and stamped his feet in rhythm to the harsh primitive sounds. Natalya took up the beat, and encouraged by this, Nicole indicated that others should join in. Although reluctant at first, several of the younger more daring members of the party proceeded to match their steps with the dancers. Caught up in the mad pace of clapping hands, stomping feet, and shouts of laughter, the group began to dance wildly while other guests murmured their disapproval.

Each rhythmic step brought Nicole closer to her husband until she danced directly in front of him, giving herself up to the intimacy of the moment—her body swaying hypnotically. A wave of jubilation swept her as sparks of desire lighted Valentin's eyes and seizing her moment of triumph, she flung her cape at his feet revealing her seductive attire to the eager eyes of the surrounding crowd. The light of passion in Valentin's eyes was quenched immediately, and he lunged at Nicole snatching her in his arms and forcibly removing her from the abandoned merrymakers.

In the outer hall, he picked her up and, ignoring her flaying arms and whispered damnations, he carried her along the corridor to her bedchamber. Once inside, he threw her upon the bed.

"Well, madame, have you enjoyed yourself?" he demanded furiously.

"And why shouldn't I? You must remember I am the daughter of a dancer." She struggled to a sitting position.

"Oh, yes, your humble origin, my dear Viscountess!" he sneered. "Does that mean I might expect further shameless exhibitions in the future?"

"I have done nothing to be ashamed of! And I shall continue to do just as I please."

"You forget yourself, madame. *I* dictate matters in this family."

"And I recall you gave me the right to lead my own life!"

"That was a mistake! You do not know the meaning of the word discretion . . ."

"You dare to talk to me of discretion after your scandalous conduct with Tessa Von Hoffman!" she stormed, jumping off the bed.

"Her again! I am tired of hearing about Tessa!" he shouted.

"Like it or not she is part of this . . . this mess!"

"Yes," he hissed menacingly. "She, too, haunts me, but whereas I have little control over her, I have you in my power."

"And what power do you profess to wield over me?" Defiantly she stepped toward him placing her hands on her hips.

"Life and death, my dear," he assured her arrogantly.

"Are you threatening me?"

"Yes, I am. It would be a pleasure to strangle you. Then again maybe I shall have you locked up in a convent . . ."

She laughed nervously.

"Or better still take my mother's advice and give you a child."

"You hateful brute!"

"It tempts me . . . especially after that provocative performance this evening." He advanced toward her. She backed away to the windows. "Why should I not enjoy the pleasures of a wife who seems to have captured the fancy of . . ." he hesitated, "God knows how many other men during my absence."

"You . . ." she gasped, her outrage nearly rendering her speechless. "You . . ."

He caught her to himself and Nicole began to struggle in his arms. "Let me go!"

"At least I shall be free of doubts during your confinement." He grabbed her writhing body more firmly.

"Why take a woman who despises you?" she cried.

"Because I am master here, and I do not think you have learned that yet! I will do whatever I damn well please with you!" he roared.

Freeing one of her arms, she slapped him hard across the face. Stunned momentarily, Valentin drew back, a black scowl contorting his handsome features as he reached out and grabbed the filmsy garment she was wearing, ripping it down the front and exposing her full breasts. She screamed in alarm, but it was stifled as his mouth closed on hers, and he bore her down on the bed. Unexpectedly a fire was lighted in her to match his own enraged passion. She clung to him only to be startled by his abrupt withdrawal. His irregular breathing was the only sound within the room as he leaned over her. Then he rose and began straightening his uniform. "Let that be a lesson to you, my love," he rasped. "I could take you anytime I want, but I shall not . . . tonight! We have guests waiting." He walked toward the door and turned to address the disheveled girl crouching on the bed. "It is interesting, my dear Nicole, although you profess to hate me, how quickly you respond to my advances."

"You . . . contemptible beast!" She flung herself off the bed and threw a vase at the retreating figure whose mocking laugh could be heard through the closed door.

Resolutely the Viscount proceeded down the stairs to the party below. His body ached with desire for her, but his pride kept him from retracing his steps and completing what he had started.

Chapter XIII

Nicole was surprised to see Valentin in the breakfast room when she came down the following morning. He eyed her silently until the servants withdrew. Then he said, "I should be at headquarters by now, but I waited to speak to you." She continued to sip her coffee. "I want you to make no further commitments without my knowledge, Nicole." Her head jerked up, eyes angry violet flames. But he ignored her defiant stare and added, "I mean it, Nicole. I do not have time to talk about it now; when I return this evening, we will discuss everything."

He got up and came around the table to her and placed a hand lightly on her shoulder, but she shrugged it loose. Valentin sighed, controlling his rising temper at her imposed silence. "Maybe we can come to some sort of an understanding if we talk it out." He did not wait for a reply.

Nicole remained seated at the table thinking over what happened the night before. She had left the bedroom dressed once again in her violet silk and reappeared below cloaking her turbulent emotions under an icy calm. It was easy to locate her husband—his burnished blond head topped most of her other guests. Nevertheless, he made no attempt to seek out her company. Several times she caught his gaze, yet whatever he was thinking was masked behind a cold exterior. Half-expecting he might lead her out in the last waltz, she was disappointed for he was nowhere to be seen.

Later Nicole thought she glimpsed him in the courtyard as she ushered out the last guests, but of that she was uncertain. Frustrated by her inability to communicate with him, she wandered about the empty rooms as the servants doused the candles and bid her a courteous goodnight.

The sound of Valentin leaving by the front door brought her out of her reverie. She got up from the table, went to the window and pushed the curtain aside in time to see him leap onto his horse. Valentin's eyes scanned the windows and rested on her for a moment, and then another. Finally, he wrenched his eyes away and rode off, leaving Nicole to stare into an empty courtyard.

Threats and reproaches. That was all he had for her! Well, if that's the way he wanted it, tonight she was going to Zarelle's with Joseph Crawley whether he approved or not.

Wellington's headquarters on the Rue Royale were a short distance from the Rue d'Anglais, but the Viscount chose to ride, taking a brief canter about the park to clear his mind and collect his thoughts. He reached headquarters in a state of depression, the ride having accomplished little.

Most of the men who formed the Duke's personal staff in Vienna were with him in Brussels, and their lively youth and good humor were as much in evidence as ever. Nevertheless, the look on Lord Ardsmore's face as he entered acted as sufficient warning and his fellow officers gave him a clear berth. He stood at a window staring moodily at the passing throng in the streets, neither seeing or hearing what took place—his thoughts filled with Nicole. Desire, anger, longing, and chagrin were tangled together in a skein of bewildering emotions. Damn the wench! She was destroying his peace! He had longed for a reconciliation. At least some sign of contrition on her part . . . but no, instead he found her as defiant as ever and—

"Colonel"—his thoughts were interrupted. "Lord Ardsmore, someone to see you."

He swung around. "Danforth! by jove, it is good to see you. How the hell are you?"

"Fine and yourself?" Gordon Danforth said clasping Valentin's hand.

"As well as can be expected," he grinned. Then added, "I thought you were in Ghent?"

"I was until yesterday, but the Duke's arrival has brought me here. I am to be a liaison officer between the court at Ghent and Brussels."

"Good, then we shall be seeing something of you."

"Yes. I heard your wife was in Brussels. How . . . how is she?"

"You shall see for yourself. You will dine with us tonight, of course?"

"I would like that."

"Good. And then you can tell me about the mysterious

201

Parisian beauty who captured your heart." A look of pain crossed his friend's face. Quickly Valentin added, "And I will regale you with tales of Vienna."

"Yes," Danforth recovered, "but now I must file my report."

"Until tonight then." Valentin escorted Danforth from the office and returned to tackle a pile of papers on his desk, stopping momentarily to wonder what had happened to his old friend and this girl Perry had written about. Perplexed still, Valentin resumed his work.

Nicole had arranged earlier in the week to have dinner with Lord Crawley at Zarelle's, a dance hall of considerable notoriety. Everyone who attended the infamous establishment disguised their appearance by wearing masks and dominos. Nicole had been half-tempted to cancel the invitation knowing of Zarelle's dubious reputation, but her curiosity, coupled with Valentin's ultimatum, spurred her on.

So, despite her husband's warning, Nicole enlisted the aid of the unsuspecting Helen Bramwell. After sending a note to Crawley advising him to meet her at the Bramwell's, Nicole concealed her domino and mask under her cloak and made her way to their home.

She was not prepared for Helen's vehemently negative reaction when she was informed of Nicole's destination. Helen remonstrated with Nicole, but to no avail for it only made her more determined to go through with the evening as previously planned.

"I do not think you should do this, Nicole," Helen pleaded as she followed her into the entrance hall.

"You make too much of it, Helen. Good heavens, you know as well as I that everyone goes to Zarelle's. I only wish to see what all the fuss is about. Now be a good friend and do not fret. I must rush. Crawley's chaise is already waiting."

And without another word, she swept from the house leaving the distressed girl behind.

The note for Captain Bramwell arrived at headquarters just as he and Lord Ardsmore were about to leave. Quickly perusing the scrawled message from his wife, the Captain raised his head abruptly and scowled at his companion.

Noticing the frown, Valentin commented, "I hope it is not bad news, Harry."

Hesitantly he held out the note to Valentin. "I . . . I think you'd better read this, Val."

The last remnants of a smile faded from Valentin's lips as he read the note. Muttering an oath, he crumpled the paper in his hand and raced from the building leaving Bramwell wondering what he should do.

Nicole's senses throbbed with the excitement of Zarelle's. The dance floor was sparsely lighted by hanging lanterns and much of the room was in semi-darkness. Tiers of private booths draped in black and red helped to create a mysterious atmosphere. Unable to follow the strange steps being performed by the costumed figures who crammed the dance floor, Nicole removed herself from Crawley's grasping arms and asked him to seek refreshments while she returned to their box.

It was cooler in the small corridor, and Nicole's agitation subsided once she was out of the crush. She was sure she had glimpsed several other socialites behind those masks and dominos; nevertheless, she could not relax. Try as she may to blame it on Helen Bramwell's forebodings, she could not shake off her uneasiness. There was a disturbing change in Crawley's demeanor tonight. He had always treated her with deference in the past, but here at Zarelle's he was behaving aggressively, and it frightened her.

Entering the box and removing her mask, Nicole breathed a sigh of relief. She had come to a decision. As soon as Crawley returned, she would ask him to take her home. She admitted to herself that it had been a mistake to come here.

"Ah, there you are, *ma chére*," Crawley exclaimed as he entered and placed their refreshments on a table. "May I offer you a glass of champagne?"

"Joseph," Nicole began nervously. "I wonder if you would think it too bad of me if I asked you to take me home . . ."

"Take you home?" He sat down beside her and clasped her hand. "But we have just arrived. The evening is young."

"I'm sorry to disappoint you, but I seem to have developed a splitting headache."

"No, no, my dove, you do not escape me so easily." He began to press Nicole back among the sprawling pillows.

"Joseph!" she exclaimed indignantly, resisting him.

"Yes, my love?"

"Do not call me that!"

"And why not, my love?" He imprisoned her in his arms.

"Stop it!" she demanded.

"Why do you thrust me away from you?"

"Why? Need you ask?" Her voice was full of reproach.

"Do not tell me you are going to remind me that you are a married woman?" He laughed mirthlessly. "That farce!"

"How dare you!"

His hold tightened as he sought her lips.

"No, you must not," she cried against his lips.

"Why mustn't I? You and I are kindred spirits. After all, we are after the same thing."

"What do you think I am after?"

"What else—the ruination of Ardsmore!"

"Oh no, you are wrong," she wailed. "Ruin my husband! Why . . . why do you hate Valentin so much?"

"I hate him for more than one reason. Ever since our days at school and later during our regiment days. Always the leader—the hero! And calling me out as a cheat over cards. But it is much more than that. Much more. Our families have detested one another ever since your husband's father killed mine in a duel." He was breathing heavily, and there was rage in his eyes.

"Killed your father?" Nicole whispered.

"Yes, killed him over a woman . . . my mother. Harrison Harcourt thought he could carry on the affair with impunity, but my father sought to avenge his honor. Didn't you know?"

Nicole shook her head numbly.

"My mother committed suicide leaving only me to redress the wrongs done my family by those damnable Harcourts. And finally I will have my revenge." He leaned toward her.

"I don't understand."

"You, my lovely, will bring us full circle. Viscount Ardsmore's wife my mistress." He threw back his head and laughed. What had she done? Why had she not listened to the warnings of so many? Bent on showing Valentin her independence, she had placed herself, the family, and her husband right in the middle of a new scandal. She must get out of here!

"And now my sweet, it is pay-up time." He pulled her back into his arms.

205

"Joseph, you are my friend." She tried to reason with him.

"Never! I am no friend of any Harcourt! I planned this right from the beginning when I first met you. Why do you think I introduced you to the maestro and encouraged you to dance? I knew your history. It is unfortunate that it had to be you. I could have cared for you. But you must be ruined along with your husband."

She struggled against him. "No, oh please, no." Gathering her last remnants of strength, she wrenched herself free and fled the box.

"So there you are!" It was Valentin who was mounting the stairs in an angry fury.

"Val!" she cried breathlessly and flung herself into his arms collapsing against his chest. "Please, take me home," she whimpered.

Instinctively his arms tightened about her, and she felt the security of that embrace, but the moment was shattered by the emergence of Crawley from the lounge.

"Ardsmore!" he snarled, dark color suffusing his face.

A man and woman about to enter their box stopped to watch the spectacle taking place.

"So, Ardsmore, the triangle is at last complete."

"I should have finished you the last time we met," Valentin seethed. He attempted to step forward, but Nicole clung to him.

"No, Val! He is mad! Nothing happened!" she pleaded. Her fear was more for Valentin than herself. "Please believe me."

"You expect him to believe that?" Crawley laughed.

Valentin's eyes narrowed dangerously and thrusting Nicole aside, he smashed his fist into Crawley's jaw sending him sprawling. "I will be back," he rasped icily, and grasping Nicole firmly about the waist, he forced their way through the gaping onlookers. He was not finished with Crawley, but this was not the place to settle the issue. First he must get his wife off the premises. Then he would take care of that menace, Crawley, once and for all. Either he or Crawley would walk away from their next encounter—but not both of them.

Valentin was not surprised to see Danforth and Bramwell hurrying toward them. Harry must have gone to Gordon. There was sure to be gossip. Helen Bramwell could not be expected to remain silent for very long, and who could blame her? Nicole's behavior had laid them both open to further speculation by the *ton*. How could she stomach Crawley? It was hard to believe Nicole despised him so much that she would make up to his most dangerous enemy. But she had! That was what was so galling!

Valentin was dragging Nicole down a side street to a waiting curricle, but she did not complain. The violent expression on his face kept her silent although she desperately wanted to explain.

Nodding curtly to the sheepish greetings of his two friends, the Viscount turned abruptly to Nicole and commanded, "Get in."

"Are you coming with me?" she asked in a whisper.

"I have unfinished business!"

"No, Val, I beg of you . . ." She clutched his arm, but he thrust her off and jeered, "You—begging? Who are you trying to save by this untimely intervention?"

There was an audible cough from Danforth which brought an end to their bitter exchange.

"I will meet you inside, Gordon," Bramwell cut in as he left them.

Watching him go, Nicole cried, "Let me explain, Val."

"Isn't it a little late for explanations?"

207

"I have been wrong . . ."

"You certainly have," he claimed in a barely controlled voice. Then he continued in clipped tones, "Gordon, will you see my wife home?"

"Think of the scandal!" she wailed.

"Nicole is right. Val, you cannot afford the scandal. Use your head," Danforth pleaded. "You would be playing right into Crawley's hands."

Before Valentin could reply, Nicole cried out and pointed behind him. Crawley had followed them from Zarelle's. All reason had collapsed once Crawley saw his ultimate goal failing and he was driven by only one thought—Ardsmore must die! Extracting a pistol from his vest, he leveled it at the Viscount.

Whirling about, Valentin stepped aside and lunged for Crawley's pistol hand, jerking it up and wrenching the weapon from his grasp. Not easily overpowered, he flung himself at the Viscount, forcing him to stagger backwards. Recovering quickly, Valentin drove into the Baron throwing a blow to his mid-section, doubling him up. Crawley gasped loudly as he was seized by the lapels and a swift sharp right, then left, landed on his chin. Crawley slipped to the ground at their feet, apparently senseless.

Quickly surveying the situation, Danforth grabbed Valentin and began pushing him toward the stricken Nicole. "You two get out of here! There will be a crowd in a few seconds. I will handle this," he spoke urgently.

"Val, look out!" Bramwell shouted, but it was too late. As Valentin turned, the Baron fired, hitting him in the shoulder. He staggered, and Nicole reached out for him.

Rushing forward, Bramwell kicked the pistol from Crawley who still knelt on the ground. "You bloody coward!" Bramwell shouted as he leveled his own gun at him. "I knew he was up to no good as soon as I saw him coming this way."

"It's lucky for me that you did," Valentin winced as he straightened and moved out of his wife's embrace.

Danforth assisted Nicole into the curricle and came to Valentin saying, "We can handle this. You must see to that shoulder immediately."

The Viscount nodded, but before joining Nicole, he instructed Danforth to make arrangements for him to meet Crawley.

"I will see to it. Now get going."

The curricle moved forward with its unhappy passengers.

"Let me see to this . . ."

Valentin shrugged loose of Nicole's hold on his injured arm. "It's all right!" he growled.

"But you are bleeding!"

"I've had worse."

"If only you would let me . . ."

He cut her off. "I'll live! In spite of your wishes. Now just leave me alone!"

Nicole's lips quivered, but she kept back the threatening tears.

Upon reaching the house on the Rue d'Anglais, Valentin managed to stumble from the curricle and steady himself beside it. Without a word Nicole offered her arm and reluctantly he accepted it.

The startled butler was told that the Viscount had sustained an injury requiring immediate attention, and that Madame Lafitte should join them in the Viscount's room. Anxiously, Nicole followed him upstairs and paused at the door wondering whether to enter his room. As if anticipating her thoughts, he said, "You had best come in and help me off with my jacket since my valet is not here." Breathing deeply, he sat down wearily and let Nicole remove his jacket. He winced, and she mumbled an apology for hurting him, but he ignored her.

"I will have to rip the shirt." Nicole waited for him to confirm her statement, but when none came forth, she repeated herself.

Vehemently he replied, "Just get on with it, will you!"

Annoyed by his curt demand, Nicole ripped the shirt carelessly. At his intake of breath, she looked down into his pain-filled eyes and was immediately penitent. How she wished to comfort him, but he wanted none of her sympathy. Unsteadily she proceeded to pour water into a basin and began to sponge the wound. Nicole suggested a doctor be called, but he insisted it was only a scratch.

"Quel dommage! What has happened?" Madame Lafitte scurried into the room.

"An accident, madame. Can you bind it for me?" he asked, pushing Nicole's shaking hands away.

As the Viscount turned from his wife, Madame Lafitte observed the crushed look on Nicole's face and the grim determination on the man's. Both were very pale.

"Nicole, *ma chère,* get his lordship a brandy and one for yourself. You both look faint."

Nicole did as she was bidden and handed the glass of brandy to him. His eyes held Nicole's for a second; then he quickly closed them and gulped down the brandy.

"Drink yours, too, *mon enfant,"* Madame Lafitte insisted as she took the bottle from Nicole's numb fingers. "And give me the bottle."

"I hope you do not intend to drink from the bottle, madame," Valentin joked feebly.

"You are too bad, *mon Colonel,"* she smiled. "This brandy will sting. Perhaps you would like to hold your wife's hand, eh?"

Hard blue eyes scorched one, then the other woman as he replied curtly, "Just do it quickly."

Nicole held her breath as he endured in silence. Madame Lafitte moved quickly and soon the wound was bound. "Ah, *fini*," she concluded with satisfaction.

"Thank you, madame." He rose and, purposefully focusing his attention on Lafitte and ignoring his wife, he said, "I can manage the rest."

"But, *non*, your valet . . . he is not here, *n-est-ce pas?*" She was undaunted by his steely blue eyes. "So your wife will help you, yes?" And she swept from the room closing the door behind her.

Unsteadily he took a step forward. Nicole, who had remained unobtrusively in the background, came quickly to his aid placing her arm about him. He stared bleakly down at her upturned troubled face. Then his eyes glazed over and he shook free of her saying, "I'm all right. I said I can manage."

"Will you not let me help you?"

"I don't understand this concern you are showing. The wildcat suits you better. Don't change character in midstream, I won't know how to deal with you."

"Will you not believe me? I never wanted it to come to this. I did not realize how outrageous Crawley could be. I thought . . ."

"Enough, Nicole, it is too late for a display of contrition. You have had plenty of opportunities up until now. But no, you blindly tore at the fabric of our relationship until there was nothing left."

"That is not true! Don't say that!" Tears sparkled in her eyes. "I know I have been headstrong, but Val, surely I am not all to blame."

He relented slightly. "I am too weary to think clearly or discuss it any more tonight. Go to bed, Nicole. That is what I intend to do." He held the door open for her, but she did not move. "Good night, Nicole," he said with cold authority.

Her head bowed, Nicole left his room and blindly found her way to her own. Dismissing the maid, she sat before the dressing table and stared at herself in the mirror. In a sudden shaft of clarity she realized what she had done. She had lost Valentin. It did not really matter about Tessa or Valentin's mockery on their honeymoon. What did Lady Eleanore or Cecily's snobbery matter? Even her mother's hatred and revenge did not matter. Nicole halted her reverie, clutching the table fiercely. It was true! The hatred and revenge instilled in her by Sylvie Harcourt had driven her to this empty pit. Nicole had always been at war with herself: loving Valentin yet hating the Harcourts. Madame Chenier had asked her about revenge being her motive, but she willfully denied it. Madame Lafitte had pleaded with her numerous times, and even the good Marquis's warnings had been ignored as she blindly persisted in destroying her chances for happiness! For what? A bitter, empty revenge she no longer desired.

Defeated, Nicole crawled into bed too miserable to weep.

Morning brought no relief from her shattering discovery, for Valentin would not receive her when she went to his room. His valet met her at the door and informed her that his lordship left strict instructions to admit no one. Anxiously she asked about his wound and was told that except for a slight fever, he was well enough. A grumbled oath from the Viscount terminated the conversation.

A dejected Nicole joined Madame Lafitte in the breakfast room.

"He does not wish to see me."

"*Naturellement*. He is ill, depressed. His pride has been injured. This will pass."

"No, I do not think so."

"Give him time. If he loves you . . ."

"He does not."

"Are you certain, *ma chère?* He does not act with indifference toward you."

"That is because he fears I will cause a scandal."

"And have you not?" Madame Lafitte asked boldly.

Nicole raised her chin haughtily, then subsided. "Yes, Fifi, I suppose I have but . . . I was provoked. I have my pride too," she pouted childishly.

"Is your pride more important than the love and welfare of the Viscount?"

"No, no, it is not," Nicole confessed. "I realize now I was wrong to allow the past to influence my judgment."

"What are you going to do about it?"

"What can I do? He will not even talk to me."

"But he will."

"When? Fifty years from now?"

"Soon, *mon enfant*. And when he does, what will you say to him?"

"I do not know."

"Then I will tell you, *n'est-ce pas?*" Nicole inclined her head and Lafitte continued, "You will be humble . . ." Nicole's face froze, but before she could speak, Madame Lafitte went on, *"Non, non,* this time you must listen, child, if you truly love this man and want to save your marriage."

Nicole sighed, "Yes, Fifi, tell me what I must do."

Lafitte patted her hand reassuringly and continued, "You must soothe his anger, assuage his feelings. Let him be master. Do not challenge him and swallow some of that pride of yours. But, of course, if you do not love him

213

enough, or your pride is more important to you than his love, then you will continue as you have been and will lose him forever. This one is a *man*." She watched various emotions chase themselves across Nicole's face.

"So, I shall be docile," she finally replied.

"Yes, but do not become a simpering idiot. That would drive him away even faster. The Viscount likes a little fire with his ice, eh?"

Madame Lafitte's advice did much to alleviate Nicole's fears for the moment; nevertheless, two days later it was difficult to remain optimistic in the face of the taciturn Viscount who appeared at breakfast. His heightened color frightened her, and she tried to dissuade him from going to headquarters for another day, only to receive a frosty retort.

"Your concern is misplaced, madame," he said and strode from the room.

Madame Lafitte smiled encouragingly at Nicole but said nothing. Several gloomy days and nights passed, each much the same. They would breakfast in relative silence; then he would leave for headquarters, not returning until late evening. If he was at home in the evening, the Viscount would closet himself in the library while Madame Lafitte and Nicole sat in the drawing room. Before retiring, he would stop at the drawing room, wish them both a formal goodnight, and disappear.

"He is drinking," Nicole whispered on one occasion.

"How can you tell?"

"Have you not noticed the look in his eyes? Oh, he begins to infuriate me! That exaggerated bow and formal goodnight speech. I am so angry. I should very much like to kick him."

"I should not advise it," Lafitte chuckled and then added, "Patience, Nicole, patience."

But Nicole's patience was beginning to wear thin as

several more days passed and Valentin continued to ignore her. She was dutifully stitching a sampler one afternoon when she became aware of his presence in the room. It was not even necessary for her to raise her eyes to know it was he. As always, his overpowering vitality communicated itself to her.

"Well, madame . . ." She jumped when he spoke. "What is the matter?" he asked.

"Nothing. I . . . I did not know anyone had entered the room," she lied.

"I am sorry if my presence unsettled you, but that is something you will have to get used to. Will you not?" he taunted.

Nicole did not reply, and Madame Lafitte breathed a sigh of relief.

"However, I will not disturb you any longer . . ."

"Why? Where are you going?"

"Do not get your hopes up, my dear wife. You are not going to get rid of me that easily. I am simply going out. Sorry to disappoint you."

"You did not," she said quietly.

"No?" he drawled.

Remembering her resolve, Nicole did not react. Controlling her temper, she shrugged her shoulders, saying, "It is for you to believe me or not."

Briefly she held his eyes; then forcing himself to look elsewhere, he said, "Do not wait up for me."

"Will you be late again?" She regretted the question as soon as it was spoken.

Turning, he appraised her coolly. "That is my business." And he left the room.

"Oh," she cried angrily, and raced to the door.

"Non, non, chérie, let him go!" Madame Lafitte urged.

Nicole clutched the door handle, then collapsed against it in resignation.

Madame Lafitte hoped the Viscount would change his tactics soon, or this private battle between these two strong-willed people would surely be lost.

Nicole knew nothing about the encounter arranged between the Viscount and Crawley's seconds. Sometime after the disastrous incident at Zarelle's, Valentin slipped quietly out of the house just before dawn on a crisp spring morning. Meeting Danforth, they rode in silence toward their destination, a copse by a small creek, a short distance outside the city of Brussels.

Thinking back over the events that had led up to this fatal climax, Valentin knew this was the only possible solution. Reining in at the edge of the clearing, he reached into his vest pocket and extracted two envelopes, one addressed to his mother and the other to Nicole. He smiled uncertainly at Danforth as his friend accepted them with a grave nod. Then dismounting, they approached Lord Crawley and his seconds. A bitter silence stalked the foursome which was broken briefly by a short protest from the attending surgeon. But his complaints fell on deaf ears as the pistols were inspected, primed, and handed to the principals. This time it would be a much quicker matter. Standing back to back in their shirt-sleeves, they waited for Danforth to begin the count. As he called out the numbers, the opponents marched in opposite directions until he reached ten. Then in the cold grey light of dawn, they faced each other and cocked their pistols. The handkerchief dropped, and the pistols exploded.

A moment's stillness followed the report. Then a glint of disbelief crossed Crawley's face as he pitched forward to the ground. Valentin's bullet had struck him in the heart and the surgeon pronounced him dead. The grimness faded from the Viscount's face and was replaced by one of sadness. At the sound of thundering hoof-beats, his features grew austere. If it were the authorities, they were too late.

"Colonel Harcourt!" One of the breathless men shouted as he dismounted.

"Here, gentlemen! If you have come to prevent the duel, you are too late."

"Is that Lord Crawley, sir?"

"It was."

"We were sent to arrest him on orders from Sir Thomas Chaldoner."

"Arrest him?" the Viscount claimed incredulously. "What for?"

"For spying sir. He was a French agent."

"Well, I'll be damned!"

"It looks like you just saved the state the trouble of hanging him. Unfortunately, the information we hoped to obtain will go to the grave with him."

"Sorry to disoblige you, gentlemen."

"Still, if we could keep his death quiet for a while, it might help us discover his cohorts. Do we have your word on this gentlemen?" The others nodded their agreement. "Then we will take care of the body, Colonel."

Valentin breathed a sigh of relief as he stared at his fallen enemy. "You have just relieved me of a tremendous burden. My thanks." Without another word, he crossed to his horse, mounted, and rode away without a backward glance.

Rearranging the pillows on her bed for the tenth time, Nicole sighed with exasperation. Closing her eyes, she tried to fall back to sleep. Why had she awakened at this ungodly hour? Why was she so tense as if expecting something momentous to happen? What could it be? The Viscount's voice suddenly echoing in the hallway below drew Nicole's attention immediately. Quickly slipping out of bed and grabbing her negligée, she raced out of her chamber along the corridor and down the stairs to the library. Bursting into the room and startling both men, she cried breathlessly, "Don't do it!"

The sight of Nicole in her night clothes reminded Valentin of their meeting some six months ago. This same violet-eyed girl with her long raven tresses had braved his wrath with such sweet bravado. Recovering from his recollections, he asked between amusement and longing, "Don't do what?"

"Fight Crawley!!"

"Why do you not sit down, Nicole," Danforth suggested.

"I do not want to sit down!" She barely spared him a glance as she turned back to Valentin watching the tightening of his facial muscles. "What is it?"

"I am afraid I have bad news for you," he said through compressed lips. "News that must not go beyond this room."

Danforth shook his head at the Viscount's choice of words. "Bad news?" She clenched the back of the nearest chair, her knuckles showing white.

"Yes, a little over an hour ago I killed Joseph Crawley.

"Oh, God," she whispered covering her face with her hands. What had she done? It was her fault. "Poor Joseph."

"Sorry, my dear," he said sarcastically. "I know how you felt about him."

Raising her head proudly, she retorted defensively, "No . . . no, I am afraid you don't!" She read the message in those icy blue eyes.

"No?" he questioned cynically. "Then perhaps you should enlighten me."

She would *never* make him understand! Tears glistened

in her eyes and rolled down her cheeks as she stared at him. Finally an inarticulate sound escaped her, and she fled from the room.

Valentin shrugged, his face full of defeat. "There you have it, Danforth."

"Have what, Val?"

"Don't be so blind!" Valentin struck the desk with his fist. "She loved the cur."

"Love? My God, Val, have you gone completely mad?" Danforth asked incredulously. "She has never loved anyone but you."

Valentin laughed mirthlessly. "You don't expect me to believe that!"

"It is true, though. As I told you . . . when I lost Geneviève it was your wife who comforted me because she understood the anguish I felt. You have been too hard on her, my friend. She has been all alone. No wonder she has made mistakes." He spoke earnestly. "Poor girl—deserted by her husband when she most needed him."

"Enough!" Valentin commanded and strode from the room.

Danforth's words rankled all day and into the night. To his chagrin the Viscount could not forget them and began feeling guilty of neglecting his young wife. By the following morning he gave into his long suppressed hopes and greeted her with unusual cordiality at breakfast.

"That shade of yellow becomes you," Valentin observed, taking in the sprig muslin dress which accentuated her dark hair and eyes. "Is it new?"

"Why yes," Nicole was surprised by the warmth in his voice and his smiling countenance. "A designer lately arrived from Paris created it."

"Bonjour, bonjour," Madame Lafitte bustled into the room and happily regarded the seated couple. "Is it

not a grand day? It gives one the appetite, yes?" She heaped her plate with food from the sideboard. "Such a day as this was made for merriment *n'est-ce pas?*"

"You're right, madame," Valentin said as he seated her at the table. "And speaking of amusement, the Bramwells' soirée is tonight. Will you come with me, Nicole? Many of your friends have been asking about you, and I am afraid I can think of no more excuses for you."

"Excuses for me?" she queried. "But I have gone nowhere because of your ultimatum." A shrillness crept into her voice.

"My ultimatum? What the devil are you talking about?"

"You warned me not to go anywhere without your permission. Remember?" she claimed indignantly.

"That was before you compromised yourself at Zarelle's," he stated flatly.

"Compromised? I? You made the scene, my lord, not I!"

"I what?" He rose from the table and crossed to her. "Why you little fool, what do you think would have happened to you if I had not arrived?"

Nicole was about to reply angrily when she felt a good, swift kick to her shin bone. Madame Lafitte frowned at her as she cried out in pain.

Brought up short, Valentin asked, "What is the matter?"

"Nothing," she gasped, "my leg . . . a sudden cramp, that is all."

"Are you sure?" He knelt down beside her as she began to rub her foot. "I thought you said 'leg'?"

"I . . . I meant . . . foot."

"Here let me." He lifted her foot onto his knee, removed her slipper, and began massaging it gently. He looked up at Nicole and caught the soft glow of her eyes on him. "Does that help?" he asked a little unsteadily.

"Oh, yes, thank you," she murmured and smiled.

"Good." He placed her foot back into the slipper and rose. Studying her upturned face, Valentin almost yielded to the temptation to kiss her. Squaring his shoulders instead, he said quietly, "Nicole, we must go out together sometime soon and squelch these rumors which are circulating about us."

"Rumors about us?"

"Yes, of course. Fortunately, Harry has kept Helen quiet about Zarelle's," he answered curtly. Then he continued more calmly, "You will come to the Bramwells' tonight?"

"I . . . I would very much like to attend the soirée."

"Fine. I shall be home early then."

Madame Lafitte sighed in relief and winked at Nicole who smiled happily.

Chapter XIV

Despite the large proportions of the Bramwell residence, the rooms were stuffy with such a crowd in attendance. Nevertheless, it did provide the opportunity for
Lord and Lady Ardsmore to mingle somewhat unobtrusively among the guests. The babble of voices in so many
languages reverberated around the room as the Viscount
calmly led the way through the many greetings retaining
the Viscountess' arm with a decidedly protective air. Nicole enjoyed being in society again, especially with her
handsome husband. She looked around the room noting
the varied little dramas being enacted. Helen Bramwell
was assisting one of her young guests to an antechamber
to repair a tear in the hem of a fragile gown carelessly
trodden by a passerby, and across the room Sophie Evers-

ly was administering a light tap of her fan to the wrist of an aspiring gallant.

Viscount Ardsmore was sought out by his many acquaintances whom he presented to Nicole with his casual but impeccable charm. It was a pleasure to sail under cover of his gallant protection, though she didn't realize how many thought the Viscount was to be envied because of the lovely picture his wife portrayed. Nicole felt a stirring of hope for their future. She looked at her husband with unconcealed admiration, and he responded with a warm smile that stopped her heart. People noted the handsome couple with delight. Valentin continued to stay at her side joining in the small talk and seeing to her comfort. It was much later when Valentin ventured to leave her for the card room. Shortly thereafter Danforth appeared to keep her company. Whatever slights there were, Nicole remained oblivious to them, for there was enough friendliness to soften the snubs of a few crusty dowagers.

One slight contretemps with Lady Raymond almost became unpleasant, but Nicole felt she handled the situation rather smoothly when all things were considered. Lady Raymond was the only person to mention Nicole's recent appearance with the dancers on the night of Valentin's arrival in Brussels. Using the guise of old age to mask her spite, the dowager flung her outrageous question to Nicole in a voice loud enough to be heard by others nearby.

"Ah, Lady Ardsmore, our accomplished ballerina," she crowed. "Society has not had the pleasure of your company these many days. I feared we had lost you for good. I hope we may expect the delight of further performances from you in the future, my dear."

"How kind of you to remember my small efforts, Lady Raymond." Nicole smiled blandly dissembling her chagrin as best she could. "I fear my poor talents are too meager to be taken seriously."

"*Au contraire,*" the dowager would not give up her sport at Nicole's expense. "You are too humble. I am sure many of the *ton* were quite impressed with your talents."

Nicole refused to be mocked further by the nasty crone. "Do you really think I showed promise?" Nicole questioned with false sweetness.

"Oh, indeed I do. You must continue your efforts to entertain, my dear."

"Well, it is no small matter when a lady of your undisputed taste gives her approval to one's efforts. You may be sure I shall place your name at the head of the list when next I entertain." With that remark, Nicole walked off having routed her adversary.

Upon returning home, Valentin commented lightly on how well they had scraped through the evening and bid Nicole goodnight. She had hoped he would make some slight gesture in her direction, but Valentin stayed away. Several other engagements were attended by the two of them, but no further progress was made in their personal relationship. At the end of an evening he would wish her goodnight and withdraw to his chamber.

When Valentin attended a bachelor dinner for a friend one evening, Nicole, who had no engagement of her own, retired early. Nevertheless, sleep escaped her. Unconsciously she was waiting for the familiar sound of Valentin's Hessians down the corridor. When it did come, she was surprised by the faltering footsteps—it was not the swift stride she had become accustomed to hearing. Slipping cautiously from bed, Nicole hastened to the door, opening it a crack, and looking out she saw her husband engaged in retrieving his sword from the floor. Spying her as he straightened, he bowed mockingly, "Ah, my beautiful wife, sorry, I did not mean to awaken you. Very clumsy of me to drop this." His speech was slurred.

"You are foxed," she commented.

"Mmmh, so it would appear. There were many toasts to old Martin. Poor old Martin! What a fool," he sneered moving close to her. "I told him so. Love 'em—leave 'em. Less trouble that way. But he would not listen. Claimed she was an angel. Ha!" He took hold of her long dark curls. "Looks are deceiving. Aren't they, my dear?"

She ignored his remark. "Let me help you to your room."

"Good idea." He smiled mischievously. "Perhaps I can entice you into my bed. Is there a magic charm that might work?"

"Don't talk nonsense," she chided. Encircling his waist with her arm, Nicole led him to his room.

"Oh, madame." The valet came forward to meet them. "I will assist his lordship."

"No, I want my wife to help me. You may go, Jenkins!" Valentin waved his hand emphatically.

"But, my lord . . ."

"It is all right, Jenkins, I will manage." Nicole dismissed him.

Valentin collapsed into a chair. "Woman, remove my boots."

Smiling to herself, she obliged by kneeling at his feet and yanking at one and then the other boot.

"That is where you belong." He studied her upturned face. "At my feet."

"You are absurd," she laughed.

Swiftly bending over her and grasping her painfully by the shoulders, he forced her to remain on her knees.

"Val, let me go," she pleaded.

"What if I don't?"

Nicole struggled to free herself, but his grip grew tighter.

"You are hurting me!"

"Perhaps if I beat you," he threatened, "you would not defy me. Maybe it is not too late." He no longer appeared drunk, just menacing.

"Take your hands off me!" Immediately he did so, and she stood up.

"I forgot." He stood up, too. "You cannot stand to have me touch you. Can you?" He seemed to have tired of the game and, removing his jacket, turned from her.

"I . . . I did not say that," she murmured.

"No? I seem to recall words to that effect on more than one occasion." Valentin unbuttoned his shirt revealing his muscular chest.

"You do not understand," she said breathlessly staring at him.

"Are you trying to tell me that I am not abhorrent to you?" He stepped toward her.

"Of course you are not! It is just that you . . . I, well, we always seem to antagonize each other," she explained lamely.

"Yes, so it seems. I wonder why?" he mused stroking his chin.

"You see what I mean? You already have that gleam in your eye."

Valentin paused, surveying her loveliness. "Forgive me. You're right." Then he added thoughtfully, "Do you think there is a chance we might be able to change?"

"I . . . I don't know," her voice was almost inaudible.

"I suppose we could try," he suggested.

"I would like that," Nicole whispered fervently. "But how . . ."

"Like this," Valentin reached out drawing her against

227

his golden chest. Then lifting her chin he kissed her lips gently. Releasing her lips and looking down into her darkened eyes, he whispered, "If love has escaped us, desire has not, Nicole."

She stiffened in his arms as he sought her lips more aggressively, molding her body to his, and conquering her will to resist. She loved him! And if desire was all he could give her she would take it. Pride be damned! With a sob she allowed herself to be lowered to the bed and felt his lean hard body upon hers, inflaming her with his passion. Deftly and expertly Valentin aroused her ardor until the moment of climax consumed them both.

Arrogantly, he looked at her before drawing away. Clearly he was the victor, she the vanquished, but it did not matter. Tonight Valentin had been hers and that was what she wanted more than anything else. If only someday he would come to love her.

A kind of tranquility settled over the Ardsmore residence after that evening. Each was content to let the situation rest where it was for the moment. No great demands were placed on either party. Both remained cautious, carefully watching the reactions of the other. The tensions which lay beneath the surface could shatter the fragile harmony that was developing between them. Because of this, their lovemaking was infrequent, but rapturous. It was only as they came spiraling down to earth out of the clouds back to reality that Nicole grew bewildered, for a triumphant mocking look would appear on Valentin's face before he relinquished his claim upon her body as its master. What did it mean? she wondered.

This shaky reconciliation continued until late one afternoon in May when their peace was abruptly ended. Nicole heard the voice of her husband in the outer corridor and the sound of voices warned her that he was not alone. The door opened and he entered looking a little harried.

"Nicole, my love," he addressed her, "see who is newly arrived in Brussels."

It was Cecily, looking flushed and happy, in the company of a pleasant faced young man who wore the same scarlet regimentals as Valentin.

Nicole rose from her seat at once and went up to the couple, extending her hand to Cecily. "How nice to see you again, Cecily."

"Dear Nicole," Cecily gushed. "Allow me to present my husband, John Tilford, to you. John, this is my cousin Valentin's wife, Nicole."

"Your servant, ma'am," he smiled charmingly and kissed Nicole's proffered hand. "The Viscount certainly has done himself proud, I must say." He regarded her appreciatively.

Nicole felt a slight blush warm her cheeks as she cast a furtive glance toward Valentin.

"Old Tilford and I cut many a caper in our Oxford days together," Valentin explained. "There was more than one occasion when we were forced to rusticate after some particularly vile escapade, eh Telly?" The Viscount gave Tilford's shoulder a comradely squeeze.

"Oh, Val, I do wish you would refrain from that obnoxious nickname," Cecily protested.

"Come, Cecily," Valentin chided amiably, "with all due respect I cannot promise that I will cry off, 'Telly,' but I do swear to forget my pet name for you, 'Peaches'."

Cecily flushed hotly. "Monster! Am I never to live that down?"

"Peaches?" Tilford questioned. "How did you come by that particular name, my dear?"

Cecily looked even more uncomfortable. "Oh, la, John,

you know how Val is always funning." She shrugged her shoulders.

"There was a fellow at school we called 'Peaches', Val. Remember? Always running to the headmaster with a tale on some poor bloke." John stopped when he realized Cecily was turning even redder.

"Nicole," Valentin intervened, "I have asked John and Cecily to stay with us. The housing accommodations in Brussels are shabby in the extreme, and since we have rooms that are unused, I assured Cecily that you would insist on their joining us here." He looked meaningfully into her eyes, and she knew what he expected of her.

Nicole picked up her cue at once and spoke with forced enthusiasm. "Of course, Val, I would not think of allowing Cecily and her husband to take up residence anywhere else." She hoped Valentin was satisfied with her response.

"You are too kind, Nicole, but I would not dream of imposing . . ."

"Nonsense," Nicole cut off further polite amenities. "Come with me, Cecily, and we will locate the housekeeper and see to the rooms at once." Nocole nodded to the men. "I am sure you will excuse us while we see to the rooms."

Cecily was not the only family member to make an unexpected appearance in Brussels. Perry Harcourt arrived unceremoniously shortly after the Tilfords. He wore a uniform and proudly announced himself a member of the Carbridge Cavalry Brigade.

"Hell and damnation!" Valentin roared. "What do you mean by this rash act? Are the Harcourts to risk extinction?"

"Egad, Val, don't be angry with me. I could not sit back and take no part in this exciting contest. Why, man, everyone is in it now—Whembley, Struthers, Addington —they are all here too. It is sure to be the grandest battle in history. You would not have me sit at home, a coward out of harm's way, would you?" Perry coaxed.

"Indeed I would, sir. This must be seen to at once. I will have you sent turnabout to England on the first return packet leaving Ostend," Valentin retorted with great heat.

"You will not do it, Val! I will not have you order me about like . . . like . . . a . . ."

"Hush, Perry," Nicole interrupted. "Val, let us have peace." She placed a restraining hand on his arm. "Your brother has just arrived and not a word of welcome." The blue eyes were piercing her own with burning anger, but she did not relent. "Perry, my dear," she said turning to him, "come give me a kiss hello. How glad I am to see you again." Nicole held out her arms to him.

"And me, too," Cecily chimed in. "La, but you are a handsome sight in those regimentals . . . I . . . er . . . mean you look, well, simply marvelous!" She ended with a defiant toss of her head in the Viscount's direction.

Even Madame Lafitte sought to check the flow of the Viscount's anger by calling for a place to be laid for Perry that he might join them at dinner.

Seeing himself outflanked in the present skirmish, Valentin relented and held out his hand to Perry. "It is not that the sight of you displeases me, for I am always glad to welcome you, Perry." And giving him a hardy grin, he clasped the younger man about the shoulders in a veritable bear hug of brotherly greeting. "And how goes our illustrious parent, Lady Eleanore?"

"Famously, just famously." Perry gratefully accepted the change of topic, realizing, however, that his brother would still have at him about his commission at a later time.

That night after Nicole had just retired, her husband entered the room. She watched him with glowing eyes as he came to her.

"You look surprised, my love," he said ruefully as he untied his robe.

"I was not expecting to see you tonight."

"Were you not?" he mused with raised eyebrows. "And why not?"

"I was afraid that encounter with Perry had put you out of temper."

Valentin frowned. "As a matter of fact it does rankle. Why did you intervene between my brother and me?"

"Someone had to come to his defense," she said rather defiantly.

"Are you suggesting my brother needs to be defended against me, and you are the one to do it?" he asked mockingly.

Nicole bit her lip, regretting the subject already, but she decided to ignore his flippant question and try to reason with him. "You must allow him to grow up, Val."

"Must I?" There was a challenge in his voice. "What for? So that he can get himself killed? He is my heir." When she did not reply, he continued, "I have no other." Once more he hesitated before adding meaningfully, "Unless you and I have a child of our own." Her downcast eyes flew to his face as he slid into bed beside her.

"Have . . . have I denied you . . . your husbandly rights?" she asked candidly as he pulled her down beside him.

His penetrating look held her. "No, but you still do not carry my child." There was a suggestion of reproach in his tone.

She gasped, and jerking away from his encircling arms, sat up. "That . . . that is not fair! Only this past month have we . . . have we . . ." She blushed painfully and turned her back upon him.

He drew himself up beside her and said quietly, "You're right, of course. I did not mean to cast aspersions. We have not had the time or inclination to discuss family matters; nevertheless it is one of our . . . obligations."

She flung about to face him, her lips trembling with emotion. "Oh, of course . . . our duty, Colonel!" she retorted bitterly and put as much space between him and herself as possible in the big bed.

"Damn it, Nicole, I only meant . . . oh, hell, let's skip it. I did not come here tonight to quarrel with you." Reaching out for her, he pulled her roughly into his powerful arms. "I only know I want you. Now."

"Don't, Val." She squirmed ineffectually to free herself from his embrace. "I do not wish to . . . not now . . . not after this . . . this conversation."

"What better time?" he demanded hoarsely, drawing her closer and kissing the tip of her ear as she averted her face and continued to resist him. "Stop struggling!" He chuckled good-naturedly.

"I will not!" she cried wrenching free.

"You will!" Valentin insisted, the humor gone from his voice as he clasped her once more in his arms and placed his burning lips on hers, forcing a response. He was determined she would yield to his will.

Battling her own desire, Nicole fought against his tightening grip, only to find their bodies more firmly entwined upon the mattress—her breast crushed beneath his hard chest. Ardently he stroked her naked flesh, and whispered intimately to her. His own body trembled with the fiery torrent of his desire for this woman. Inevitably Nicole's love for him swept away any of her lingering resistance, and returning his passion, she yielded completely to the ecstasy of his demanding body.

Afterward, as she lay within the circle of his arm, Nicole wondered if she could be with child. There was nothing she would like better than to present this arrogant Viscount with a son and heir. On this happy thought she drifted off to sleep.

Morning light was streaking the sky when she woke to the light touch of Valentin's lips on her shoulder. She blinked and turned bewildered eyes on him. This was the first time he had ever remained with her through the night. Pleased by this, she greeted his smile with one of her own and wound her arms about his neck as he rose above her. This time she did not struggle against the tumult of his desire but reveled in the glory of their union.

Later, emboldened by her new found contentment, Nicole snuggled next to him and felt his immediate response in another breath-crushing embrace. Finally, releasing her, he sprang from the bed.

"Enough, woman," he chuckled. "I promised to report to headquarters early, and I have Perry to see yet."

"Val," she sat up tugging the sheet above her breast.

"Mmh?" he smiled at her disheveled appearance.

"W . . . will you grant me a favor, please?" she coaxed.

"Anything in my power, my love." He came over to her and began stroking her cheek gently. "What is it you desire?" His eyes danced mischievously as he brushed a kiss across her lips.

Thrilled by his affection, Nicole reluctantly put her request into words. "It . . . it is about Perry."

His reaction was immediate. The contented smile faded from his lips. "Well?" he asked sternly then removed himself from her vicinity.

Unhappily she continued, "Do not be too harsh with him, Val. Let him explain how he feels . . . and . . . and do not scorn his opinions."

"Scorn his opinions? You intimated something like that

last night," he claimed, puzzled and exasperated. "Is that what you think I do?" He folded his arms across his chest and leaned against the bedpost.

"Well . . . sometimes," she faltered.

His eyes gleamed coldly as he strove to control his annoyance. Seeing his reaction, Nicole quickly slipped from the bed affording him a captivating view of her full breasts and long limbs. Momentarily he forgot her insinuations as a more primitive urge flared and burned through him. Covering herself and pulling her dark tresses from her negligée, she came to him, and placing a tentative hand on his arm, Nicole looked beseechingly up into his brooding face. Shaking his head to clear his mind, he asked pensively, "Why does it mean so much to you how I treat Perry?"

"He was so good to me when . . ." Here was another subject she did not wish to speak of; nevertheless, she went on, "when I was in Paris. And I grew very fond of him. I do not wish to see him hurt. Do try to understand, Val."

He sighed deeply controlling a momentary jealousy of his own brother. It was absurd to react this way just because the boy held a place in her affections which he himself did not. "Very well, it shall be as you wish." He managed to smile slightly.

"Thank you," she whispered and pressed a light kiss on his cheek.

"Nicole?" He reached for her.

"Yes?"

Checking himself abruptly, he answered curtly, "Never mind, it was nothing." And he quickly left the room.

If only he could tell her how he felt. But no, not yet! He could not stand another rejection as he had in Paris. They might be sleeping together, but there was more to love than that. Nevertheless, things were beginning to look hopeful. She didn't even protest when he took her this morning after having forced her to submit to him last night. Yet he would have to learn to be patient. Valentin laughed. A patient Harcourt! Well, he could try.

Nicole was not sorry for her intervention on Perry's behalf, for later that same afternoon Valentin's brother burst into the drawing room and swooped Nicole into a bear hug lifting her off her feet. "Nicole!" he yelled, "Val's relented! I am not to be sent packing!"

"Oh, Perry, I am pleased." For more than one reason, she thought ecstatically. Valentin had listened to her and complied with her request.

"Actually, there was not much else he could do." Perry swaggered.

"Perry, never underestimate the power of your brother to make things go his way."

"Oh, ho!" he jeered, "so, my dear sister-in-law has finally come to know her husband."

"Never you mind," she replied sternly before returning his smile. Then changing the subject, she invited him to join the ladies for tea. Hastily he remembered another engagement and fled from the scene.

In Brussels there was the certainty that war must come, and yet everywhere there was the disbelief that it actually would come. It was as if only constant activity could convince the people that life was normal and not about to tumble headlong into chaos.

Reports of minor skirmishes between Napoleon and the Allies were duly circulated, embellished, distorted, and dissected. Once more Napoleon was assuming the shape of invincibility. Everywhere he passed the countryside defected to him.

But, of course, there was Wellington who knew how to deal with the Corsican ogre. There was nothing to fear with such as he to command the Allies. Wellington would settle Napoleon once and for all. Would he not?

So the city of Brussels continued to swell with the influx of men who prepared for war while the ladies filled their days with a flurry of social activities.

At Lady Barclay's card party Nicole found herself in the presence of Tessa Von Hoffman, but unlike past encounters, Nicole detected a change in her regard toward Valentin's former mistress. Noticing the lady's voluptuous curves, she decided that the woman was over-ripe—an overstatement of the provocative *femme fatale* who shamelessly drew attention to herself at every opportunity.

"The men in their uniforms are such a thrilling sight. I vow I never expected to find Brussels so enchanting." Tessa was rhapsodizing about the current military scene. "What is it about a man in uniform that makes him so irresistible?"

"I think it must be that men are at their best in war," Sophie Everly, a romantic featherbrain, chimed in. "All that manly strength and courage marching so valiantly to face death and destruction. It makes me quiver with admiration."

"My dear Sophie," Maria Bellington adjured, "I see nothing to admire in men cutting each other to pieces and spilling their life's blood in the carnage of war." The note of censure in her voice attracted the attention of others.

"Oh, but I did not mean that at all," Sophie replied abashed.

"Then just what is it that you think they march to, child?" Maria pursued.

"I did not think. I only meant they look so grand in their uniforms, as Madame Von Hoffman remarked."

"Madame Von Hoffman's reason for being in Brussels

237

is not the necessity that has brought many of us here. Since she has no one dear she fears to lose on the field of battle, it must make for a perspective somewhat more careless . . . ," Caroline Revington added with ill-concealed malice. Justin Revington was whispered to be the latest object of the Von Hoffman charm.

"Oh, but you do me an injustice, Lady Revington," Tessa returned smugly. "There are many I hold dear among those gallant defenders."

What had started as a mere exchange of pleasantries was threatening to become a verbal battle.

"Can it be half past the hour already?" interposed Laura Plendell with a mind to sidetrack a dangerous conversation. "I do declare my husband gave strict instructions for me to be in attendance when he arrived home this evening. Dear Lady Barclay, I must leave. Such a lovely party."

Lady Barclay cast a grateful glance to Lady Plendell for her timely intervention which led the way for the breaking up of the party. Soon all were making their compliments and leaving for home.

Nicole went to look herself over before the Viscount arrived to escort her home. When she opened the door to the powder room, she was confronted with Tessa Von Hoffman who had just risen from the vanity. Nicole hesitated on the threshold. Although they traveled in the same circle, they were never alone together or spoke to one another. But now Tessa faced her, a challenge in her eyes.

"Don't leave on my account, Lady Ardsmore."

"I won't."

"No?" Tessa drawled. "But then why should you unless you still see me as a threat."

Nicole sat down in front of the vanity ignoring Tessa while the older woman studied the Viscountess's reflection in the mirror. Then she startled Nicole by asking, "Do you love him very much?"

Nicole swung to face her. "That is none of your affair!"

"Yes, you love him. Who would not, eh?"

"I do not have to listen to this!" Nicole stood up as if to leave, but Tessa's next words arrested her.

"Why he prefers you to me I do not understand. I would have remained his mistress even though he married you."

"How dare you say these things to me!"

"Why not? If the chance comes for me to get him back, I will not hesitate to take it."

"That you will never do!" Nicole retorted triumphantly. "You've lost him to me forever."

"You think so?" Tessa taunted.

"I don't think so, I know so. I don't fear you any more, Madame Von Hoffman." Nicole was surprised at the conviction in her words. "If anything, I feel sorry for you."

"Feel sorry for me?" Tessa was flabbergasted.

"Yes, you're rather pathetic—having to seek out other women's husbands—never finding a man who will desire you for himself alone. I really see it now—you are pitiable."

"Pitiable! Why you little beast, I could tell you stories . . ."

"Not anymore," Nicole cut her off. "You've already done your worst, and you've failed. If only you had some pride and would stop chasing after a man who no longer wants you, you would cease being an embarrassment to all of us." Nicole sat down and turned her back on her adversary, but her knees were shaking.

Speechless with rage and frustration, Tessa stalked from the room muttering darkly, "We shall see."

Still trembling with anger and nerves, Nicole determined that Tessa would never get Valentin in her clutches again, and forgetting her toilette, she raced along the corridor to the staircase, stopping abruptly to witness the scene below.

Valentin was crossing the deserted hallway to greet Tessa who had just descended the last stair. He was bestowing a charming smile on the lady as he raised her hand to his lips and kissed it briefly. "Ah Tessa, looking as lovely as ever, I see."

"And you, *mon brave,* handsome as the devil himself."

He bowed slightly in acknowledgment of the compliment. "Come tell me, how are you?"

"I go on, but I still miss you, *Liebchen.*" She made as if to encircle his arm, but he stepped away.

"I do not like to contradict a lady," he said lightly, "but with all those adoring swains at your feet, how could you miss me?"

"Well, one must have some diversion, *n'est-ce pas?*"

"To be sure," he responded with a laugh. But noticing Nicole poised at the top of the stairs, Valentin sobered and walked past Tessa. "Ah, there you are, my sweet." Then remembering the lady, he turned and bowed saying pointedly, "Goodbye, Tessa."

"Goodbye, Valentin." Tessa watched him turn to Nicole, her eyes full of bitter resignation.

Nicole took Valentin's outstretched hand as his gaze swept her face looking for her reaction. To his relief she betrayed nothing.

Smiling she said, "I'm ready, my love."

On the way home they spoke little, and Nicole knew that Tessa figured in his thoughts as well as hers. But Nicole no longer considered the older woman a rival. She had passed beyond that stage of jealousy where Tessa was concerned. This afternoon she saw the woman clearly for the first time. And she had observed the Viscount's casual handling of her, too. Sighing, Nicole snuggled closer to her husband who seemed surprised, yet responded with aplomb by kissing her lightly on the cheek.

"Behave," he scolded affectionately, "or those passing soldiers will think I am escorting a *chère amie* instead of my wife."

"Valentin!" she exclaimed indignantly as he began to shake with suppressed laughter. "You are incorrigible."

"Am I, love?" He winked at her wickedly.

"Yes, but I . . . I like you that way."

He stared at her, slowing the horses to a sedate walk before remarking, "You never cease to amaze me, Nicole."

"Good, I like to keep you guessing," she responded playfully.

He threw back his head laughing and grasped her about the waist with his free hand.

"Val, watch where you are going." She squirmed from his encircling arm. "And remember the passing soldiers."

He bent his head toward hers and growled next to her ear, "To hell with the soldiers."

"No, you are right and we must behave. I acquiesce to your better judgment."

"Why, you little minx, when have you ever acquiesced to me?"

"Right now, my lord," she answered sweetly.

She was rewarded with a bark of laughter. How she loved that handsome face with its endearing, flashing smile. Nicole reached up touching his cheek with her fingers, and his hand closed over hers drawing it to his mouth where he placed a kiss on the palm. His eyes blazed down at her, and she melted against him.

"Ah, ah, my girl." He shook his head negatively. "Remember your willingness to acquiesce to my better judgment."

She blushed. "Very well, my lord, I shall sit here sedately, and watch the handsome soldiers in their splendid uniforms."

Valentin eyed her suspiciously until she giggled. "Jade!" He winked and turned his attention to the horses to hurry them on their way.

Watching the passing parade, Nicole had to admit to herself in all honesty that she was not entirely opposed to Tessa's rhapsody about men in uniform. She, too, found them a gallant sight. Her pulses could be stirred by a martial tune as well as the next. And there was something noble and inspiring about a soldier's willingness to face battle. But her heart stopped when she tried to imagine the man seated beside her on the battlefield. Dear God, what would that be like? She cut off the thought midstream before the horror of it could grasp her fully.

"Here we are, my love, home at last." His deep voice intruded on her disturbing thoughts. She gave him a wistful smile, and let him lift her out of the curricle.

Chapter XV

Taking a mid-morning stroll, Nicole and Cecily walked along the River Dender to watch the military contingents from the Allied countries gather for parade maneuvers in the Parc de Bruxelles. The sight of so many splendid young men in their colorful uniforms flashing with gold and silver and marching to the stirring martial music was a thrilling occasion for the ladies. It reminded Nicole of the recent conversation at Lady Barclay's. It was true that men in uniform were inspiring to see. And the military pageantry was an effective antidote to the creeping fear of war.

"Are they not magnificent?" Cecily claimed breathlessly.

"Indeed they are," agreed Nicole. "If the music and

marching continue much longer, I shall join ranks with the men and march to battle along side of them."

"Gracious, Nicole, but you do get carried away. It must be the French blood that causes such emotional tendencies." Cecily could never resist a sly thrust if the opportunity presented itself.

Nicole was just about to snap back at her when she noticed a dark gentleman in the crowd whose general bearing seemed familiar. Almost at once he looked up and caught her eye. Beauchamp! What was he doing here? The sight of him was displeasing, and already he was heading in their direction.

"Cecily, we have spent far too much of the morning here. We shall be late for luncheon if we do not start back at once." Nicole turned to leave.

"Oh, pooh! I want to see everything." Cecily resisted Nicole's tug on her arm. "Oh look, Nicole. Is that gentleman not seeking to gain your attention?" Cecily nodded toward Beauchamp who was shouldering his way through the crowd.

Nicole ignored her question and exclaimed, "Cecily, I really must insist. Valentin especially wanted me to be present for luncheon today, and I would not want to disappoint him." She turned on her heel and headed on the path homeward.

"Oh very well," Cecily pouted. "If you must spoil the fun, I suppose I have no choice but to follow. Nevertheless, I feel there is plenty of time, and besides that dark man was trying to reach us, I am sure."

"What man was that?" Nicole asked while keeping up the hurried pace she had set for them.

"The one I just mentioned." Cecily stopped and pointed behind them.

"I am sure you are mistaken, Cecily. Now do come along." Once again Nicole tugged on Cecily's arm commandeering her homeward. It took a measure of self-control to resist a furtive glance over her shoulder to see if Phillippe Beauchamp were following. She could not say why, but the sight of him in the park seemed to hold a menace of some kind.

Nicole fretted the rest of the afternoon. All she needed was Phillippe to upset her life. A French cousin! Just a few days ago Lady Raymond had suggested to Nicole that her world must be topsy-turvy, living all those years under Napoleon as a French citizen and now to find herself an English Viscountess. Nicole wished to avoid any encounters that might seem suspicious, however innocent.

Unfortunately her hopes faded the very next morning when Phillippe Beauchamp's card was presented, and he strolled into the drawing room.

"You are early for a morning caller, cousin," Nicole greeted him coldly.

"I desired to see you *en particulier*. I have a matter to discuss which must preclude other parties," Phillippe stated arrogantly.

"I cannot imagine anything you would have to say to me which must be spoken of in private," Nicole answered just as arrogantly.

"Can you not?"

"What could you possibly be hinting at, Phillippe?"

"Eh bien, I shall inform you. Lord Crawley . . . I know the circumstances that led to his death."

She sighed unhappily. "I do not know how that concerns you."

"Vraiment? Joseph, he was how shall I say . . . your *bon ami* . . ."

"I find your suggestions insulting in the extreme!"

"Me, I suggest nothing. I am aware that the Viscount, your husband, has had cause to . . . question your fidelity, *non?"*

"If you think our being related will allow me to stand here and listen to your vile insinuations, you are terribly mistaken, Phillippe. I think you had better leave at once, and do not trouble yourself to retain the connection between us any further. *Adieu!*" She turned to leave the room.

"Do not play the *grande dame* with me, Nicole. You will listen to me or have much cause for regret."

Nicole could not walk away. Her guilt over the past held her captive to his threats. "Very well, Phillippe, get your nasty business over with so I can be rid of your presence."

"*Doucement, cousine, doucement.* You will change your haughty tone when you have heard all I have to say."

Nicole did not reply further, but faced him stolidly, awaiting the harm she feared he intended.

"So now I proceed, eh? You have been very indiscreet, my little one." She blanched as he went on. "I have here from you a note to Lord Crawley."

"A note?"

"*Oui.* Written in your own hand. I shall read a most interesting portion to you. 'I will be happy to assist you in this endeavor which must endear you to any true Frenchman!'" Phillippe lifted his eyes from the note and regarded her smugly.

"That was an acceptance note concerning the ballet company," she explained.

"So you say."

"What do you mean?" She was frightened now.

"This note that you allege concerns the ballet . . ."

"It does!"

"Ah, as I said before, 'so you say'." He held up his hand as she was about to protest. "But others might see it in a different light, *non?*"

246

She refused to respond to the sneering man standing over her.

He continued. "It could so easily be interpreted to show your willingness to assist Napoleon Bonaparte."

"Bonaparte? What absurdity are you talking about?"

"I'm talking about your helping Crawley betray the English."

"What?" she asked incredulously.

Impatiently Phillippe insisted, "Crawley was in the pay of the emperor."

"No, I do not believe you!"

"He was deeply in debt and was quite agreeable to our plan. As an Englishman he had access to places otherwise closed to us, *oui?* Crawley was able to glean much valuable information for us. *Malheureusement,* he lost his head and let the Viscount force him into that fatal duel. *Imbécile!* His hatred cost him his life and us a very useful contact."

Nicole shuddered in revulsion.

"We planned it so carefully, and he ruined everything." He sighed contemptuously. "So now we must begin again. And you, *ma chère,* must aid us."

"You must be crazy," she stormed rising to her feet, "to think I would help you! I will see that you are arrested for the spy that you are."

"*Au contraire.* This packet of notes is all the assurance I need that you will do no such thing." He slapped the packet between his hands. "It was so good of Joseph to entrust them to me, *n'est-ce pas?*"

Nicole felt herself sinking into an abyss, but she tried to hold it off. "Packet?" She swallowed convulsively.

"*Oui,* it contains many interesting items. Here is one requesting a closed carriage and a large sum of money."

"Geneviève," she whispered. "You cannot mean this."

247

"Ah, but *ma petite,* I do. What do you think your husband would do if he received a *billet* mentioning the Ardsmore earrings?"

"You despicable . . ."

"Now, now, *ma chère.*"

"I always knew there was something particularly vile about you!"

The leering smile was wiped from his face. "How would you like your initialed handkerchief to be found at a suspicious meeting broken up by British agents? It could be easily arranged."

Nicole felt her legs trembling and sat down quickly. In a weak, strained voice she asked, "What is it you want of me? Money?"

"My, my we are direct. I hate to disillusion you, but money is not what I want." Beauchamp stepped closer to her, and she recoiled as he hissed, "I want information."

"Information?" she questioned in wide-eyed disbelief.

"Naturellement. Your husband is a Colonel on the staff of Wellington. Valuable information passes through his hands. I want it!"

A cold fear crept up her spine even as she answered defiantly, "Never!"

"No? Are you so sure of that? What do you think your chances would be of explaining these *billets* to an already wary husband? Or better still, a few words to the Duke suggesting Colonel Harcourt's wife is a spy?"

"They would not believe it," Nicole wailed, terrorized by the thought of Valentin's reaction.

"Would they not?" he asked cynically. "With your French ancestry, this packet of notes, your friendship with Crawley, not to mention your floundering marriage to an Englishmen? Shall I go on?"

"No, no, you cannot be so cruel."

248

"I have no intention of being cruel, little one, if you are reasonable and follow my instructions."

"The Viscount tells me nothing."

"But he will. Have you not learned to use those so charming feminine wiles on him yet? Plenty of opportunities must present themselves to go through his desk."

"No, no! I cannot!" She was becoming desperate.

"Eh bien, you leave me no choice." He turned as if to go.

"No, wait!"

He turned and smiled. "I thought you would come to your senses."

"I . . . I need time to think."

"It will change nothing."

"Please," she pleaded, hating herself.

He contemplated her distress. Sure of his victory, he decided to be lenient.

"Very well, you will have twenty-four hours. If you think to betray me, remember I am not alone in this. And I will deal more generously with you than the others. Tomorrow I ride in the park between two and three. If you are there, I will know you have agreed to help us."

Numbed, she stared at him until the door was opened abruptly.

"Oh, excuse me. I did not realize you were having a private *tête-à-tête,* Nicole," Cecily said slyly.

Still too stunned to react, Nicole quietly introduced her two least favorite relatives to one another.

"Why, of course, the charming gentleman I saw beckoning to you in the park yesterday. You never told us about your French cousin, Nicole," Cecily smirked.

"My charming *cousine* has had much more important things on my mind, have you not, *ma chère?"*

Nicole murmured something noncommittal. Phillippe

decided it would be wise to distract Cecily's attention from Nicole and led her across the room chatting in an intimate fashion, his head bent close to Cecily's.

Nicole watched them nervously but was allowed no further action as the Wexfords were announced, shortly followed by Lady Barclay and Maria Bellington. The morning passed quickly in a steady stream of arriving and departing callers. Phillippe Beauchamp had taken his leave, but his absence did nothing to lessen the agitation within Nicole's bosom. She found Cecily watching her speculatively and was determined that the girl should not be allowed the pleasure of tormenting her further.

Somehow Nicole managed to get through the day, but the evening still lay ahead. Since Perry and Telly were both on duty and Madame Lafitte had retired with a migraine, only Cecily and Valentin would join her for dinner.

Not wishing to face her husband alone, Nicole was the last to come downstairs. As she was about to enter the drawing room, she heard the Viscount laugh.

"Come on, Peaches," he chided. "You are up to your old tricks again."

"Laugh if you will, but I tell you they were very confidential."

"And so might we be, cousin, but it does not necessarily mean anything."

Cecily frowned and seeing the Viscount's wife she became silent.

"There you are, my love. Cecily was just telling me you had a visit from a cousin of yours." He crossed to her.

"Y . . . yes, quite unexpected. I had no idea he was here in Brussels."

"Didn't you?" he questioned, and Nicole wondered if there was a note of suspicion in his voice. No, of course not, she chided herself.

Changing the subject, Nicole asked, "Did you happen to see Gordon today?"

"No, he is being run ragged between Brussels and Ghent."

"Poor man. I do hope he has time to join us tomorrow evening."

"I think so. By the way, your mentioning Ghent puts me in mind of something I have been meaning to tell you. I might have to accompany the Duke to the Court for a few days this week myself."

"Why? . . . Oh, no, I do not wish to know!"

"What?" He eyed her in puzzlement.

"I mean I do not want to pry into things which do not concern me."

"Well, I would like to know," Cecily intervened. "Why are you going to Ghent?"

"Because the Duke wants me to accompany him," he mocked, and Nicole relaxed. "Come ladies, I see the butler is about to beckon us to dinner."

To Nicole's relief, the conversation remained light and frivolous during the course of dinner, and it was not until they rose from the table that Valentin had a moment alone with her.

"Come into the library, will you Nicole?"

"Is . . . is anything the matter?" she asked tremulously as she accompanied him to the library.

"I do not know. That is what I was about to ask you."

"Me? Why no. What could be wrong?"

He shrugged. "I just wanted to be sure."

"Everything is fine." Nicole assured him eagerly. Then, "What made you ask?"

"You are not acting like yourself."

"How am I acting?" Nicole asked warily.

"I am not sure . . . jumpy."

"You are imagining it." She laughed.

Ignoring her comment, he added, "And you are pale." Valentin took hold of her chin. "Are you ill?"

"Oh no," she protested. "A trifle fagged perhaps. All I need is a good night's rest."

"We have been going pell-mell," he agreed. "I hope you feel more yourself in the morning." Lightly brushing his lips against hers and then studying her upturned face, he said, "Sleep well, my love." As he was about to leave, he paused. "By the way, Nicole, I would not become too friendly right now with your cousin. His being French and turning up here at this time does not make him exactly *persona grata.*"

Nicole bristled and without thinking asked, "Does the same then not apply to me?"

"You? Why should it? You are my wife!"

"I happen to be French too!" she said defensively.

"And what is that supposed to mean?"

"Oh, I don't know what it means." Miserable, Nicole sank into a chair and covered her face with her hands.

"Nicole?" Gently he removed her hands from her face, but she kept her eyes closed. "Look at me," he commanded.

Half afraid Nicole did, noting the concern in his face.

"What is troubling you?"

For an instant she almost blurted out her calamity. Then the fear of losing him rose up. Their relationship was too fragile yet to withstand the resurrection of Crawley and what had happened, so she lied. "I told you I am tired, and tomorrow I will be fine."

He was not convinced. "Can I not help you?"

"Really, Val, it is nothing."

"Very well, my dear, if you insist. I shall not trouble you further."

"Enjoy yourself tonight." She touched his cheek lightly with her fingers.

"I shall return early."

"Then I will wait up for you."

"No, I want to see the color back in your cheeks tomorrow. So get to bed early and sleep well. I'll see you in the morning."

Valentin continued to be perplexed by his wife's behavior. She was still pale and agitated the next day when he casually asked what her plans were, and he was struck by the look of panic in her eyes. She insisted everything was all right, and he sensed her desire to resist his scrutiny. Frustrated by his inability to communicate with her, he stormed out of the house without a goodbye.

Nicole was all but oblivious to her husband's irritation and concern, so involved was she with her private fears. The hour had come for her to meet Beauchamp in the park and no plan to thwart his designs had presented itself to her. Somehow she had to find a way to get her letters returned to her before Valentin discovered the truth. Would it be possible to search his rooms for the incriminating articles? It was extremely dangerous, but so far it was the only idea that had occurred to her.

"You have not heard a word I have been saying," Cecily protested as they rode their mounts through the park that morning.

"What . . . uh . . . I am sorry, Cecily, I was lost in my own thoughts."

"So I noticed. I was trying to tell you about my gown. The one I ordered for the Richmonds' ball. Have you decided what you will wear?"

"No, I have not given it much thought. Balls, regattas, picnics, soirées . . . to tell the truth, they interest me less all the time."

"Well, there is something that seems to interest you more!" Cecily pointed her riding crop toward Phillippe Beauchamp who immediately came to them.

"Ladies, it is pleasing to see you. May I accompany you on your ride?"

"By all means," Cecily demurred. "I know you and Nicole must have much to discuss. Please do not let me stop you. I see my friends, the Wexfords, just ahead and I shall ride with them."

"That is not necessary, Cecily!" Nicole retorted.

"Is it not? If you had not said so, I should say Monsieur Beauchamp would like nothing better. Besides, I really must speak to Karen Wexford." Before Nicole could protest further, Cecily had spurred her horse ahead.

"That deceitful shrew! She would do anything to create trouble!"

"Let her go. She thinks to promote a love affair, eh? Perhaps it could be arranged?"

Nicole stared at him with open contempt. "You? I loathe you!"

"Why you little . . . " Phillippe caught himself. "Never mind that now. Have you brought information for me?"

"What? Of course not!"

"Then we shall meet again tomorrow."

"That is impossible! If I ride out every day to meet you, Cecily is sure to inform my husband. And if he were to grow suspicious . . ." She looked at him meaningfully.

"*Oui,* we do not wish to jeopardize the situation. I ride here each morning. When information comes your way, meet me. Do not let too many days pass before I hear from you, *ma petite,* or I might grow impatient and have to come to your home, eh?"

"Don't do that! I will come to you!"

He nodded his agreement.

"How shall I get in touch with you if something urgent comes up?" She swallowed convulsively, afraid she sounded too eager. He must not suspect her true motive for asking.

"You grow impatient to help?" His eyes narrowed, doubt registering in their depths.

"I . . . I just wish to be prepared . . . in case . . . just in case something unexpected should happen."

"Send a message to the Hare and Hound, room eight. I usually can be found there in the early hours of the morning. It would be best to get a message to me then."

"I will remember."

"*Bien,* I shall see you soon, *n'est-ce pas?*" He doffed his hat and left her to catch up to Cecily.

Chapter XVI

By dinner time Nicole had decided that she must carry through her dangerous idea. Tomorrow she would not go to the theater with her husband and the Tilfords but would beg off by claiming a headache. Once they were gone and Madame Lafitte was in bed, she would go to the Hare and Hound and search Beauchamp's room for the notes, handkerchief and earrings. With luck she would discover them and be home before anyone suspected anything.

At first Nicole was anxious for the next twenty-four hours to pass, but when the time came, fears shook her resolve, and when Valentin rejected the idea of going to the theater without her, she almost gave up her plan. But then the dread of his discovering the truth reasserted itself, and Nicole pleaded with him to attend. He finally capitulated to her entreaty and left for the theater with the Tilfords.

After Madame Lafitte and the household had settled down for the night, Nicole donned a black velvet cape and hood, placed a small mask over her face, and stealthily crept out of the house. She made it to the street without mishap. Before finding a hack, however, she had to walk the entire block. Several people stared, and one man even attempted to talk to her, but she kept her head down and resolutely walked on until he gave up and went away. She gave the driver directions to stop a short distance from the inn. Then Nicole settled back for what seemed like an interminable ride to the Hare and Hound.

By promising the driver a handsome sum of money for the return trip, he agreed to wait for her. If he thought her behavior peculiar, he gave no sign of it and slouched down in his seat to wait. Nicole scurried away toward the shabby inn.

Her heart pounding violently, Nicole peered through a dirty window into a small waiting room which seemed deserted. As her eyes scanned the dimly lighted lodging for any occupants, she noticed a closed door behind a reception desk, and to the right an archway leading to a parlor. At the far left was the staircase. The unoccupied room presented the perfect opportunity for her to enter unseen and get up those stairs, yet her legs would not move. Reminding herself of the consequences of failing to obtain the correspondence, Nicole forced her shaking limbs to respond. The inn door was ajar and she slipped through undetected. Proceeding cautiously toward the stairs and gaining the first step, Nicole almost cried out as they creaked beneath her feet. Alarmed at possible discovery, she dashed madly up the winding stairs and reached the first landing. Catching her breath, she started down the ill-lighted passage scanning the numbers until she reached number eight, Beauchamp's room. Earlier she had taken the precaution of sending a message to Phillippe at the Hare and Hound to make certain he was out for the evening. Unfortunately, Cecily had caught sight of the unopened missive on its return, but Nicole could not worry about that now. She put her ear to the door and listened for any sounds from within. Hearing nothing, she placed a trembling hand on the knob and turned it, but the door did not budge. She groaned, realizing it was locked, but she was prepared for this, and yanking a large hairpin from her head, she applied it to the flimsy lock. Silently thanking a former school mate for such knowledge, she opened the door and stole inside.

After growing accustomed to the dark, Nicole lighted a candle and stepped to the center of the chamber. Glancing about the room which contained only a chair, a bed, and a bureau, she decided to investigate the contents of the bureau first. Casting her muff up on the bed and crossing to the chest, she managed to open the top drawer after a brief struggle with a loosened handle. Neckcloths and handkerchiefs were all that it contained. Nicole was careful not to disturb the contents. Then she opened the next drawer. Again nothing. Frantically she pulled at another . . . then another. Still nothing. Whirling about she cast an anxious eye toward the bed. Kneeling beside it, she searched underneath the mattress and then below. Here she discovered a trunk. Dragging it out and flinging it open, Nicole found a compartment crammed with papers.

At that moment her attention was drawn to a sound at the door. With trembling hands she reached for her muff and secured the small silver-handled pistol inside. Then she rose to face the intruder as the door flew open.

"Val!" she screamed and collapsed on the edge of the

bed. "Oh no, no," she moaned pounding her hand against the bedpost.

Holding his gun poised, Valentin strode into the room and demanded savagely, "Where is your lover?"

"You have it all wrong—all wrong!"

Coming to her and lifting the pistol from her numbed fingers, he eyed the small weapon and then her. "Have I indeed, madame?" His voice was a cold whiplash. "Apparently a clandestine meeting in the middle of the night should not be construed as anything out of the ordinary."

"But . . . how did you know that I was here?"

He stared at her. It would not be wise to tell her Cecily had come to him that evening bearing her tale of malice . . .

"So, cousin, you go to the theater after all, leaving your wife alone."

"Nicole insisted. She is fatigued . . ."

"Oh, Valentin!" she spat at him cutting him off. "She deceives you!"

"You better explain that remark!" he warned her hotly.

"Val, are you so blind that you don't see what is going on between Nicole and Phillippe Beauchamp?"

"Tread softly, Cecily, you impugn my wife's good name!" he spoke quietly.

"You still wish to protect her, don't you? After all that happened in Paris and here in Brussels with Crawley!"

"That is enough! I don't want to hear another word from you about the Viscountess!"

"Very well, it shall be as you wish. But answer me just this one thing. Why does she send and receive secret communiqués from Beauchamp?"

"You are mistaken!"

"Am I indeed?" she continued sarcastically. "Then I did not see with my own eyes just some half hour ago your loving wife, the Viscountess, with a letter in her hand marked 'Phillippe Beauchamp' on its envelope."

Shaking his head, Valentin brought himself back to the present. Ruthlessly he took possession of Nicole's chin forcing her head back. "When I think of how sweetly you pleaded for me to go on to the theater without you . . ."

"Valentin, do not prejudge me, I beg . . . "

He cut in, "Of course not, madame! I am anxiously waiting to hear how you explain this all away." He laughed cynically, dropping her chin suddenly, as if he had been burned. Then scornfully he continued, "Actually I am surprised, my dear, I thought you had more . . . sensibility. Crawley . . . perhaps . . . but Beauchamp?"

"How dare you!" she cried outraged by his insinuations. "How dare you imply that I . . . I have never been unfaithful to you! Never!"

"Then how do you explain this?" He swept his arm around the room.

"What difference will it make? You will not believe me anyway."

"Try me."

"And if I can not convince you?" She met his cold gaze.

He reached out for her, his eyes narrowing as he encircled her throat with his hands. "Then so help me I will strangle you here and now." For an instant the strong hard fingers tightened meanacingly about her throat. She did not struggle or cry out but closed her eyes and whispered in despair, "So be it." Immediately his fingers slackened their hold on the long white column and slipped away.

He studied her closely. Unshed tears glistened in her eyes, and her lips trembled involuntarily. Quickly crossing to the window before his inclination to comfort her got the better of him, he clenched his hands behind his back and stood facing her. "I am waiting!"

She could no longer hold back the tears, and seeing them he turned his back to her and stared out of the window until she regained her composure. Then she whispered, "Where shall I begin?"

Facing her, he uttered angrily, trying to cover his own pain, "Beauchamp! You love him?"

"No! I loathe him!"

Relieved, but not convinced, he asked bitterly, "If it is not Beauchamp, then what are you doing here?"

"He . . . he was blackmailing me," she blurted it out.

"Blackmail? Why? Whatever for?" Disbelief rang through his words.

"A packet of notes . . . foolish notes I wrote."

"Notes? To whom?" His face darkened.

"To . . ." she paused reluctant to tell him anymore, dreading his reaction, "to Lord Crawley."

"Crawley!" Valentin thought he saw it all now. "And in them you wrote of your love for him," he mocked icily covering the jealous rage which was about to consume him.

"No! no, it was nothing like that I swear!"

"Then what?" he demanded.

"Different things. Foolish things. The ballet for one."

"The ballet?" He shook his head. "What does the ballet have to do with it?"

"The notes are vague and can be easily misinterpreted." She looked directly at him. "I could appear to be a spy."

His eyes narrowed and his facial features hardened as the import of her words struck him. "You better tell me everything that has passed between you and Beauchamp."

And Nicole did including Geneviève, the Ardsmore earrings, and the initialed handkerchief. When she finished some time later, Valentin paced the room in silence for several minutes. Then he demanded, "Why did you not tell me all this days ago?"

"Because you always think the worst of me."

"That is not true!"

They stared at each other uncomfortably until the Viscount broke the silence. "What did you think to accomplish by coming here tonight?"

"If I could have found the notes and freed myself from Beauchamp, you would never have had to know what a fool I have been."

"Do you realize what could have happened if Beauchamp had surprised you here instead of me?"

"But I have to find those letters, Val!"

Torn between his concern for her and the enormity of the situation just thrust upon him, he did not answer her immediately. Finally he said, "I doubt whether they are here."

"There is still the trunk." Nicole bent to it and began rummaging through the papers. "Nothing," she cried hopelessly.

"I didn't think so." He pushed the trunk under the bed.

"I have to find them!" she insisted.

"Never mind. I have an idea. Come on, let's go." He grasped her arm, but she shook free of him.

"But the letters . . ."

"Hang them! I have a plan."

"You do? What is it?" she asked eagerly.

"Not now! I'll tell you on the way home. Right now let's get out of here before someone sees us." This time he held her hand firmly as he drew her through the doorway and quickly along the passage. As they came to the bend in the stairwell, Valentin saw the proprietor leaning over the registration book. He stopped abruptly holding Nicole to him. They remained frozen in each other's arms until the owner disappeared into the back room. Almost reluctantly Valentin disengaged himself from his wife and led her quickly out of the inn. After securing his horse to the back of the hack, Valentin joined Nicole inside. Once he was seated, Nicole questioned him about his plan. He smiled at her eagerness but sobered soon enough as he began to explain.

"After Crawley's death, I discovered that he was about to be arrested as a spy. With his help the Foreign Service had hoped to find out who the other agents were. Unfortunately, their hopes were dashed by his demise. Now, however, this might give us another opportunity to discover who those men are."

"I still do not understand."

"I have not had time to consider all the details as of yet, but just suppose Beauchamp and his colleagues could be trapped at some clandestine meeting. Through your assistance we might be able to arrange it."

"You are suggesting that I act as a go-between?" Her eyes were wide with astonishment.

"Something like that. Then I should be able to retrieve the correspondence and the other things without difficulty once you have proved your loyalty."

"Proved my loyalty?" she cried in disbelief.

He realized his error. "I should not have put it that way."

"But that is what you meant! You still do not trust me!"

"Have you made it easy for me to trust you?" he retaliated, and she turned from him. "Look at me, Nicole!" But she refused to do so. "I will not talk to the back of your head!" He seized her and turned her so that she was pinned between him and the side of the hack. "It is not important at this moment whether I believe you or not!

264

But if those letters fall into the wrong hands, you do know what it could mean!" He released her, and she sank into the corner of the dark coach.

It was quiet for several minutes, and then almost inaudibly she spoke. "I will do whatever you wish."

"Good." Realizing that he had been unduly harsh with her, Valentin slipped his arm around her shoulder. "I am sorry, my dear, I did not mean . . ." Nicole shrugged free of his embrace unwilling to accept his apology. By the time they arrived home each was suffering from a sense of injury and had retreated into a shell of hurt pride.

Deploring his behavior of the night before, Valentin approached Nicole in the morning with misgivings. At his request she reluctantly accompanied him to the library where she now stood stiff and aloof. He offered her a chair, which she accepted disdainfully. Deciding he had to make his peace with her before broaching the subject of Beauchamp, he began, "Nicole, you have every right to be angry with me. I behaved badly last night."

Surprised by his admission, she unbent a little and admitted, "You only stated the truth."

"I went too far, and I ask your forgiveness."

She was flustered by his apology. "Please, let us not talk of it further."

"As you wish." He nodded his agreement.

The arrival of the butler with coffee helped to alleviate the strain between them.

"Will you pour a cup of coffee for me?" the Viscount asked his wife when the butler withdrew from the room. As she handed him the coffee, he said, "I suppose you are anxious to know what I was able to accomplish after leaving you last night." He went on to tell her that he had gone to the Duke of Wellington and explained the coil they were in. The Duke called in Sir Thomas Chaldoner, a member of the British Foreign Service and a plan was formulated by the three of them to ensnare Beauchamp and his cohorts. Nicole's part would be to deliver messages to her cousin and arrange a meeting with the others. At that point she gasped.

"Do not let it worry you," he assured her. "Certainly, you will not be expected to attend the meeting. When the time and place are set, your part is done. You will be home when we break up that gathering."

"But you will be there?"

"I will go as a representative of the Duke. Your name will never be mentioned. It should work out very well. I can't wait to get my hands on that loathsome cousin of yours."

"Val, you will not do anything rash?"

"Of course not, my sweet, have you ever known me to do so?" he asked mischievously and hugged her. Valentin noticed the worried frown that creased her lovely brow. "The best part of it is that no one but Wellington and Chaldoner will ever know that you were involved in this intrigue, and your correspondence will be discreetly returned to you. Do not look so gloomy," he chided. "Everything is going to work out, I promise you."

"I hope so," she managed to smile.

On the night that Valentin had unexpectedly left the Tilfords at the theater to search out Nicole, Cecily's hopes of replacing Nicole in Valentin's affections had foolishly risen. Despite her marriage to John Tilford, Cecily could not give up her secret yearning for Valentin, stubbornly clinging to the notion that in his heart he did not truly love Nicole.

In the days that followed Cecily could glean nothing of the private turmoil masked behind the Ardsmores' polite, but withdrawn, exteriors. She cared nothing about Nicole's coolness toward her, but Valentin's rebuffs upset her. His continued reserve made her aware that she had wounded him deeply when she revealed Beauchamp's involvement wth Nicole.

But why had he been so disturbed, Cecily asked herself as she paced the empty drawing room. The answer she had been blindly resisting thrust itself through to her unwilling conscience—Valentin really loved Nicole! It wasn't merely a marriage of convenience—for either one of them. Regardless of all that had happened between them, Nicole and Valentin loved one another, and it was useless to hide from that fact any longer.

So where did that leave Cecily Fairfax . . . Tilford, she asked herself.

Out in the cold.

And what could she do about it?

If she persisted in fighting the truth, she would succeed in estranging Valentin completely. And as she faced that fact, she discovered that the prospect didn't frighten her as much as it once had. If the full truth were known, John Tilford had something to do with it. Maybe he meant more to her than she realized.

All at once Cecily knew it wasn't going to be as unbearable as she had thought. She could relinquish her hidden desire for Valentin at last.

What would Nicole think when she stopped baiting her? Cecily laughed and determined to improve her relationship with the Viscount's wife before another day passed.

But if Cecily ceased to be a problem, Phillippe Beauchamp remained to plague Nicole's peace, even though the first message delivered to him brought Nicole his praise when next they met.

"*Très bien, chère cousine,* your information was interesting."

267

Nicole tried to hide her agitation behind a small tight smile, remembering Valentin's advice to appear natural and friendly. The only bad moment occurred when he asked how she was able to obtain the intelligence. Somehow she managed to prevaricate speaking evasively until he seemed satisfied and let the subject drop. During the following days several other communications were passed on to him, each containing enough truth to appear useful to the enemy and establish Nicole's importance as an accomplice. Because Beauchamp seemed well satisfied with the arrangements, Nicole was unprepared for his sudden demands at their next meeting.

"We need a schedule of the Duke's plans for the coming week. I want specifics—times and places. I will meet you here in two days. Have it for me then."

"But that is impossible!"

"Pourquoi?"

"I cannot do it . . ."

"What do you mean? Have you forgotten your vulnerability so soon?"

Conquering the desire to take her riding crop to him, she replied between compressed lips, "No, I have not forgotten, but it will take time to get what you ask. As you have so often reminded me, my husband is a wary man. Do you wish to arouse his suspicions?"

Beauchamp pondered her words before replying shortly, "Very well, see what you can do. I will ride here every morning. Come as soon as you can."

When Nicole relayed Phillippe's demands to the Viscount, he immediately went to see the Duke of Wellington. Late that night he returned and awakened her from a sound sleep. Not remembering the urgency with which he left her earlier, Nicole smiled invitingly up at him, winding her arms about his neck, but he kissed her briefly then

268

withdrew from her arms. "I must talk to you about your cousin."

"Now?"

"Yes, it is important. The Duke and Chaldoner feel this may be what we have been waiting for."

"And what have you been waiting for?"

"Until now Beauchamp has accepted the information you have been willing to supply. Suddenly, however, he is demanding specific facts. It may be very important." He stood up.

"I see."

"Chaldoner thinks this is the time for you to demand to see Beauchamp's superiors."

"I will have to give him some reason for wishing to see his superiors."

"You'll have one."

"What is it to be?" She looked up at him innocently as he paced the floor in front of her.

"Tell him . . ." He stopped pacing. "Tell Beauchamp you will give him exactly what he wants if you are no longer treated as an outsider but as one of them."

"He'll never believe that!" Nicole claimed from her lounging position among the pillows.

"You must convince him it is true. Explain . . ." he faltered, "that the situation between us has become . . . impossible. Say you wish to return to Paris. That you believe Napoleon will win and you want to be presented at the French court. Tell him you wish to meet with his superiors to discuss your future."

"You . . . you want me to tell him that?" She stared at him in disbelief.

Ignoring the implication of her remark, he added grudgingly, "I don't think he will find it too hard to believe. After all, he is aware that we have had our differences. It seems everyone is aware of our past difficulties, including the Duke and Chaldoner."

Deeply wounded, Nicole continued to stare at him. Then swallowing her misery, she replied bitingly, "I agree with you. He probably will believe it. Is that all?"

"My God, isn't that enough?" He ran his fingers through his hair.

"Is there anything else I should know?"

"After you make the arrangements for the meeting, that's it."

"Well then, if you don't mind, I will go back to sleep. I am extremely tired." She proceeded to yawn, roll over, and bury her face in the pillow.

Valentin stared down at the inert form of his wife. He knew it would be impossible to talk to her while she was in this frame of mind. Grinding his teeth together and swearing an oath under his breath, he snuffed the candles and left the room. Nicole then cried herself to sleep.

Phillippe's eyes narrowed as he listened to the Viscountess's tale, but his only comment when she finished was that he would see what could be done. When next they met, he told her that everything had been arranged for three days hence.

"I will meet you outside your home at ten o'clock."

"No, just tell me where to go. I do not think we should risk being seen together." My God, I can't go with him to that meeting! Nicole thought.

He laughed derisively, "What kind of a fool do you take me for?"

Frightened, she replied, "I don't know what you mean."

"You do not think I am stupid enough to trust you?"

Astonished, she stared at him. "But . . . but I told you it is imperative that I get away from my . . . my husband."

"That may be and then again . . ." he shrugged his shoulders, "who knows what game you perhaps play, eh?"

"I am in deadly earnest," she said with conviction. "If I do not get the reassurances I need, I will never give you the information you want. And you can do your worst because I no longer care to save my marriage. All I want is to be free of it."

"You are very convincing, little *cousine*." He eyed her speculatively before adding, "You wish to return to Paris. I wish for the schedule of the Duke. So we shall strike a bargain, *n'est-ce pas?* Come with me, and you shall have your assurance and I . . . I will have the schedule, *oui?*"

Nicole hesitated trying to think of some way out. But further protest on her part might only make him more suspicious. "Very well, I will go with you . . . under one more condition."

"And that is?"

"My correspondence must be returned to me at the same time I give you the schedule."

He did not answer her immediately. Then he nodded in agreement and after a few more words left her.

Nicole did not have the opportunity to speak to the Viscount about her encounter with Beauchamp until much later. By then she was quite composed and related the surprising turn of events in a detached manner. She would have to go to that meeting.

"Impossible!" he stormed. "Other arrangements must be made."

"But what can they be, Val?"

"I don't know yet, but I am going to see Chaldoner about it right now."

Calling for his groom to saddle his horse, Valentin hurried from the house. Nicole's spirits revived immeasurably. That was not the reaction of an indifferent man.

She waited impatiently for his return, peering out of the window every time a horse passed by. But the hours dragged on interminably, and still he did not come. Just when she had given up hope and was about to retire, she heard his horse's hoofbeats on the cobblestones. Racing to the door to meet him, Nicole was immediately subdued by his appearance. Frowning moodily, he mumbled a greeting. Then taking her arm, he led her into the library.

Nicole waited quietly while he poured himself a brandy; however, she already knew what he was about to say.

"Nicole," he broke the stillness that surrounded them.

"You want me to go with Phillippe?" She placed her hands to her breast to quiet the tumult of emotions which cried within her, Not enough! He does not care enough!

He nodded abjectly and took hold of her hands. "There seems to be no feasible alternative. I have been over it a dozen times with both the Duke and Chaldoner." He knelt beside her chair. "But nothing can go wrong. I will be there along with Perry and Danforth. That was definitely decided. Then no one else need know about this."

She withdrew her hands from his tight grasp.

"Nicole, if you do not want to do it, I will understand."

"Will you?" She looked at him blankly.

"Whatever you say," he encouraged. "I will tell Chaldoner and the Duke to go to the devil."

"Do you want me to go?" she asked matter-of-factly.

He rose and walked to the fireplace before answering. "It is your decision."

"I see." She stiffened. "Very well, then I will go. I suppose it doesn't matter anyhow."

"What do you mean it doesn't matter?" he asked gripping the stem of his glass until his knuckles showed white.

Shrugging her shoulders, she replied, "Let's not discuss it further. I said I will do it." Nicole rose from the chair.

"Nicole!" Valentin reached out for her, but she shied away.

"I am very tired. If you don't mind, I will bid you goodnight."

"Nicole." Again he tried to embrace her.

"Please, Valentin, don't!" His arms dropped in defeat, and he watched her cross the room and close the door quietly behind her.

"Damn it!" he swore out loud. If only she had refused. But he could not do it for her. Wellington had extracted a promise from him when he saw his reluctance to comply with the scheme. "State the facts simply. Then let her decide. I do not need to remind you how vital her decision may be to this entire campaign." The Duke had been clever, playing on the Viscount's loyalty to England. And now he was trapped. He continued to pace back and forth for several more minutes until he released the tension by smashing the crystal brandy glass on the hearth.

Chapter XVII

Pale but composed, Nicole reached the library where the Viscount, Gordon Danforth and Perry Harcourt waited for her the night the assignation with Beauchamp was to take place. Raised voices within the room stopped her from entering.

"I don't give a damn!" Valentin swore, "I cannot let Nicole do it."

"Val, you have no choice," Danforth adjured. "You gave the Duke your word."

"I will not jeopardize the life of the woman I love!" he said angrily.

Nicole grasped the nearest hall chair for support. Sinking into it, she repeated the words, 'the woman I love.' He loves me! she whispered incredulously. A wild elation seized her, and jumping to her feet, she rushed toward the library entrance only to be arrested again by the ensuing conversation.

"The Harcourts have always lived on the brink of scandal. What is one more? Right, Perry?"

"I am with you, Val!" Perry agreed.

But Danforth denounced them. "And honor? Would Nicole wish you to sacrifice that?"

"She will not know. Besides, I will think of another way to make that despicable cousin of hers give us the information we want."

"How?" Danforth insisted.

"Yes, Val, how?" Perry reiterated Danforth's question.

"I do not know yet," Valentin answered impatiently.

Nicole retraced her steps, deep in thought. What was she to do? Valentin would never listen to her once his mind was made up. She had to do something. There was only one thing she could do.

Snatching a piece of paper and a pen from the escritoire in her room, she scribbled a note to Beauchamp stating that he was to meet her a half hour earlier than planned. Quickly sending it off with a servant, she sat down to write a much more difficult note to her husband. There was so much to say, and it could not be written. Not now! Next she sought out Madame Lafitte and enlisted her aid. Shortly thereafter she left the house by a side entrance and walked to the street corner where she would meet Phillippe.

As soon as Nicole was out of the house, Madame Lafitte presented herself to the Viscount, handing him his wife's note. Recognizing the handwriting, Valentin quickly tore open the envelope, a premonition of fear seizing him. He read of the changes his wife had made in the plan and groaned, "My God," as he handed the note to Danforth. Then rounding on Madame Lafitte, he noticed she was clutching a small box. "What is that?" he demanded savagely, tearing the box from her trembling hands.

"Not now, my lord, it is only to be opened if . . ." Her voice trailed off.

Ignoring her protest, he opened it. The moment he discovered the glittering stick-pin he realized its significance. That day at Uncle Maurice's chateau! With mounting dread he read the attached note:

Forgive me for disobeying your wishes once again, my darling, but there truly was no other way. I have always loved you. Your adoring wife, Nicole.

Reflecting momentarily, his eyes glittered as brilliantly as the sapphire he held. Then purposefully he hastened from the room with Danforth and Perry behind him. He could not lose her now!

The Viscount's quick pursuit of his wife soon brought them within range of Beauchamp's curricle which they were shadowing at a discreet distance as it headed toward the outskirts of Brussels. In town Beauchamp might not notice them, but once they reached the country roads there was little likelihood of remaining hidden.

Sitting beside her cousin, Nicole realized that danger as she tried to parry his questions about her departure.

"Since the Duke's schedule for the coming week caused your hasty departure, let me relieve you of it."

"No . . . not until I have seen your superior."

"Peste! Do you think I ever had any intentions of letting you meet my superior?"

"But you promised!"

He laughed maliciously. "You believed I would trust you?"

"Why . . . why should you not trust me?" Nicole tried

to sound defiant although her voice began to shake. "Have I not given you the information you desired?"

"So it seemed at first. Your fear of your husband discovering those letters, it was genuine enough. That is why your later story, it had to be a fabrication."

"But I told you why . . . I changed my mind . . ."

"Then why were you still so desperate to get your hands on those letters? *Naturellement,* I had to ask myself that question. And, of course, the reason, it was quite obvious. You see, *chère cousine,* I always believed that you loved the Viscount. But me, I did not calculate his devotion to you. So, I look again at the situation. The Viscount, was he helping you to keep me informed—*est-ce possible* he too was a spy? That is very doubtful; therefore, I find it *nécessaire* to do some investigating. It was not too difficult to discover that the Duke, Chaldoner and your husband confer secretly. Tut, tut, *ma chère,* such a complex game you play. You expect me to be so gullible, eh?" His bantering tone changed suddenly to one of malice. *"Traitresse!* I should dispose of you here and now!" He flicked the reins, and the horses moved ahead quickly.

"You would never get away with it." Her voice quaked.

"Why? Because your husband follows us?" he scorned.

She gasped, and he laughed once more assuming his bantering tone. "Ah yes, I know that, too. It is as I planned. Why else do you think I insisted you come tonight?" At her puzzled frown he explained. "To ensure my escape."

"Your escape?"

"Mais oui. The Viscount will not endanger your life. So I am assured safe conduct through the lines. And my superior, he remains secret."

"If you suspected, why did you wait until tonight to escape?"

"Because there was always the chance that I am wrong.

Ah Nicole, if you had been *fidèle,* what my friends and I would have accomplished."

"What *would* you have accomplished?" she prodded.

He laughed contemptuously. "You still think to lure me? But no difference. It is too late. Our plan will no longer be possible. It could have worked but for you." Again the light mood was overshadowed by hatred.

"What would have worked, Phillippe?" she pressed for that piece of intelligence. "If it is all for naught . . ."

"It was a truly magnificent scheme . . . to kidnap the Duke of Wellington. Then the emperor would have marched through Brussels perhaps without a shot being fired. *Maintenant,* the battle will come. And the loss of many French lives with it. All because of you and your lover! So we will put an end to this charade and attract the attention of our gallant escort, *n'est-ce pas?*"

Abruptly halting the curricle, he seized Nicole, and before she realized what he intended, he gave her two resounding slaps across the face making her cry out involuntarily.

Valentin heard his wife scream and spurred his horse forward.

"That is far enough, monsieur!"

The Viscount drew rein as he eyed the gun pointed at Nicole's head. "Hold up!" he called to Perry and Danforth who were directly behind him.

"Bien. Now that I have your attention, gentlemen," Beauchamp purred, "we will come to terms, *n'est-ce pas?"*

"That depends." Valentin shrugged, assuming an indifference he was far from feeling.

Beauchamp was scornful. "Do not play with me, Colonel, unless you wish to see this pretty piece of womanhood drenched in her own blood."

Valentin's face paled.

"So, this baggage," Beauchamp nudged Nicole with

279

the pistol, "does matter, eh? Very well, you will now oblige me, gentlemen, by dismounting."

"Do as he says," Valentin ordered as the others hesitated.

"Remain mounted, Colonel. You, I will need." Beauchamp smiled confidently. "You ride with your wife and me to the frontier. And once I am safely through the lines, I shall set her free to return with you. Try to stop me and I kill her without the slightest hesitation. *Comprenez-vous?* Get out!" He thrust Nicole from the curricle. "Out of my way!" he demanded of Perry and Danforth as he edged himself and Nicole toward the horses.

In a daze she allowed herself to be pushed in the direction of the pawing animals. Danforth and Perry backed away in the face of the waving weapon while Valentin sat motionless waiting for an opening. With a shove from Beauchamp, Nicole stumbled against a horse that reared and snorted, diverting her cousin's attention long enough for Valentin to spring from his saddle and knock the pistol from Beauchamp's hand as it went off. The startled horses leaped and plunged entrapping Nicole, Phillippe and Valentin among them. Perry and Danforth raced to the horses attempting to control the frightened animals while the Viscount battled Beauchamp in their midst. Nicole tried to scramble out of the way of the brawling men and thrashing horses only to be struck in the back and sent sprawling head first on to the ground. She was knocked senseless.

"Nicole?" She heard her name called from what seemed a long distance.

"She is opening her eyes," Perry's voice drifted above her.

"Sweetheart." A soft brush of lips touched her cheek.

"Val?" she murmured hazily.

"It's all right, darling." Valentin smiled down at her. "Can you stand?"

"I think so. I don't know which is throbbing more—my head or my back." She placed her hand to her head as Valentin helped her to her feet. She swayed against him, and he lifted her into his arms and carried her to the curricle.

"What happened?" she asked as he placed her on the seat and climbed in beside her.

"The horse caught you . . . "

"Phillippe?" She interrupted him.

"Nothing to worry about on that account. Gordon's got him neatly tied up. He and Perry will deliver him to headquarters while I get you home." He flicked the reins, and the others followed.

Suddenly she burst into tears burying her face in his shoulder. "I failed," she cried.

"No, you did not." Valentin soothed, holding her against him. "Listen, Nicole, Beauchamp will talk. We will find out who is behind this spy ring."

"But they will get away by then."

"The important thing is that the ring will be destroyed, and Beauchamp will tell us why they wanted Wellington's schedule."

She sat up and gave him a watery but triumphant smile. "I know why, Val. They were going to kidnap the Duke."

"Good God! Gordon, did you hear that?" he shouted. "Nicole, you will be a heroine once the Duke hears of this."

"But my letters! Oh Val." Dejectedly she sank against him, her head aching with the effort to speak.

"Here, my dear, I think this is what you were worried about."

"The letters!" she shrieked. "Where did you find them?"

"On Beauchamp."

"I am free, Val!" She kissed him impulsively. Then she fell limply against him mumbling, "Oh my head." And fainted.

When Nicole awoke, candles flickered on a nearby table, and Valentin sat on the edge of the bed. At her bewildered expression he chuckled softly. "That is right. You are home in your own bed." He touched her chin lightly with his knuckles. "You gave me quite a scare, passing out on me like that, but Madame Lafitte assured me you would be all right."

She sat up. "I am." Then placing her hand in his, she asked, "Is it really all over?"

"It is, my darling wife, all over." He bent to gently kiss her soft lips.

Clinging to him, silent tears slipped down Nicole's cheeks. "Forgive me, Valentin, forgive me. I love you so much," she whispered brokenly.

"Don't cry, my darling. Please don't." He held her tightly against him until the stiffness flowed out of her, and she relaxed in his arms. "Nicole, it is you who must forgive me for being such a blind idiot." He held her even tighter.

"Oh no, no, Val. It was all my fault. I was so full of imagined hurts that I could not see or think straight. I was letting my mother's past destroy my life."

"I did much the same thing. When I thought you did not love me, my pride took over with a vengeance. That is why I left you in Paris."

"And I thought you did not care for me," she murmured.

"I love you, my darling," he whispered kissing her trembling lips.

"And I have loved you ever since I can remember."

"Nicole," he whispered huskily tightening his grip on her. His lips held hers with deepening desire. The driving hunger of his love for her so long held in check could finally be given full rein. All his restraint gone, he gave vent to a torrent of raging passion which could not be denied. Carried along by his consuming desire, Nicole trembled under the demands of his questing hands and caressing lips. Against Valentin's taut frame and burning heat her own body flamed and ached with mounting desire for his possession of her. It came in a crescendo of surging ecstasy and consuming fire. Valentin looked into her loving eyes, and she saw the same triumphant expression upon his face that once used to disturb her. No doubts about it could plague her now, for it was the fulfillment of love's dream she saw. "I love you." They spoke the words simultaneously, and cradled in his arms she slept peacefully.

A light kiss on her lips awoke Nicole. Languidly she stirred beneath the sheet and opened her eyes to see her husband grinning down at her. "Hey, sleepy head, I am off to headquarters."

"Val, must you rush off?" she cried encircling her arms about his neck.

"Yes, I must." He gave her a quick kiss. "Do you know, I have already breakfasted and seen Perry. I thought you might be interested in what took place after Perry and Danforth took Beauchamp to headquarters last night. But if you are not . . ." He smiled mischievously and began to remove her arms from his neck.

"Valentin!" she screeched. "You would not dare to leave me in suspense!"

"Oh, would I not?" He grinned playfully and started across the room.

"Val!" She jumped from the bed heedless of her undressed state and flew into his arms. "Do not tease me."

"Tease you, madame? I think it is you who teases me shamelessly," he said stroking her curves and kissing her lips. "Egad, Nicole, get something on before I forget myself."

She snuggled next to him. "I will, my lord," she smiled provocatively up at him, "if you promise to tell me about Phillippe."

"Why you little minx." He laughed and lifted her into his arms. Then throwing her onto the bed, he claimed, "I think, madame wife, you need a further lesson in heeding the advice of your husband."

"I . . . I was only joking, Valentin," Nicole responded somewhat flustered as she became aware of his intention.

"Well, I am not," he smiled arrogantly stripping himself of his clothing and coming to her. "I do not intend to resist the temptations of your lovely body ever again."

"I am yours to command, my love." Nicole pulled his head down to meet her lips, yielding to him.

"God, I want you, Nicole."

"Yes, Valentin, oh yes," she replied breathlessly as he began to weave his magic over her again.

Sometime later she stirred from his embrace, and he rose to dress. She sat up and asked, "What *did* happen to Beauchamp?"

He smiled and replied, "He was more than willing to talk. It seems they hoped to delay the Allies' preparations by kidnapping the Duke. And Boney is about ready to attack."

"Must it come to that?"

"I am afraid so, my dear." Noting the fear in her eyes, he changed the subject. "I will try not to be too late, so that I can escort you to the Richmond ball tonight."

Attempting to match his light tone, she said, "I have a new gown for the occasion."

"Good. Then wear these, my dearest." He dropped the Ardsmore diamonds into her hand.

"The earrings! Where did you find them?"

"Danforth got them from Beauchamp last night."

"Thank you." She blushed painfully remembering all her foolishness again.

"My love, that episode is behind us. From now on all we will have to remember are the good times."

"There have not been too many of those."

"But there will be. Here is one I will always cherish." He dangled the emerald and sapphire stick pin before her eyes.

"You do remember?"

"How could I forget."

"Oh, my love, it is so hard to believe all my dreams are coming true."

"They are as long as they include me."

She laughed gaily. "Every one!"

"That is all I want to hear."

It was a great disappointment to Nicole when the Viscount's note arrived expressing his regret that he would be unable to accompany her to the Richmonds' ball after all. In the note he promised to meet her there as soon as possible.

Perry willingly waited upon his brother's wife that evening. She wore a diaphanous yellow chiffon with delicate threads of gold woven throughout the low-cut bodice and slightly flared skirt. It swayed and clung to her exquisite figure as she came across the room to greet her brother-in-law. She smiled as he kissed her hand and said, "Ravishing! You are absolutely ravishing! If you were not my brother's wife . . ." he teased, eyeing her appreciatively from her Grecian curls to her satin slippered feet. "Not a man will be able to take his eyes off you this evening."

"Oh, dear," she said with a touch of concern, "your brother will never approve."

"He would be a fool not to."

She stood before the fireplace mirror and tried to adjust the bodice to cover more of her bosom.

"Speaking of my brother, I know he was terribly disappointed not to be able to escort you himself."

She met his eyes in the mirror—a worried frown creasing her lovely brow. "Those dreadful rumors of war . . ." Perry shifted his weight uneasily as she turned from the mirror to grasp his fingers. "Will it come to that?"

He shrugged his shoulders. "Don't know for sure, luv. But don't look so worried." Perry added proudly, "We will have old Boney beat before you can bat an eye."

Nicole's protest was interrupted as Cecily and John Tilford joined them.

"Oh I say, Nicole, that is a most stunning gown," Tilford surveyed her admiringly.

"Why thank you, Telly," Nicole smiled flirtatiously.

Catching the jealous gleam in Cecily's eyes, Perry quickly slipped a matching shawl over Nicole's shoulders and led her from the salon.

The élite of Brussels society was already assembled in the salons of the Richmond home by the time Nicole and her party arrived. It was apparent, however, that the Duke's staff was still absent, for the smiling guests arrayed in their splendid finery were tense beneath their carefree façade. Nicole chatted lightly with Helen Bramwell while each scanned the room anxiously watching for the Duke's party. Maria Bellington joined them looking calm and serene.

"How can you be so collected at a time like this, Maria?" Helen accused.

"Do cheer up, my dears. I hear the Duke is on his way."

"Have you heard if it is war or not?" Nicole asked.

"Gossip and rumors. Nothing definite. We must await the Duke."

"This waiting is unbearable," Helen cried.

"Hush, my dear child," Maria scolded. "You do not wish to show such fears to Harry, do you?"

Tears sprang into the young girl's eyes. "Come with me, Helen, you must compose yourself," Maria said soothingly leading Helen away.

"Foolish chit!" Lady Barclay commented. "I am glad to see you are not allowing circumstances to crush you down."

Nicole did not have time to respond. The Duke was announced, and his party entered the ballroom.

Immediately Nicole saw Valentin, his blue eyes searching the ballroom for her. But before he could catch sight of her, the Duke of Wellington was surrounded by a mob of the curious and the anxious who questioned him about the rumors of war. His quick terse reply was in the affirmative. It would be war! Nicole, whose limbs were already shaking in anticipation of those fateful words, remembered Maria Bellington's stern warning just moments earlier. Fleeing the ballroom, Nicole sought the privacy of a small salon where she could compose herself before facing her husband. Only seconds after reaching the sanctuary, the door opened and closed softly behind the Viscount.

"Nicole?" he questioned, crossing the room to take her outstretched hands in his own. "What is it, darling?"

Her eyes were misted. "Hold me, Valentin," she whispered unsteadily, staring at the glittering medals and gold-trimmed scarlet uniform.

He crushed her against him, his brass buttons digging into her flesh, and he whispered her name softly several times. Then he was holding her at arms' length, smiling boyishly. "You are looking very fetching tonight, my sweet."

"Oh, Val . . ." her voice quavered.

"Shh." He placed his fingers to her lips. "The night is still young, and I want to hold you in my arms. Will you dance with me?"

He was being deliberately casual, and she must make every effort to do the same. She could not let him down now. Striving for an inner composure to carry on the charade, she answered, "I am yours all evening if you want me, my lord."

"Want you—you know I do." He held her gaze then added lightly, "Turn around, and let me see all of this delightful creation you are wearing."

"Do you like it?" She pirouetted around him.

"Enchanting. What there is to it." He stroked his chin thoughtfully.

"I decided against dampening the underskirt . . ."

"You better had!"

"Oh?" She eyed him provocatively. "And what might you have done if I had?"

"Need you ask, you minx?" He raised his hand playfully letting it come to rest on her cheek.

Nicole snatched it to her lips, kissing it. "I love you," she murmured.

Overwhelmed, Valentin quickly took her by the hand and commanded, "Come on, my dear, let us get out of here before I forget where we are, or you shall be quite embarrassed."

She flushed in spite of the delight she felt. Decorously accepting his arm, they returned to the ballroom.

Melting into his arms, Nicole was oblivious to everyone

else, her violet eyes shining up at the man she loved. They danced time and again with one another until some of the Viscount's friends and fellow officers began to protest. It was impossible to refuse their requests to dance with his wife. Reluctantly he relinquished his claim on her. As Nicole danced by him in another's arms, she would meet his loving gaze, and immediately the music ended, she would hurry to his side. Valentin would draw her close to him, the pressure of his hand on her arm reassuring as he joked with one or two others dressed in scarlet.

The mad frenzy among many of the guests bent on forgetting the impending crisis contrasted sharply with others who had grown pale and quiet, clinging desperately to their loved ones as the evening drew closer to its climax.

"So, Lord Ardsmore." Valentin turned to meet the sardonic eyes of the Duke of Wellington. "I found it expedient to come and introduce myself since you seem to have forgotten my express wish to meet your lady."

"My lord Duke, I . . . I . . . forgive my oversight."

Nicole was amused at her husband's discomfort.

Catching the humor in her eyes, Valentin quickly made the introductions. The Duke took her hand in his and kissed it while she curtsied.

"My dear Viscountess, how can I ever express my gratitude for your efforts on behalf of our cause."

Nicole was flattered at the Duke's pointed recognition of her efforts. They chatted amiably for a few minutes until the Duke took leave of her announcing, "You must excuse me, dear lady, but I think it is time we prepared for our departure."

The time had come for final goodbyes!

"Dearest," Valentin smiled, "I must rush. Stay a while, and let Danforth see you home."

"No, Val! Do you think I could stay at a time like

this? You must let me come with you to the house." She clasped his arm.

"It will only be more difficult."

"Every second with you is precious to me. Please, darling, do not deny me this."

"As you wish, my love."

Upon arriving home, they were met by Valentin's valet who had the Colonel's military gear packed. "All ready, Colonel."

"Fine, Jenkins. Have the horses saddled. I will be along directly."

"Very good, my lord." He dashed off.

Drawing Nicole into the unlighted library, Valentin buried his face in her hair breathing in her fragrance. Then allowing his lips to wander over her face, he whispered, "Did I tell you how especially beautiful you looked tonight?"

"Yes." She choked back a sob.

"And how very much I love you."

"Oh Val, Val." She clung to him as his hands dropped to her hips pulling her next to him.

"I will be back, Nicole. This is only the beginning. Just remember that, darling."

"Yes, my dearest. I shall pray . . ." She did not finish her words as his lips found hers—bruising in their intensity. Then gently disengaging himself from her embrace, he gave her one of his more tender looks, touched her cheek with his hand and was gone.

Chapter XVIII

Colonel Harcourt, astride his great black stallion, was on a ridge overlooking the countryside of Waterloo as he watched the Allies and the opposing French form themselves for battle. On the opposite side of the valley a sea of blue uniforms hovered in the morning light growing in size and number until the horizon seemed aquiver with the motion of human bodies.

The first and second rounds of fire came from the French artillery, and small puffs of smoke began to appear along the line of battle. Gradually the sound of heavy cannon filled the air with a deafening roar. A thick smoke hung heavily over the battlefield making it impossible to see clearly. The sharp crackle of musketry punctuated the general din with increasing regularity, while shells screamed overhead and crashed into the sodden earth sending up great showers of mud and stones.

The call to charge sounded, and a great horde of French cavalry was racing through a storm of whistling bullets, sabers held high, straight toward a counter-force of British cavalry no less eager for the pitch of battle.

They met, a great thudding of horses and clashing of arms. To the awful screams of the instruments of war were added the screams of men in the throes of hate and lust, fear and pain. And the grand designs of the generals lost their shape and became formless. There were no longer set patterns of infantry columns and cavalry flanks moving in majestic order. Instead there evolved an inferno of men and animals and weapons snarled together.

It was into the midst of that heaving horror of death that Colonel Valentin Harcourt, Viscount of Ardsmore, plunged his stallion. He was carrying a message to General Comstock requesting reinforcements to support the right flank, which was in serious danger of being overcome by French troups.

The Colonel wheeled his stallion violently through the wild fracas of shouting men and thundering horses, whipping his sword skillfully before him, seeing first one then another blue uniform crumple before the vicious thrust of his powerful arm. They were not the bodies of men that received the piercing of his weapon, but merely obstacles to be cleared from the path of destruction he was hacking between himself and the enemy. Nevertheless, his luck faltered. A hot, searing pain struck him in the chest, and Valentin swayed, almost losing his seat astride his heaving horse. With a sharp curse damning all French hides, he clamped his jaws together and held on. He was through the worst and made his way into the woods surrounding Hougoumont to General Comstock's entrenchment. It was only after delivering Wellington's message that he slipped from his horse and lost consciousness.

*   *   *

The sounds of cannonade shook the city since dawn, shattering windows and frightening much of the populace into a state of panic.

"Oh my God," Cecily wailed. "I should have left the city with the Wexfords when I had the chance."

"It's too late for that now, Cecily. We must try to be brave," Nicole urged.

"No, no, Nicole, I cannot. We can still gather a few of our belongings and escape to Antwerp."

"Are you mad, Cecily? Have you looked out of the window in the last hour? The streets are mobbed with people attempting just that."

"I don't care! If they can make it, so can we."

"Don't you remember that our carriage has been stolen? Besides, you might consider John."

"Oh Lord, Nicole, John is a soldier—it is his duty, but I am not obliged to remain here." The girl was close to frenzy.

"Cecily, you are overwrought. I'm sure you don't mean what you are saying."

"But I'm so scared, Nicole, I beg you to come to Antwerp with me."

"Never! Do you think for one minute I would leave while Valentin is in danger? They can destroy the whole city, but I will not leave without him! Don't you care what happens to John?"

Cecily hesitated, making an effort to stem her hysteria, but she could not. "I see no need to sacrifice my life as well as his."

"Don't say that!" Nicole shook with fear and anger. "How can you be so callous!"

Their conversation was interrupted by the arrival of Gordon Danforth.

"Gordon!" Cecily sprang at him. "Surely you can get us out of here—you're a member of the British Legation."

"It is too late, Mrs. Tilford. The people are running wild in the streets, and every sort of conveyance has been commandeered. It is best to remain inside. I had a terrible time getting here."

"But there must be some way. What about the river barges?"

"Impossible. Wellington has secured every one of them for the wounded."

"What are we to do?" she cried.

"My dear lady, remain calm. There is nothing for you to do but wait."

"For what? For Bonaparte to enter the city?"

"That's not very likely to happen . . ."

"Is it not? I heard he has beaten the Duke and is already marching on the city."

"Don't believe everything you hear, my dear. The city is rife with rumors. We can't be sure at this point whom to trust. I'm afraid our Belgian hosts are just too frightened right now and waiting to see which side of the fence to jump on."

"It's as bad as that?" Nicole questioned.

"Don't give up hope, Nicole. Louis is still in Ghent. He hasn't seen fit to take flight yet. Besides, Wellington has saved the day more than once. Did he not do it at Torres Vedras in Portugal? We must have faith he can do it again."

"I have, oh I have," Nicole claimed fervently as Cecily fled the room.

When the bodies of the wounded and dying began to arrive from the battlefields, Nicole could not sit idly by hoping for news of Valentin and the others to reach her. Waiting passively for the daily lists of battle casualties was beyond her nature to endure. The awful dread which greeted those postings was made bearable only by her secret belief that her husband's name would not appear on those fearful lists and that her love would protect him from harm. She tried to close her ears to the shocking tales of the sufferings of the wounded on the battlefield. One report told of the agony of dying men plundered by looting soldiers who sometimes killed them as they stripped away their valuables.

Nicole's need to take action found release in joining the scores of women who went to nurse the injured and dying soldiers beginning to crowd the city. At first the awesome sight overwhelmed her, and the horrors of gaping wounds and bloodied limbs and screams of pain almost drove her away, but the thought that these could be Valentin or Perry gave her the courage to remain and face the task before her. Gritting her teeth, she went among the wounded offering whatever assistance was demanded whether it was trying to find space for torn bodies in the overcrowded houses turned into makeshift hospitals, or offering the comfort of prayers, or most appalling of all, the dressing of the hideous wounds crying out for attention. Gradually Nicole became inured to the ghastly sights of shattered limbs as she feverishly worked to staunch the flow of blood from the pitiful human flesh mauled by the brutal weapons of war.

As time passed even the streets of Brussels were turned into hospitals with row upon row of wounded lying on the sidewalks in an endless sea of suffering. The most heart-breaking cries were those of the men for water, and many were actually maddened by pain and thirst. When Nicole could no longer force her weary limbs to further effort she dragged herself home to snatch a few hours of tormented sleep.

The sounds of bombardment awoke Nicole abruptly

the next morning. She shuddered at the prospect of another frightful day like yesterday facing her; nevertheless, bracing herself, she prepared to leave for the hospital.

Cecily was further alarmed as Madame Lafitte declared her intention of accompanying Nicole. Crying that she would be left alone and unprotected, Cecily demanded that the women remain with her. Nicole refused to be moved by Cecily's fears and was about to leave with Madame Lafitte when Danforth arrived escorting Perry who was limping.

"Perry," she cried.

"Didn't mean to frighten you, Nicole, but I took a shot in my leg. Damn Frogs! Sorry to put you to all this trouble."

"Hush, dear," Nicole soothed him placing her hand in his. "You know I could not bear to have you in anyone's care but my own. You are my family."

"You're a trump, Nicole. Should have known you have the heart of a lion."

"Do not overrate my courage, dear Perry," she claimed smiling with effort. "But enough about me, you are the one requiring attention. Let's get you upstairs where you can rest."

After seeing to Perry's comfort, Nicole returned to Gordon Danforth. "How did you find him, Gordon?"

"Perry came to my lodgings this morning. He didn't want to come here and worry you unnecessarily, but, of course, I knew you would want him here. His wound is not serious, but he will get more attention here."

"Thank you, Gordon. You have been such a good friend to all of us."

"It has always been that way between the Harcourts and me," he replied with embarrassment.

"I only wish I could have helped you and Geneviève

296

more when you needed it." She touched his hand impulsively.

"No, Nicole, it was not meant to be for Geneviève and me—just as it *was* meant for you and Valentin to come together." There was a significant pause as she accepted his statement. "I must return to headquarters, but I will stop by later."

"Gordon," she still held his hand, "has there been any word of Valentin?"

"None." He patted her hand. "At the first word, I will let you know."

"Please," she whispered as he departed.

Cecily joined Nicole in the drawing room shortly after Danforth left. A worried frown marked her brow as she paced nervously about the room. "Nicole . . . I . . . I'm sorry about the other day. John . . . John is out there somewhere. I did not realize how much that silly man meant to me until I saw Perry. What if I should lose him?"

"I understand, Cecily, but you must not think like that," Nicole replied calmly enough, but her own fears made it impossible to console Cecily further. How much longer before she would know Valentin's fate?

When the news of Napoleon's defeat spread through Brussels, by the nightfall of June 18, 1815, forty thousand men lay wounded or dying in the Belgian fields surrounding Waterloo. On the very next morning an overwhelming effort to rescue the wounded was launched. Once the Belgians no longer feared backing the wrong side, the houses of the rich were thrown open to the victims of that terrible battle, and little distinction was made whether a soldier had been enemy or ally.

Nicole still had no word of Valentin and her alarm grew uncontrollable. For days she had been harboring a secret plan, and it took only the news of Napoleon's defeat to precipitate her into action. She would go find Valentin herself, and there was no stopping her.

"But *chérie,* this is madness!" protested Madame Lafitte. "Where shall you begin to look for the Viscount in the swarming confusion in the streets. You will not reach the city gates."

"You cannot stop me, Fifi. So cease your prattle. I am determined."

"My dear Nicole, how can you hope to endure the rigors such a search must entail?" This was from John Tilford who had arrived minutes ago in the wake of Gordon Danforth, both bearing the news of Bonaparte's rout to the household. They were gathered in Perry's bedroom. Cecily clung happily to her husband's arm.

"You talk to me of rigors when I do not know if my husband is alive or dead!" she choked. "He may be wounded! Suffering! Oh, do not stare so, but help me instead, please."

There was a pause. Then Perry quietly injected, "She is right."

Madame Lafitte and Danforth looked at each other, and realizing the futility of remonstrating further, looked back to Nicole.

"Very well, my dear," Gordon agreed. "I shall prepare a carriage and see you through this hazard and supply whatever assistance I may."

"Thank you once again, my dear, good friend."

It was at the Namur gate, amidst the throngs of returning wounded that Nicole spied Valentin. She was anxiously hailed by Harry Bramwell who was directing a path for the stretcher bearers through the crowd. Danforth held Nicole back when she attempted to climb from the wagon. Bramwell approached them as they alighted. Grasping Nicole's hand, he urged her, "Prepare yourself, Lady Ardsmore. He looks . . . bad."

"Oh, Valentin, no!" she cried faintly.

"But his chances for recovery are good. The surgeon removed the ball from his chest and bound it. I was told that the Colonel's constitution is strong . . ."

"I must go to him," she interrupted Bramwell.

"Nicole," Danforth cautioned. "For his sake you must not give way. You must be strong."

She nodded, bracing herself, but her heart was beating wildly with fear as she approached her husband and knelt beside him. At the sight of Valentin her resolve weakened. The gray pallor of his skin, the matted golden hair and the dirt-streaked face caused her to tremble violently. But pressing a shaking hand against her mouth, she held back the anguished cry which sprang to her lips. Valentin groaned and opened lackluster eyes.

Nicole placed her hand on his brow as he continued to mutter incoherently. "Valentin," she barely whispered his name, but his head jerked in her direction, and his lips soundlessly formed her name, wrenching her heart. "Oh my darling." She took his hot hand in hers and felt the fingers move feebly.

"He has been given some laudanum to help him rest and ease the pain." Bramwell spoke behind her. "Get the Colonel into the wagon," he ordered the stretcher bearers who moved as quickly as possible with their burden to the conveyance and lifted him in. "He is to be kept cool and quiet, and a new poultice is to be applied every few hours. The surgeon is worried mostly about his fever."

"We'll never be able to thank you enough, Harry," Nicole murmured fervently, clasping his hand before Danforth assisted her into the wagon beside her husband.

"I'm glad I could help. I pray to God he recovers Now if you'll excuse us, we'll be getting back. There are many others who need our aid."

Nicole heard no more of the discussion between the two men as she bent over her husband, wiping the dirt and grime from his face.

The jostling wagon moved slowly through the masses toward the house on the Rue d'Anglais, all the while Danforth fearing the damage the ride was doing the injured man. His moaning had increased, and Danforth threw an anxious look over his shoulder at his friend. Nicole lifted her tear-stained face to him.

"Not much farther, my dear," he assured her.

She placed a cool cloth on Valentin's forehead and whispered lovingly to him. "Oh, my dear. My dearest love." Her words floated through the miasma of his pain and suffering, for he needed nothing so much as the comfort of his upon wife after his passage through the hell of battle, and hearing her voice, his agitation lessened.

The entire household watched as Danforth and Tilford carried Valentin to his room. Cecily wept while Perry cursed, but it was Madame Lafitte who took charge of the near chaotic situation. Shouting orders, giving instructions and supervising the entire matter, she soon had the Viscount settled. Then Nicole, along with Danforth at her side, began her vigil beside Valentin's fever-racked body.

Later, when she removed the bandages so that a new compress could be applied, she gasped at the sight of the torn and inflamed flesh. But forcing down her weakness, she worked quickly binding the injured area of his chest. Suddenly Valentin cried out wrenching free of her. As he struggled to sit up, Danforth clasped his arms about his, subduing him while Nicole completed her ministrations.

Straightening from her position, Nicole found her legs too weak to support her. Sinking to her knees and burying her face in her husband's hand, she began to weep.

"My God, Nicole, you must rest, or you will be no good to him later on when he is fully awake and in pain. Let me call Madame Lafitte."

Realizing the truth of his words, Nicole allowed herself to be put to bed where she fell into an exhausted sleep.

Several hours later she returned and remained with Valentin through the nightmare hours of his agony. When the doctor arrived, Valentin was in a state of semi-consciousness, but the doctor's words were encouraging. The fever had dropped, and if Colonel Harcourt continued to improve for the next twenty-four hours, he saw no reason why the patient should not recover completely. Nicole breathed a sigh of relief but never relaxed her care of Valentin during that crucial time.

The sun was rising on a new day, and Nicole was adjusting Valentin's blankets when his eyes opened and focused on her.

"Nicole?" he whispered weakly.

"Valentin?" She felt his forehead and discovered that the fever was gone completely, and his eyes were no longer clouded. "How do you feel?"

He grimaced, furrowing his brow, but replied steadily, "Much better."

Taking the wan face between her hands and gently kissing his lips, she said, "Liar." Then slipping her arm under his shoulders, she lifted him so he might drink to moisten his parched lips.

"Did I dream it, or did you tell me earlier . . . that the Allies had routed Napoleon?" He frowned.

"It is true. Tilford and your brother, Perry, have already rejoined their regiments in pursuit of the fleeing army."

"Damn! . . . I shall miss it."

"According to Gordon . . ."

"Gordon?"

"Why yes, he has been in constant attendance since we found you, but you were not clear-headed at the time." She smiled at his confusion. Valentin sought her hand, and she grasped his, holding it to her breast. Swallowing tears of joy and relief she said, "They informed me that this would be a clean-up operation, and no doubt by the time you are well, the Allies will be in Paris. Does that relieve your mind, my love?"

"Immensely, but I still wish I could be with the Duke when . . ."

"Hush! You have done your duty. You must get back your strength, and that will only come with peace and quiet. You must rest."

"I am tired," he agreed as he closed his eyes and drifted off to sleep, images of a violet-eyed girl dancing seductively before him in his dreams.

From that moment his progress was rapid, and the doctor, when he visited a few days later, assured the Viscount it would not be long before he was up and around.

One afternoon sometime later as Nicole was rebandaging Valentin's wound, she felt a tug on one of her curls. She looked up and frowned at him, then proceeded with what she was doing. Once again he pulled at the loosened curl.

"Valentin, don't," she insisted shaking her head free of his fingers as the curl came tumbling down. "Now see what you have done," she scolded as several more tresses fell about her shoulders and breast.

He only laughed.

"Oh, I can see you are going to be a naughty patient." She smiled indulgently and straightened away from him.

"Now I will have to leave you and go repair the damage you have wrought."

"Nicole, don't leave me," he pleaded sweetly, sitting up among the pillows.

"But I must. It is your own fault you know," she chided and turned her back to him.

Valentin moaned loudly and flopped back among the pillows, thrashing about in pain.

Immediately she was at his side. "Valentin! What is it, my love?"

He reached up with his good arm and pulled her down alongside him on the bed.

"You wretch! You scared me. I thought you were in pain!"

"I am, Nicole. In more ways than one."

She caught his meaning but ignored it saying, "Shall I bathe your brow?"

"No, my love, just promise to stay with me." He snatched a quick kiss.

"I . . . I would willingly if you promised not to exert yourself," she temporized, eyes flashing with mischief.

"Since I am too weak to do no more at present than hold you and kiss you," which he proceeded to do arousing her own longing for him, "you have my promise to behave."

"Very well." Nicole smiled helplessly, returning his kiss.

"You see, my love," he said triumphantly. "The Harcourt luck has finally had its way." He settled her more firmly within the circle of his arm.

Nicole sighed contentedly, snuggling closer to the man she had loved since her childhood. She knew that she and Valentin would never be separated again. Not by anything. Ever.